Fu George smiled. His hand strayed to his breast pocket. His smile froze on his face. His hand plunged into the pocket. There was nothing there.

Fu George remembered the brush with Maijstral, the man's uncommon civility. Vanessa perceived his agitation. She put a hand on his arm. "What's wrong, Geoff?"

Soundlessly, the steel doors irised back. The room was bathed in the light of one star devouring another.

There was no applause. The sight was too awesome.

Fu George glared across the room at Maijstral. He was sitting next to Advert, and both were smiling as they tilted their heads back to watch Rathbon's Star being eaten.

Maijstral, Fu George thought, *this means war*.

Walter Jon Williams
HOUSE OF SHARDS

A TOM DOHERTY ASSOCIATES BOOK
NEW YORK

HOUSE OF SHARDS

Copyright © 1988 by Walter Jon Williams

A TOR Book
Published by Tom Doherty Associates, Inc.
49 West 24 Street
New York, NY 10010

Cover art by Don Brautigam

ISBN: 0-812-55783-2   Can. ISBN: 0-812-55784-0

Library of Congress Catalog Card Number: 88-50629

First edition: November 1988

Printed in the United States of America

0 9 8 7 6 5 4 3 2 1

To Françoise Auclaire le Vison
"the Chef"
and Baron le Vison of Milwaukee
"the Waiter"
l'appétit vient en mangeant

. . . One false move and we could have a
farce on our hands.

—Tom Stoppard,
On the Razzle

CHAPTER 1

When one star gobbles another, the universe may be forgiven if it pauses to take breath. Imagine the sight: the smaller star a bright-haloed emptiness, a nullity that draws into itself vast ruddy flares of stellar matter until it consumes the very heart of its companion. People might well stop and stare. Some may even pay for the privilege.

Thus Silverside Station, a small asteroid held within view of the phenomenon by mighty anchors of self-generated gravitational energy. Small, hence exclusive. With exclusive rights to the view.

And about to have its grand opening.

A private media globe hung inconspicuously over the control console. Recording every word.

"Imagine it. Everyone on both sides of the border wanting to have a ticket. Salivating for one. Offering *anything* to get one. And the two of us, flying into Silverside on our own private racing yacht."

A doubtful frown. "I'm not certain of this rule banning the media. It seems extreme." A glance at the private globe. "I can't record myself. That's a little absurd."

"The ban only applies to *most* of the media, Pearl. Some will be there. Kyoko Asperson, for one."

"*That*," the Pearl said, her ears flattening, "will guarantee catastrophe."

Pearl Woman was tall and dark-haired. Her shoulders and arms bulged with transplanted muscle: in her youth she hunted daffles from proughback, and that takes upper-body strength. Her hair shagged from her head like the mane of a lion. She wore a single pearl hanging from the left ear, an object balanced artfully by a duelling scar on her right cheek. Both were her trademarks within the Diadem, never duplicated by others of that exclusive organization, though they were often imitated by her admirers across the Constellation.

The enthusiasm of Pearl Woman's companion was undimmed. "Only three of the Diadem were invited. Three of the Three Hundred. You and the Marquess Kotani and Zoot. Imagine that."

Pearl Woman gave her a look. "Advert. I need to dock the ship."

Sulkily. "You *could* put it on auto."

"Not my way, Advert."

Advert, with a self-conscious glance at the media globe, fell silent. She was young and pale and willowy, with wavy brown hair that fell halfway down her back. She had dropped her second name, hoping the Human Diadem might notice and consider her for the next vacancy. She wore silver rings on every finger, including the thumbs, and fondly hoped they (and perhaps the hair) might one day become her own trademark. Pearl Woman knew better, but had not as yet disillusioned her.

Advert was new to this sort of existence and still felt a little uncertain. Her remaining illusions, Pearl Woman thought, made her charming, though in an unformed sort of way. One day Advert's particular brand of charm would cease to hold its attraction; but that day had not as yet arrived.

Throughout their conversation, the awesome sight of one

star consuming another had been splayed across the ship's viewscreens. Neither paid it the slightest attention.

The entry concourse was a long, low room, carpeted in dark green. Darker tapestries flashed winks of silver thread from the walls. The lighting was subdued, and a small orchestra played brisk tunes in the corner. People in uniforms stood behind desks; robots carried bags in efficient silence. Disembarking passengers took their time strolling toward the desks. It was not done to seem in a hurry.

"Pearl Woman. You are looking very dashing."

"Maijstral. It's been years."

"The matched swords are very elegant. What are they, small sabers?"

"Cutlasses. I thought they'd add a swashbuckling touch." Pearl Woman snicked one sword from its scabbard, performed a figure, returned it. Like the claws of a kitten, a touch of fear moved along Maijstral's nerves. Someone had tried to hack him to bits with a sword just recently, and the presence of edged weapons made him more than usually nervous.

He and Pearl Woman clasped hands (three fingers each) and sniffed one another's ears as, around them, the entry concourse bustled on. Maijstral was slightly taller than average, but he had to raise his head to reach the Pearl's neck.

Drake Maijstral's dark hair waved to his shoulders. He was dressed in grey. Lace floated casually at neck and wrists. He wore a large diamond on one finger, and leather buskins on his feet. His eyes were green and heavy-lidded; they gave an impression of laziness, or at least languor. He seemed to be in his mid-twenties.

Maijstral turned and indicated a restless young man dressed in violet plush. "My associate, Mr. Gregor Norman."

"Charmed, Mr. Norman," said Pearl Woman, "This is Advert, my companion."

Hands were clasped all around, but High Custom sniffing was avoided—the entry concourse was a little too common for High Custom unless rank and previous acquaintance demanded it. Maijstral and Advert offered one another two fingers, indicating a certain presumed intimacy through their common acquaintance with Pearl Woman. Pearl Woman and Advert gave one finger each to Gregor. Gregor gave two to Pearl Woman and three to Advert, the latter indicating a degree of hopefulness far above his station.

Advert sniffed and drew herself up. Gregor, who had spoken his greetings in a provincial accent that could only be described as cheeky, declined to be properly abashed and instead grinned.

The custom of hand-clasping, after an interval of several thousand years, was now a rage. It had been rediscovered by the Constellation Practices Authority, who recommended it a "natural, human gesture," and suggested it replace the elegant ear-sniffing of Khosali High Custom.

Traditionalists and Imperialists denounced the revival as vulgar. Pro-Constellation partisans adopted it eagerly. Saying hello had suddenly become a gesture fraught with political import.

That, and the issue of how many fingers to offer, had all society dizzy with new possibilities.

Pearl Woman took Maijstral's arm. They strolled lazily toward the customs desks.

Behind them, Gregor offered Advert his arm. She ignored it and followed the Pearl, her head high. Gregor gave another cheeky grin and then put a hi-stick in his mouth.

"Do you like the way Laurence is playing you in the vids?" Pearl Woman asked. "I didn't like him at first, but I think he's growing into the part."

"I've not seen him," Maijstral said. Pearl Woman gave

a disbelieving grin. "People never believe me," Maijstral said equably, "but it's true."

"Is Roman with you?" Pearl Woman asked.

"Yes. Taking care of the baggage."

"Please give him my compliments."

Maijstral nodded. "I will. He will be pleased that you remembered him."

"You are out of mourning, I see."

"It's been over a year."

"That long? I had no idea."

"Thank you, by the way, for your condolences. That was kind of you."

"Are you His Grace of Dornier now? Should I be mi-lording you?"

Amusement sparked in Maijstral's lazy eyes. "Heavens no," he said. "I'd feel foolish being the Duke of This and the Viscount of That, considering the family's lost almost all the estates during the Rebellion and there's nothing to be his grace the Duke *of*."

Pearl Woman smiled. "I understand."

"The most ridiculous title, of course, is Hereditary Prince-Bishop of Nana. My father prevailed upon me to preach a sermon at my investiture, and I felt damned silly standing up in front of a packed cathedral. I'd just taken out my burglar's ticket, so I preached on tolerance." He cocked his head in remembrance. "It was well received, at least," he said. "And it entitled me to a small stipend. So it's not all bad."

The way ahead was clear, and they stepped to the customs counter. A Khosali female looked at them from behind the clean ebon surface. Eyes glittered from beneath the polished brim of a narrow cap tailored with notches to allow her pointed ears full movement.

"Mr. Maijstral," she said, pointing. "Your desk is over *there*."

Disembarking from second class, a nondescript, portly man named Dolfuss picked up two heavy suitcases from the robot baggage carrier and began moving toward customs.

"Excuse me, sir," the robot said. "I will be happy to carry those."

Dolfuss ignored the robot and moved on.

The room glowed blue. Mr. Sun, sitting in his padded chair behind a U-shaped console, found it a soothing color.

He looked with satisfied eyes at his security monitors. Individual media globes had tagged everyone who had just disembarked, and images of each decked the walls. A hologram projector set into Mr. Sun's desk showed a file labelled *Known Associates*.

Gregor Norman, it said. *Human male, age 20 yrs*. The picture was an old one and showed Gregor wearing vulgar earrings and a grossly offensive hairstyle. A short arrest record was appended.

Next to Gregor floated the hologram of a Khosalikh wearing a subdued dark suit with a fashionable braided collar. *Roman*, it said. *Khosali male, age 46 yrs. Bodyservant. No arrests or convictions*.

Mr. Sun touched an ideogram on his console. Two of the video monitors flashed. *Match*, the console reported, and made a pleasant chirring sound.

Mr. Sun smiled. He touched another ideogram to transmit the pictures to Khamiss at the entry concourse.

Acknowledged, flashed the response.

Mr. Sun looked down at his uniform, brushed away a speck of lint. A simple touch, he thought. A simple gesture like *this*, he thought, and like the lint, the thieves are brushed away.

In his view, this set of burglars had a lot to atone for, and he intended the atonement start now.

"Mr. Norman," said Khamiss. "Your line is over there."

"I'd count those rings if I were you," Pearl Woman said.

Advert glanced in surprise at her fingers, and Pearl Woman smiled. Advert was so *easy*.

"Sometimes they'll take the jewelry right off you, right in public," Pearl Woman said. "It's vulgar, but sometimes Allowed Burglars like to show off."

"That Gregor person was vulgar enough, heaven knows." Advert looked dubiously at the trademark that dangled from the other woman's ear. "Aren't you worried, Pearl?"

Pearl Woman touched the matched silver hilts of her swords. "Not at all, Advert," she said. "It's for other people to worry, not me." She looked at Advert. "If Maijstral ever bothers you, there's something you can do to get rid of him."

"Yes?"

"Ask him if his mother is well."

"That's all?"

"It's always worked for me."

Dolfuss waited in a queue with the other second-class passengers. (Second-class passengers weren't expected to mind waiting in line.) The others were either servants of the first-class passengers or people who actually worked at Silverside, late arrivals come to take up their new jobs. Dolfuss was the only guest.

Dolfuss didn't care. He was enjoying himself.

* * *

Annoyance flickered across Maijstral's face. A tall, thin, grimly satisfied sort of person was looting his luggage. Gregor, a step back, gazed on in astonished dismay.

"Darksuit," said the man, a human named Kingston. His ears fluttered in disapproval. He lifted the object from Maijstral's trunk, and handed it to a robot. "Illegal onstation. It will be returned to you on your departure."

"The point of a darksuit," said Maijstral's servant, Roman, "is to blend in with the darkness. There is no darkness on this station. The suit would be useless."

Roman was a tall Khosalikh, erect, dignified, his ears folded in an expression of cold fury. He spoke Human Standard without accent and, considering the circumstances, with admirable restraint.

"You may complain to Mr. Sun if you wish," Kingston said. "He's head of security. I only enforce the regulations."

Roman's nostrils palpitated in anger. Maijstral gazed in cool annoyance at the sight of his belongings strewn over the concourse. He frowned.

"I see no need to appeal to underlings," he said. "I will complain to Baron Silverside in person."

"Nothing, sir, would give me greater pleasure," Kingston said, radiating grim happiness. He looked down at Gregor's trunk, then reached into it. He picked up a small gadget and held it up to the light.

"An electronic device of the sort referred to as a 'black box,' " he said. The quotes were clear in his voice. "Commonly used to interrupt alarm systems." He wagged a solemn finger at Gregor. "Very naughty, Mr. Norman," he said. "You'll get it back when you leave."

Gregor turned red. Maijstral folded his arms. "Must we be subjected to this amateur stand-up routine while you search our baggage?" he asked. "Let's get it over with, shall we?"

"Certainly, your worship," said Kingston. He handed the black box to his robot with an elaborate gesture. "Now let's see what Mr. Norman has in his gadget box, shall we?"

There seemed to be a delay in disembarking the second-class passengers. Dolfuss waited patiently, glancing over the concourse. There were supposed to be members of the Diadem here, and Dolfuss had always been a big Nichole fan.

The lounge bar, called the Shadow Room, was dark, quiet, scarcely inhabited. A woodwind quartet readied their equipment in a corner.

"Marquess."

"Your grace."

"I enjoyed the recordings of your last play. I only wish I'd had the chance to see it live."

"Thank you, your grace. The play did wonders for my share. I believe I saw you in that race on—Hrinn, was it?" The Diadem's researchers had given the Marquess Kotani current facts on every prominent person scheduled to be at Silverside, the better to be ready for informed conversation. The Marquess always did his homework.

"Yes. I did fairly well in the Hrinn race."

"Second only to Khottan."

The Duchess smiled. "Khottan," she said, "was lucky."

Kotani returned the smile. He was a spare, cultivated, brown-skinned human with a brief mustache, greying temples, and a distinguished profile. He had been born in the Empire and had made his reputation with the naturalness of his languor. He was one of the older members of the

Diadem—their first lord—and his share had always remained in the top twenty.

The Marquess cast a careful glance over the lounge bar, seeing no one he cared to talk to other than the Duchess. "Will you join me at my table?" he asked.

"Alas," said the Duchess, "I am here to meet someone."

"Some other time, your grace." He sniffed her and withdrew.

Her grace Roberta Altunin, the Duchess of Benn, was nineteen and a gifted amateur athlete. Her hair was dark red and cut short, her eyes were deep violet, and she moved with grace and confidence. She had first-rate advisors, and they had suggested Silverside as a perfect location for her debut.

She stepped to the bar and ordered a cold rink. She nodded to the man standing next to her.

"Mr. Kuusinen."

"Your grace."

They clasped hands (one finger apiece) and lightly sniffed one another's ears. Mr. Paavo Kuusinen was a slight man with an unexceptional appearance. He wore a green coat laced up the sides and back.

"The coat suits you, Kuusinen."

"Thank you. I discovered that my wardrobe marked me too easily as an Imperial citizen, so I had a new one made. Your gown is quite becoming, by the way."

Roberta smiled lightly. Her drink arrived, and she put her thumbprint on the chit.

"The *Count Boston* has arrived," Kuusinen said. His forefinger circled the rim of his glass. "I understand that Zoot is aboard. And Drake Maijstral, the burglar."

"Have you seen them?"

"I have seen Maijstral. He seemed to be having difficulty at customs."

Lines appeared between Roberta's brows. "Will that be a problem for him?"

"He seems a man of considerable resource. I'm sure he will rise above the difficulty."

She raised her glass, put it down again. "I don't want this to go wrong, Kuusinen."

"Geoff Fu George is already on station. Perhaps he would be more suitable. He has more resources to draw on."

"I want Maijstral." Firmly.

Kuusinen assented. The woman's mind was made up. "Your grace," he said.

Roberta glanced behind her, seeing Kotani in conversation with a short woman in bright clothes and a funny hat. "We shouldn't be seen together for very long, Kuusinen. Perhaps you should make your congé."

"As you wish, your grace."

They clasped hands, still one finger apiece, and sniffed. Kuusinen passed the woodwind quartet on his way to the door. Roberta took her drink and drifted in Kotani's direction. She noticed silver media globes hovering over Kotani's conversation.

". . . I'm still looking for something suitable," he was saying.

"I understand," the short woman agreed. She spoke a broad provincial accent that seemed less comically non-U than, somehow, a deliberate provocation. "It must be difficult finding a part nowadays that features the sort of old-fashioned character you favor."

Kotani stiffened slightly. "Not old-fashioned, my dear," he said. "Classical, I should think." He turned to Roberta. "Your grace, may I present Kyoko Asperson. Miss Asperson is a *personality journalist*." He gave the words an unnecessary emphasis that indicated his distaste. "Miss Asperson, may I introduce her grace the Duchess of Benn."

Roberta offered the journalist a cautious finger during the handclasp, receiving two in exchange. Kyoko Asperson was a head shorter than Roberta, with straight black hair and a round face. She dressed in bright reds and yellows, and wore a odd mushroom-shaped hat. A loupe stuck over one eye allowed her to see through the lenses of her hovering media globes.

"Congratulations on your Hrinn race," Kyoko said. "You gave Khottan a run for his money."

"Metaphorical money, of course. An amateur event."

"Will you be turning professional anytime soon?"

Roberta sipped her drink. "Probably not. Though I haven't quite decided."

"You don't need the money, of course, but on the professional level the competition is more intense. Do you find yourself intimidated by the prospect?"

Roberta, having never considered this question, was mildly surprised. Amateur contests, in her circle anyway, were far more fashionable than professional competition. "Not at all," she said, truthfully, and then wondered if she'd said it convincingly enough. But Kyoko had already moved to the next question.

"Do you feel any pressure to turn professional simply in order to have people take you more seriously? Do you think that people take amateur sports *seriously* enough?"

The quartet began to play, starting with a high-pitched screech from the ristor. Roberta glanced at Kotani in dismay. He smiled at her and nodded, happy to be out of it.

Roberta resigned herself to a very long afternoon.

"Mr. Drake Maijstral?" Maijstral's interrogator was a slight man in a brown jacket.

"Yes. May I be of assistance?"

"Mencken, sir. VPL."

Mencken held out Maijstral's Very Private Letter. Throughout Maijstral's life, the appearance of a VPL courier would have been an occasion for dismay. Maijstral's father had used VPL almost exclusively, and his letters were either long lectures concerning Maijstral's faults, or requests for money in order to honor an old debt. Maijstral restrained his reflexive annoyance, signed for the letter, glanced at the seal, then broke it.

"Will there be a reply, sir?"

"Not now. Thank you."

"Your servant." Mencken bowed and withdrew. Maijstral looked at the card, then handed it to Roman. "We're invited to a wedding. Pietro Quijano and Amalia Jensen will be getting married on Earth in six months' time."

Roman read the card. "Will we be attending, sir?"

"Possibly. We're heading in that direction. I've never seen Earth."

"Nor have I."

"Perhaps it's about time we did. But I'll need some thought before I decide."

"Very well, sir."

The orchestra was packing up and heading for the main lounge. Dolfuss had finally arrived at the customs desk. "I feel so lucky," Dolfuss declared. "I won my ticket in a lottery. Otherwise I'd never have a chance to visit a place like this." He glanced around the room. "I'm impressed already!" he said.

The uniformed Tanquer closed her nictitating membranes, as if to deny what she was seeing. "Yes, sir," she said. "I understand just how lucky you feel."

"And I was able to schedule my ships so as to work in a business trip. Stop at Ranc on the way home. That's why I'm carrying my sample case."

The Tanquer's bushy tail twitched. "The exit is that way, sir. Your room is programmed to receive you."

"Thanks. I'm going to have fun here, I know it!"

Dolfuss laughed as he picked up his suitcases and walked for the exit. He was the only person carrying his own luggage. As he moved into the corridor, he saw Maijstral asking directions of a robot.

"Mr. Maijstral," he said.

"Mr. Dolfuss. I hope your journey was pleasant."

"It was. Very. I even made some sales."

"How fortunate."

"See you later."

Dolfuss bustled away. His head swivelled left and right. He was enjoying the scenery.

The robot was a latest-model Cygnus, a dark, polished ovoid that hovered a precise sixteen inches from the floor and did all its work with grappler beams. Its dark carapace bore an ideogram meaning "Advanced Object."

"As I was saying, sir," it said. "Take the second left, through the arcade, then your first right."

"Thank you," Maijstral said. "I don't know how I could have got lost so easily." A frown crossed his face. "I believe your carapace has something on it. Let me see."

As he leaned over the robot, he made a brushing gesture over the carapace with his hand. A programming spike was inserted into the robot's input connector. Maijstral brushed again. The spike was removed and palmed.

"There," he said. "Much better."

"Thank you, sir."

Stepping lightly, Maijstral began to stroll in the opposite direction from that which the robot had indicated.

* * *

The orchestra had moved from the entry concourse to the main lounge, appropriately called the White Room. The music was muffled by dazzling white couches, chairs, and carpeting, but the music was also echoed pleasantly by a sixteen-foot length of natural impact diamond that hung overhead. The stone had been discovered during the excavation; it wasn't gem quality, but it resonated well, and added a lustre to the room.

Overhead was a window, its view fixed at the sight of one star devouring another. The shutters were resolutely closed, awaiting the grand unveiling.

"Pearl Woman."

"My lord."

Kotani and the Pearl stood on the white soft carpet, sniffed, and gave each other three fingers—Diadem members were *de facto* intimates.

"Have you met Advert?"

"I don't believe so." (Sniff. Three fingers. Sniff.) "Charmed."

"Pleased to meet you, my lord."

Kotani cast a glance over his shoulder. "I just made my escape from Miss Asperson."

The Pearl gave a sniff. "I understood she was to be here."

"She is currently fashionable. Fashions pass, thankfully."

"One may hope her vogue will be of short duration."

"Have you seen Zoot?"

Pearl Woman shook her head. "Perhaps he's waiting to make a grand entrance."

"Perhaps," archly, "he's hiding from Asperson."

The orchestra came to the end of its piece. Those in the lounge tapped their feet in approval. The carpet absorbed the sound entirely.

Above, the diamond still rang.

"Shall we sit down, my lord?"

"Certainly." They found a settee and settled in. "Her grace Roberta is here," Kotani offered. "The Duchess of Benn."

"Ah. The racer."

"There will be a race tomorrow. Before the Duchess's coming-out ball."

"Perhaps I'll enter the race."

"She's very good."

"Perhaps I'll cheat." Smiling, a little too whitely.

"In that case," said Kotani, "I'll have to be very careful of my wager."

". . . then take the first right."

"Pardon me, but I think there's something on your carapace."

Mr. Sun looked with satisfaction at the piles of burglar equipment that had been confiscated from Maijstral's party. "That should serve to slow him down."

Kingston, his tall assistant, gave him a look. "You don't think it will stop him entirely?"

"I think he will have to steal *something*. After all, Geoff Fu George is here. Neither of them can afford to be shown up by the other."

"I suppose not."

"And there's another factor." Sun gave his assistant a significant look. "The Shard is here."

"Virtues!"

"We may *hope* the Virtues will prevail. And no swearing, Kingston."

"Sorry." He looked thoughtful. "Perhaps the rivalry will make them careless."

Sun's face split in a thin smile. "Yes. That's precisely what I'm counting on."

"Excuse me."

Kotani looked at the rotund figure, then blinked at the eye-scorching pattern of the man's jacket. "Yes? Mr.—"

"Dolfuss. I'm a big fan of yours. I was wondering . . ." Holding out a notebook and pen.

"Oh. Certainly." Kotani took the objects and turned to give Dolfuss the benefit of his noble profile.

"Do you suppose Nichole will be here?" Dolfuss asked. "I'm a particular fan of hers."

"I believe Nichole is touring with her new play." Kotani scrawled his signature, then looked at Dolfuss over the pen. "Mr. Dolfuss, I don't think I've seen you before. How came you here?"

"I won a raffle."

"I thought it must have been something like that."

"The first right, you say? Oh. I believe you have something on your carapace."

The woodwinds chortled away, laughing in their lower registers. Roberta passed them on her way out of the lounge. Behind her, Kyoko Asperson was interviewing one of the waiters.

"Your grace."

"Mr. Fu George." Roberta's lips turned up in an amused smile. "I have always expected to meet you sooner or later. I'm relieved the suspense is over at last."

Geoff Fu George offered her two fingers and delicately sniffed her ears. He received two fingers in return. A certain object of mutual interest assured them of a degree of intimacy before they had ever met.

"I suppose—" he smiled "—it would be pointless to ask whether you have the Shard with you."

Her violet eyes sparkled. "I suppose it would," she said.

He bowed easily, conceding the point. Geoff Fu George was a compact, assured man of forty. His long blond hair (some of it, by now, implanted) was held with diamond pins and trailed down his back. He had been on top of the burglars' ratings for six years, since the Affaire of the Mirrorglass BellBox had put him solidly on top. His hairstyle was almost trademarked. He had once been asked to join the Diadem, and he had declined. The resulting sensation had assured him more celebrity than he would have received had he accepted.

"Will you take my arm?" he asked. "I was about to head for the Casino."

"With pleasure."

"I noticed that the station network ran a history of the Eltdown Shard earlier this afternoon. I suppose that could be a coincidence."

"I daresay." Smiling.

Through his jacket, Roberta could feel the outline of his gun against her arm. The corridor to the Casino was covered in a deep carpet woven of Kharolton moth wings. The wallpaper was patterned on the Cerulean Corridor in the City of Seven Bright Rings. The molding was blanchtree from Andover. Clearly Baron Silverside had spared no expense.

"I understand the customs people are unusually strict here on station," Roberta said. "I hope you haven't been inconvenienced."

"Only slightly. Still, I thought they were more officious than necessary. I shall speak to Baron Silverside when I see him."

A Cygnus robot passed them on its silent repellers. Its carapace gleamed in the subdued light.

"I understand you're racing tomorrow. I hope to watch, if circumstances permit."

Roberta gave him a sidelong look. "You don't want to take advantage of my being busy?"

He seemed offended. "Your grace," he said. "I wouldn't dream of interfering with your debut."

"Thank you." Surprised. "That's a kind thought."

"Just because I steal," said Fu George stiffly, "doesn't mean I'm a cad."

"Robot," said Gregor Norman. "I wonder if you could direct me to the Casino."

"Certainly, sir. Follow this corridor to the main lounge. Take the third arch on the right. It's marked with the ideogram for 'luck.' "

"Thank you. Excuse me, but I think you have something on your carapace."

"Thank you, sir."

"Only too." Meaning, only too happy.

Gregor deftly inserted the programming needle, gave the carapace a pat, then slipped the needle out. He and the robot parted company. At the first turning, he met a man in a loud jacket. The man was holding a notebook and looking at something therein with apparent delight.

"Mr. Dolfuss," Gregor said, and nodded.

"Mr. Norman." Nodding back.

Both went on their way, smiling.

Zoot paced back and forth in his room, then stopped and looked at himself in the mirror. His ears twitched uncomfortably. His diaphragm throbbed in resignation, and he resumed his pacing.

What the hell should he wear? That was the difficulty.

All the Diadem's advance people were humans, that was the problem. They didn't understand.

The advance people wanted him to wear his exploring togs. In the *lounge!* Before *dinner!*

His conservative Khosali soul was appalled by the idea. Wearing the environment suit seemed like an insult to Silverside and all it stood for: restraint, elegance, High Custom. But yet the Diadem people had seemed so certain that the suit was what his public expected from him.

A leaden distress settled in his soul. He looked at himself in the mirror again, seeing the trademark dark-grey environment suit with its pockets, its analyzers, its force-field repellers. His nostrils flared; his ears turned back.

"Room," he said. "What time is it?"

"Twenty-five thirteen Imperial Standard," said the room.

Zoot growled happily. Dinner would begin in just over an hour: there wasn't time to be seen in the lounge before he'd have to come back to the room to change. His hesitation had saved him.

"Room," he said. "Send a robot to help me dress."

He could have asked for one of the Diadem people, but they'd do nothing but set his nerves on edge.

The Casino featured the cool, respectful sound of money being lost. Not much money yet: the night was young and many guests had not yet arrived.

"Your grace," said Geoff Fu George, "may I present Pearl Woman and Mr. Drake Maijstral. Sir and madam, the Duchess of Benn."

"Your very obedient, your grace," said Maijstral. Roberta thought she could see a gleam of interest in Maijstral's hooded eyes before he sniffed her ears.

"Another man I've always expected to meet. My pleasure, sir."

"Your grace." Another set of sniffs. "May I present my companion, Advert."

"Miss Advert."

"Your very obedient, your grace."

Pearl Woman gave Roberta a calculated look. "I understand you will be racing tomorrow."

"Yes. A small amateur field."

"Perhaps I will enter."

Roberta smiled inwardly. A Diadem member would attract more attention to the race, hence to herself. The whole point of being here, after all, was to be noticed.

"I hope you shall. The company will be all the more distinguished by your presence."

"Perhaps you might be interested in a small side wager?"

"If it wouldn't compromise my amateur standing."

"I'm sure it would not."

"In that case, yes. Five novae?"

"Let's make it twenty."

"If you like."

Pearl Woman showed delicate incisors that matched her earring. "Done," she said.

Maijstral and Geoff Fu George exchanged handclasps while Pearl Woman spoke with Roberta. Maijstral offered two fingers and got one in return. It was, he reflected, nothing more than what he had expected.

Both men smiled. Their smiles lacked warmth.

"Maijstral," said Fu George, "have you heard the rumors coming out of the Constellation Practices Authority?"

"Referring to Allowed Burglary."

"Yes. They're considering an outright condemnation."

"That," said Maijstral, "could be unfortunate."

"They could put us in prison. Just for practicing our profession. We'd all have to move to the Empire. And I don't know about *you*, Maijstral—" smiling, a bit more warmly "—but I *like* being a member of the majority species. Call me parochial if you like."

"The Constellation suits my temperament as well, Fu George."

"Then you'll join in the Burglars' Association? We're going to try to head this off before it gets out of committee."

Maijstral sighed. "I suppose I must."

"This is no time to be a maverick, Maijstral. Personal style is one thing; survival is quite another. Aldiss is holding the treasury. I hope we can count on a generous contribution." A thin smile. "The Sporting Commission has agreed to count it for points."

Another sigh, this one purely internal. "A generous contribution. Yes."

Geoff Fu George smiled again. Maijstral fancied he could feel its warmth on his skin. "I knew you would understand, once this was put to you in person. Aldiss told me he had the damndest time getting ahold of you by post. Even Very Private Letters seemed not to get through."

"My life has been irregular, of late."

Fu George glanced at Roberta. "I wonder if the Shard is on station?"

"I've no idea."

"I am very interested in the answer to that question, Maijstral. Very."

Maijstral gave him a look. His green eyes seemed less lazy than before. "Does that mean I am supposed to be uninterested?"

Fu George shook his head. "Not at all, old man. I was just talking to myself." He stood on tiptoe and craned his head across the Casino. "Ah. I believe I see Miss Runciter. Have you met her? Oh. I forget. Sorry, Maijstral. Tactless of me."

"No need to apologize."

"I should join her. You will excuse me?"

"Certainly." He offered Fu George his hand. One finger, as was no doubt proper.

Mr. Sun sat quietly in his blue heaven, awaiting information. He pictured himself as a spider in its lair, his fingers dancing on threads, each thread a monitor, a functionary.

The spider would never leave its home. Information would flow in, the spider would weigh it, judge it, define a response. Mr. Sun felt himself centered, ready, alive.

"Third ship's arriving, sir. *Viscount Cheng.*"

Khamiss's sharp Khosali face hovered holographically to one side of Mr. Sun's monitors. Mr. Sun turned to face his assistant. There was a congregation of thieves in the Casino, and he was reluctant to face away.

"The Drawmiikh is aboard this one, sir," Khamiss said.

"I am aware of that, Miss Khamiss," Sun snapped. His irritation was feigned: he really didn't mind her reminding him of things he hadn't actually forgotten, since this gave him a chance to impress listeners with the acuity of his memory.

"I want you to take charge of the Qlp party personally," he said. "I don't know what the creature is doing here, but I don't want incidents."

"Yes, sir."

"Take particular care, Khamiss."

"Very well, sir."

Her head vanished. Sun, with a happy sigh, returned to his monitors.

The burglars were talking as if they were old friends. Sun felt a grim satisfaction. If he had anything to say about it, talking was all they'd ever do.

Sun was on a mission, he considered, from God. Since the Rebellion, humanity had been asserting itself in the reaches, and had also been rediscovering its own suppressed heritage. Along with other rediscoveries—Shakspere, Congo Veiling, Sherlock Holmes, and so on—ancient philosophies had been recovered. Mr. Sun had absorbed two of these. Besides becoming an ardent Holmes fan—the Manichean duality of Holmes and Moriarity appealed to him—Sun had become an adherent of a recently excavated creed called the New Puritanism.

Refined to its essence, the New Puritanism believed that every act had its cost, that everything had to be paid for. Sin was the occasion of a cosmic imbalance, and if the sinner didn't commit some act to compensate, the Almighty would do it for him; and the Almighty didn't care who got hurt in the process—God, according to the New Puritanism, didn't much care who got squashed when the Sin Balance was sufficiently out of alignment: He'd flatten anybody, sinner and nonsinner alike.

Mr. Sun hoped, in the small matter of Allowed Burglary, to be the Almighty's instrument in the business of flattening the wicked. Fu George and Maijstral had been sinning far too long; it was time, Sun was certain, they paid for it before some innocent party did the paying for them.

Khamiss watched her superior's face fade away, replaced by a holographic ideogram meaning "may I be of assistance?" She told the machine that it couldn't, and the ideogram disappeared.

Behind her, a woodwind quartet was setting up for the arrival of the next ship. Tuning, a bassoon bubbled away.

Khamiss straightened her uniform and squared her cap, awaiting the next ship and its cargo. She was young for the amount of responsibility she bore—she had just grown her first nose-rings, which proclaimed her age as twenty-five— and she was acutely aware of the burden of Sun's trust. She was second-in-command of security at the most exclusive resort in the known universe, and she fully intended to prove worthy of the task.

She glanced down at her medal and brushed it lightly with her fingers. The Qwarism Order of Public Service (Second Class), awarded her when she had stopped a fleeing burglar and held her prisoner for the authorities.

Khamiss had been a student at the time, studying to follow her parents' footsteps as an insurance broker for the three-century-old firm of Lewis, Khotvinn, & Co. How could she have known, when she was strolling home from school and happened to notice a small hologram-shrouded figure ghosting over the wall of the Reed Jewelry building, that it was an incident that would change her life forever?

It *was* luck that she happened to be carrying a briefcase heavy with insurance forms. It *was* luck that her first swing caught the camouflaged burglar square on the head and knocked her unconscious. But still, it wasn't the capture of just *any* thief that awarded her the Order of Public Service (Second Class).

Khamiss had caught (complete with a satchel full of gemstones that included the famous Zenith Blue) none other than Alice Manderley, renowned Allowed Burglar listed third in the ratings, a burglar whom the security services of fifty worlds had been unable to apprehend. Khamiss suddenly found herself a civilization-wide celebrity. Offers of employment appeared, and some of them were too good to pass up.

The most interesting had come from Mr. Sun, who was assembling a top-notch crew of security people which would offer its combined expertise to the elite throughout the civilized stars. Sun promised quick advancement, that and commissions for some of the most exotic and influential people in the Human Constellation.

Khamiss had done well in Sun's employment, though she hadn't caught any more top-ranked Allowed Burglars. But now, on Silverside Station, she had a very good chance.

Silverside Station had been designed partly as a deterrent to Allowed Burglary. Sun, who viewed Allowed Burglars with a particularly thoroughgoing aversion, had convinced Baron Silverside that Allowed Burglary ought to be abolished, and Silverside had given Mr. Sun a free hand in designing the station's security systems.

Sun was going after the burglars with all his cunning, all his intelligence, all the techniques he had created and savored over the years. Khamiss was going to help him.

But still, Khamiss couldn't find it in her soul to pursue the matter with quite as much alacrity as her employer. Had she known it was Alice Manderley in the darksuit and not some local thug, she might, in fact, have passed the woman by. She bore the institution of Allowed Burglary no grudge, nor any of its members.

But still, duty called. And tracking the burglars, she admitted, *might* just be fun.

Holograms announced the *Viscount Cheng's* successful docking. The woodwind quartet began to play. Khamiss nodded in time to the beat, and waited for the first wave of passengers.

"You'll excuse me, ladies, I hope." Geoff Fu George gave his formal congé to Advert, the Duchess, and lastly to Pearl Woman. As he sniffed her left ear, his lips closed delicately over the dangling pearl and the sonic cutters in his white implanted incisors neatly severed the dangling link. He slipped the pearl under his tongue, smiled, and stepped across the Casino toward Miss Vanessa Runciter.

Vanessa looked up at him and gave a near-imperceptible nod. Fu George knew that she'd caught everything on the micromedia globe she was wearing in her hair.

Satisfaction welled in him like warm water from a volcanic spring. He had practiced the stunt for months, ever since he had conceived the idea of separating Pearl Woman from her trademark, in public, without her knowledge. He had been a bit clumsy at first: Vanessa had lost a part of her earlobe, and even after surgery restored her appearance Fu George had a difficult time persuading her to resume practice. But return she did, and now he could perform the trick flawlessly.

The most satisfying part of his maneuver was that, since both he and Maijstral were present at the time, Pearl Woman wouldn't know which had done it. Her temper was famous, but he doubted she'd challenge without proof.

Fu George would sell it back to her, of course, through the most discreet agent he could find, assuming of course that she bid higher than any of her fans. But he wouldn't sell the trinket before everyone in the Constellation had taken note that the Pearl had lost her trademark, and the speculation concerning who had done it reached its height. At that point the video would be released, and it would be obvious to whom should belong the credit, and the points.

The Ratings Authority gave a full ten points for style. Geoff Fu George had it in abundance.

He wasn't on top by accident. He was very good at his work.

"Maijstral. I fancy a round or two of tiles. Will you join me?"

"Certainly, your grace." Mildly surprised at her suggestion, Maijstral offered Roberta his arm. Perhaps, he thought, she was just sizing up the opposition.

"I understand the customs people here are very rigorous," Roberta said. "I hope you are not entirely inconvenienced."

"I'm on station simply for the company."

Roberta shot him a look under her lashes. "Yes? How unfortunate. I hoped we might discuss . . . business matters."

Maijstral absorbed this. His lazy green eyes glowed. "I am entirely at your disposal, madam," he said, and sat her at the tiles table

"Five a point?"

His voice betrayed a slight hesitation. "Very well," he said.

Lord Qlp *oozed* onto a concourse that echoed to the sound of a woodwind quartet.

Oozed, Khamiss thought. There was no other possible word. She tried very hard not to shudder.

Lord Qlp was one of the Drawmii, a particularly enigmatic species living almost entirely on Zynzlyp. Though the Drawmii were undoubtedly intelligent and (in their own opaque fashion) cultured, it had never been entirely established whether the Drawmii had ever *noticed* their conquest by the Khosali, or understood entirely what it meant. Very few of the Drawmii travelled off their native planet, and when they did their travels were obscure, their motives doubly so.

The Drawmii looked like glistening, eight-foot-long sea slugs. This one was green below and bright orange above, with mottled off-white warts scattered about its body. Five eyestalks sprouted along its back. It left a trail of slime as it moved.

Accompanying it was a female Khosalikh, about thirty, in the uniform of a Colonial Service diplomat. She wore a translation stud in one ear.

Khamiss stepped forward to offer her assistance and was promptly staggered by Lord Qlp's appalling odor. Her nostrils slammed shut, and she only opened them by an act of will.

This, she realized, was the down side of working with the public.

"Khamiss, ma'am," she said in Human Standard, her voice a bit denasal. "Silverside security. I have been put entirely at your service. If you could give me its lordship's documents, I will process them directly."

A cigar, she thought. If I smoke a cigar, perhaps I won't have to smell this.

"I am Lady Dosvidern," the Khosalikh said. She spoke Khosali Standard. With polite restraint, she sniffed Khamiss's ears. "I am Lord Qlp's translator and assistant."

Lord Qlp raised its front end and made a series of blurting sounds. Lady Dosvidern listened, then translated. The voice she used when translating was different: deeper, more polished but less expressive, as if she felt it wasn't her place to interpret its lordship's remarks by means of locution. Her formality verged on High Khosali without quite losing the communicative ease of Standard.

"The temporal affinities have been propitiated. They are sound," she said.

Khamiss glanced from his lordship to Lady Dosvidern and back. "I am gratified to hear it, my lord," she said. A cigar, she thought. No. Wrong. *Lots* of cigars.

Lord Qlp spoke again. Its breath made its normal odor seem pleasant. "Silverside is an appropriate contextual mode," Lady Dosvidern said. "The requirements of the continuum are clear. The Protocol of Mission demands the location of the Duchess of Benn.''

Khamiss's mind swam, but she understood the last sentence well enough. "I will see if I can locate her grace, my lord. If you will excuse me?'' She turned on her heel and marched back to one of the desks. Never had station air tasted so sweet.

She shouldered aside the customs agent at the second-class counter—the second-class passengers would have to wait—and touched the ideogram for "security central.'' Sun's holographic profile appeared above the desk. His eyes were fixed ahead of him, presumably on his monitors.

"Mr. Sun,'' she said. "Lord Qlp wishes to meet the Duchess of Benn. Can you locate her for me, please?''

The answer was immediate. "She's in the Casino, playing tiles with Maijstral.'' Mr. Sun's tone made it clear that he had no respect whatever for Roberta's scale of values.

"Thank you, sir. Would you have a robot meet me there, and bring a box of cigars?''

"I didn't know you smoked, Khamiss.''

"I have started, sir.''

Sun's expression was indifferent, yet resolute. Khamiss thought that Sun made a point of being indifferent to anything unusual, presumably in the hope this would demonstrate his own omnipotence. "As you like, Khamiss,'' he said. The hologram vanished.

Khamiss turned back to the Qlp party and saw Lady Dosvidern approaching on silent feet. While Khamiss waited she inclined her torso slightly to the left in order to peer around her ladyship and make certain that Lord Qlp wasn't up to any mischief. Apparently it was not: it was undulating slightly, perhaps with respiration, but not moving anywhere.

"Miss Khamiss,'' said her ladyship.

"Yes, my lady?"

Lady Dosvidern's voice was tactful. "Have you been provided as, ah, a full-time escort for Lord Qlp and myself?"

Khamiss was cautious. "If necessary, ma'am."

"I don't believe any such necessity exists," said her ladyship. "I have been travelling with Lord Qlp for some time. It is inactive most of the time, and although its, ah, olfactory presence can be overwhelming, it has never acted in such a way as to prove a hazard to other beings."

Relief bubbled in Khamiss's mind. "As your ladyship suggests," she said.

"And now," said Lady Dosvidern, "if I might trouble you to escort us to the Casino?"

Cigars, thought Khamiss.

"Certainly, my lady," she said.

Lord Qlp burbled a greeting as the two Khosali stepped toward him. Khamiss's nostrils clamped shut. She couldn't get them to open.

Afterward, she was denasal for hours.

"Drexler and Chalice will have everything ready by tonight," said Vanessa Runciter. She dressed in cool colors that emphasized her clear, pale skin; her hair was the color of smoke and piled on top of her head in an old-fashioned way, and she smoked a cigaret from a silver-banded obsidian holder. Her father had cornered the dither market on Khorn and left her the entire pile when he died: to others it seemed perfectly unfair that she was lovely as well as implausibly wealthy.

While waiting for Fu George to make his move, she had lost a cool four hundred novae at the markers table. Even the croupier had been impressed.

Vanessa put her arm through Fu George's. They began strolling toward an exit. "I've been making lists. We've got a lot to choose from. Kotani's diamond studs, Baroness Silverside's famous art collection, the Baron's cape, Madame la Riviere's antique necklace, jewelry of one sort or another from Lord and Lady Tvax, Colonel Thom, the Waltz twins, the Marchioness Bastwick, Adriaen, Commodore and Lady Andric . . ."

Fu George delicately raised his handkerchief to his lips, folded the pearl within it, put the handkerchief in his inside breast pocket. "And Advert," he said. "She's got a minor fortune and likes to display it."

Vanessa looked dubious. "It might be a bit dangerous, going to that quarter again."

"Ten points for style, my dear."

"True." Dubiously. She frowned as she concentrated on her list. "There's an antique store—expensive, some nice items, but nothing truly exciting. A rare book store. Drexler will have to look at that: I'm not enough of an expert. A jeweler's, but it would have considerable security. The main hotel safe."

"The Eltdown Shard," Fu George said.

Vanessa stopped in her tracks. "You're sure?"

"No. But the new Duchess is here, and this is her debut."

Vanessa took a languid puff on her cigaret as she glanced over the room. One of the many holographic ideograms for "good fortune" paraded over her head. "They had a history of the Shard on the station feed, did you notice? But perhaps that's just publicity. It's a long journey from the Empire. Providing security for that entire distance . . ."

"She can afford it."

Vanessa's eyes narrowed as she focused on the tiles table. "She's playing tiles with Maijstral. I don't like the looks of that."

"It means nothing. She is young, a social being. She conversed as pleasantly with me."

"I *still* don't like it, Geoff."

Vanessa and Maijstral had a history. Fu George, knowing this, discounted her objection and began moving in the direction of the exit once more. A Cygnus moved by on silent repellers, holding a tray of drinks in its invisible force field.

"We'll know for certain tomorrow night," Fu George said. "If she has the Shard, she'll wear it then."

"And until tomorrow?"

He thought for a moment. "The Waltz twins, I think," he said. "Both at once should be good for a few style points."

"Pardon me. I believe you have something on your carapace."

"Yes. He's got all the family titles now; he had his father declared dead a little over a year ago." Pearl Woman gave Advert a knowing look. "That was just before the new inheritance law came into effect. Maijstral saved himself a lot in taxes by getting the job done when he did."

Advert glanced over her shoulder. She could see Maijstral chatting to the Duchess as they bid their tiles. "Horrible," she said. "One hears of such things, but one never knows the people involved. It gives me a chill to look at him."

"No more a chill than Maijstral's dad got." Pearl Woman grinned and tossed her hair. Advert looked at her in horror.

"Pearl," she said. Pearl Woman looked at her, then frowned.

"What's wrong?"

Panic wailed in Advert's veins. "Pearl," she whispered desperately. *"Something's missing!"*

* * *

Mr. Paavo Kuusinen walked out of the Casino, the tip of his walking stick making a casual touch upon the mothwing carpet at every second step. He was keeping Vanessa Runciter and Geoff Fu George in sight. They seemed to be heading toward the main lounge.

A happy awareness tingled in his nerves, and he allowed himself a satisfied smile. He was pleased to discover that, of all the people in the Constellation, Fu George and Miss Runciter shared a secret with him alone.

Kuusinen knew where Pearl Woman's trademark was. He had been watching the party from the cashier's table, and had, by a stroke of fate, looked up just at the instant of the theft. Elegantly done, he had to admit.

The observation, lucky as it was, hadn't been made purely by chance. Kuusinen had a permanent, professional interest in Drake Maijstral and Geoff Fu George, and he had been watching them closely.

Unlike Roberta, he sensed something potentially catastrophic in the situation here. Silverside Station was a small place, two first-rank thieves like Maijstral and Fu George were unlikely to coexist happily, and the presence of other inflammatory characters like Pearl Woman and Kyoko Asperson wouldn't help.

For the present, however, Kuusinen was happy to possess his secret.

For a long, pleasant moment, he wondered what to do with it.

"Pardon me. I believe there's something on your carapace."

"Oh, no." Pearl Woman was appalled by the sight of the approaching mushroom-shaped hat surrounded by eight bright, bobbing media globes. The Pearl raked her fingers through her hair, drawing strands down over her left ear in hopes of concealing the empty chain. Advert clutched her other arm.

"Miss Asperson," Pearl Woman said, and bowed. She turned her head slightly, offering the globes a three-quarter profile.

Kyoko Asperson grinned up at her. "Pearl Woman," she said. The Pearl offered token sniffs; Pearl Woman tried to keep her head turned casually away. "So pleased to see you again. I believe this is Miss Advert?"

"Yes. Advert, allow me to introduce Kyoko Asperson."

"Your servant, miss."

"Yours."

"I'd be delighted to stay and chat, Miss Asperson," Pearl Woman said, "but I'm late for an appointment."

Kyoko's bright birdlike eyes flicked from one to the other.

"I understand entirely, Pearl. It was, however, Miss Advert whom I was hoping to interview."

Advert cast a cool glance at the Pearl and received a nod in return. She would cover Pearl Woman's retreat.

She took a breath and gazed into the awful loupe over Kyoko's eye. Terror touched her nerves with its delicate sable brush. "My pleasure, Miss Asperson. Shall we walk toward the lounge?"

"As you like."

Never, Advert thought, had a provincial accent sounded so ominous.

"Zoot! I hardly recognized you."

A surprised reply. "Sir?"

"Without your jacket, I mean."

"Oh. It's not really suitable for this lounge, I thought."

"I suppose. But I really expected to see you in it. My name's Dolfuss, by the way. Your obedient."

"Yours."

"Could I have your autograph?"

"Honored, sir."

"I was very disappointed Nichole isn't going to be here. She's one of my biggest fans. I mean—well, you know what I mean."

"I liked her last play very much."

"Saw that. Didn't care for it myself. Didn't seem to be the real *Nichole*."

A short beat's pause. "Rather thought that was the point."

"Well. Shouldn't keep you. Thanks so much."

Zoot watched the man bustling away. His ears were down, and his diaphragm spasmed twice in resignation. Were his public *all* like this?

Perhaps, he thought guiltily, his advance people were right, and he should have worn the jacket.

Too late now. He adjusted the laces on his (perfectly conventional) dinner jacket and strolled toward the lounge.

"Don't alter your arrangements in any way," Maijstral said. "Just keep me informed of what they are."

"At present," said Roberta Altunin, the Duchess of Benn, "my arrangements consist of six very large Khosali with guns."

"Presumably they will not be on duty tomorrow night."

"No. They won't." She looked at him with a smile and clicked a pair of tiles together. "This is fun, you know."

Maijstral's expression was opaque. "Sixteen, your grace," he said, and placed a tile.

Roberta's smile broadened. "I was waiting for that." She turned over tiles. "There's thirty-two, and forty-eight, and sixty-four. And here's the Pierrot, so that's doubled to a hundred twenty-eight."

Maijstral surveyed the table and let out a long breath.

"I'm afraid that's consummation." He turned over his remaining tiles. Resigned to his loss, he picked up a polychip from its rack, then touched to its smooth black surface a stylus that permanently rearranged its molecules. He wrote the amount, an ideogram that stood for "I.O.U.," then pressed his thumbprint to the back.

"Your grace," he said, offering it.

She accepted it. "I'm very good at things I care about," she said. "One of them is winning."

"I am beginning to understand that."

"Another game?"

Maijstral smiled thinly. "I think not, your grace. People in my profession shouldn't use up their quota of luck in games of chance."

She laughed. "I suppose not. Good lord. What's that smell?"

People in the Casino began exclaiming and pointing. Maijstral leaned back in surprise at what he saw over Roberta's right shoulder. Roberta turned around to observe the astonishing sight of Lord Qlp oozing toward her, accompanied by two Khosali, a tall, expressionless female with a translation stud and a small female in the uniform of station security. The smaller of the pair was craning her head, turning left and right. An expression of relief entered her face. "Robot!" she called, and waved a hand.

Lord Qlp undulated to Roberta's side and made a squelching noise. She tried not to shrink back from the appalling smell.

"Your grace," said the tall Khosalikh, "allow me to present Lord Qlp." She was speaking High Khosali.

"Your servant," returned Roberta, denasal. She looked for ears to sniff and found none. She made an approximation and dipped her head twice. To inhale at all required a steely act of will that excited Maijstral's admiration.

The tall Khosalikh spoke. "I am Lady Dosvidern, Lord Qlp's translator and companion."

"My lady."

Lord Qlp lifted its forward half and burbled briefly. Lady Dosvidern folded her hands and translated. "The Protocols are in accord. Movement is propitious. The time of delivery has arrived."

Roberta looked at Maijstral for help. His ears flicked back and forth, indicating his own bafflement. "How nice," Roberta finally said.

Lord Qlp lowered its end to the floor and made loud, moist noises. Roberta felt warm breath on her ankles and drew them back. The Khosalikh in the security uniform, thankfully standing away, was lighting a cigar with a relieved expression.

Something thudded onto the carpet. "Oh," said Roberta. Lord Qlp had just disgorged a hard, moist, glistening lump, about the size of two fists placed side-by-side.

Roberta stared at it. Lord Qlp reared up again and made a loud bellowing noise which Lady Dosvidern declined to translate.

There was a long pause. Maijstral observed a general movement toward the Casino's exits. He longed to join the crowd, but knew it would seem impolite to leave Roberta in the lurch.

It apparently occurred to Roberta that Lord Qlp was waiting for something. She looked up at it.

"Thank you," she said.

Without saying anything further, Lord Qlp turned and began to move toward the exit. It was followed by Lady Dosvidern and the security guard, puffing smoke.

Roberta called to a robot. "Please have this . . . object . . . delivered to my room," she said. The robot lifted the thing in its beams and moved toward an exit.

Maijstral stood and offered an arm. "Perhaps," he said, "we might look for some fresh air."

Roberta rose. "Thank you," she said.

"You handled that very well, your grace."

Roberta was surprised. "You think so? I just . . . reacted."

"Your instincts, if you don't mind my saying so, were impeccable."

"Well," she said, putting her arm through his, "let's hope this sort of thing doesn't go on all the rest of my stay."

The Cygnus delivered its burden into the reluctant hands of Roberta's lady's maid, and then began its return to the Casino.

On the way, it suddenly stopped, turned toward the wall, and used its beams to manipulate several hidden catches. The wall swung open, revealing a passage. The robot entered.

Alarms called urgently from Mr. Sun's console. He scanned his board and noticed that both Maijstral and Geoff Fu George had left the areas covered by his monitors. A tight smile moved across Mr. Sun's countenance. He pressed the ideogram for "general announcement." It was time for the Almighty to get a little of His own back.

"Strawberry Section, Access Tunnel Twelve." His voice was triumphant. "Watsons," he said, "the game's afoot!"

CHAPTER 2

K hosali High Custom allows people, within certain well-defined limits, to steal for a living; and the societies of the Human Constellation, for lack of anything better after several thousand years of Khosali rule, follow High Custom. The Constellation Practices Authority exists for the purpose of altering High Custom in the image of redefined humanity, and the reason the Authority is necessary is that the Human Constellation lacks the self-generating regulatory apparatus possessed by Khosali custom.

The Empire's regulatory apparatus is, in fact, the Imperial family. Whatever is done by the Pendjalli, and in particular by the Pendjalli Emperor, exists *de jure* and exclusively within the context of High Custom. The Emperor himself can do no other: his behavior *dictates* High Custom.

The accepted reason for Allowed Burglary is that High Custom, besides reflecting the Khosali reverence for tradition, high-mindedness, and idealism, should also reflect another, more occult aspect of Khosali character, namely their (largely unacknowledged) admiration for individuals of low repute: thieves, charlatans, murderers, adulterers, self-slaughterers, drunks. Social xenologists have noted that High Custom not only allows these individuals to exist within the context of accepted society, but regulates their behavior, thus minimizing its negative effect upon society at large. Thus is a killer transformed into a duellist, a depressive into an idealistic suicide, an adulterer into an adventurer, a char-latan into an entertainer, and a burglar into a sportsman.

The regrettable truth is that these acknowledged reasons for Allowed Burglary are either window dressing or *post facto* rationalization. The real reason for this one particular aspect of High Custom is that Differs XXIII, the last Mon-tiyy Emperor, was a kleptomaniac, driven by some inner compulsion to lift small, valuable objects from the apart-ments of his friends and ministers. Once this was observed, kleptomania and the Imperial ideal had to somehow be rec-onciled in the minds of his subjects: somehow Montiyy honor had to be preserved. The result was Allowed Bur-glary, permitted and regulated through the Imperial Sporting Commission under the benevolent sponsorship of His Im-perial Majesty. Differs graciously withdrew his name from consideration in the rankings; and after knowledge of his thievery became semipublic (though never officially ac-knowledged), the negative effects of a breach of Imperial honor were buffered. In another victory for High Custom and the Imperial bureaucracy, an Imperial embarrassment had become, instead, a new fashion, and in time an industry.

One wonders if Differs' functionaries could have antic-ipated the results of their little effort at damage control: burglars recording their crimes so as to sell the recordings to the media; thieves making endorsements of alarm sys-tems, shoes, jewelry, and nightwear; the rise of theft as a popular entertainment comparable to portball or hand vol-leys.

But that is a fact of existence: minor actions can have major consequences. An offhand remark at a party can end in two people facing each other with pistols, Imperial idio-syncracy can result in the expansion of bureaucracy and the rise of a minor industry, the abstraction of a bit of nacre dangling from a chain can change the lives of everyone involved.

Just watch.

"Mr. Maijstral."

"Mr. Dolfuss."

Dolfuss straightened, adjusted his appalling jacket. In spite of the jacket he now seemed dignified, poised, almost elegant. He even gave an impression of being thinner. "Thus far it's been a delight, sir," he said. "I've no idea when I've enjoyed myself more. Oh." He reached into a pocket. "My room key," he said. "The doorplate's keyed to my prints, but I suppose you won't want it to register your own."

"No. I rather suppose not." Maijstral pocketed the key. "Thank you, sir."

"See you later, Mr. Maijstral."

"Mr. Dolfuss."

Maijstral walked to Dolfuss's room, picked up the sample case that waited in the closet, then continued down the corridor to his own room. He declined to thumbprint open the lock—such things could be used by station security to keep track of people—and instead used his own key.

Maijstral's four-room suite was decorated in shades of brown. A holographic waterfall, silver and gold and bright diamond, cascaded down the center of the front room. Gregor Norman sat behind it, his feet on a small table, a histick in his mouth. His hands beat a complex rhythm on his thighs. He straightened as Maijstral came in, looked at the case in Maijstral's hand, and grinned.

Maijstral put the case on the table. "I hope you won't mind opening this," he said.

"Only too." Meaning, only too pleased. Gregor touched the locks, then opened the case. He began unloading black boxes, alarm disruptors, dark suits, communication equipment, holographic projectors.

Gregor told the room to play a Vivaldi woodwind concerto adapted for Khosali instruments. Though baroque music was a passion with him, and he listened to it whenever possible, the concerto now had another function: Gregor wanted a lot of background noise in case Maijstral wanted to talk business. Sometimes, he had discovered, people were crude enough to put listening devices in their rooms.

Roman, Maijstral's Khosali servant, appeared on silent feet. He was tall for a Khosali—had he been human, he would have been a giant. He was forty-six years old, and his family had served Maijstral's for generations.

Maijstral looked happily at Roman. Roman was the only constant in his inconstant life. Roman combined the benevolent functions of parent, cook, valet, and (when necessary) leg breaker. In short, Roman was home. Life without Roman was unthinkable.

Roman took Maijstral's guns and knife, then unlaced his jacket and trousers. High Custom insisted on clothing that was difficult of access: it demonstrated the need for servants, or at least for cleverly programmed robots. Roman took the jacket and placed it on a hanger. Maijstral flexed his arms, rotated them, then stripped off his empty shoulder holster, sat down on a chair, and held up his feet. Roman drew off his buskins and trousers.

"We shall have to alter our schedule, gentlemen," Maijstral said. He planted his feet on the floor, dug his toes into the carpet. "Tonight's plan may proceed, but we should postpone our plans for tomorrow."

Gregor had strapped on goggles that allowed him to perceive energy field formations. He looked up at Maijstral with silver insect eyes. "Something has come up, sir?" The hi-stick bobbled in his mouth as he spoke.

Maijstral paused, enjoying the suspense. "The Eltdown Shard is onstation," he said. "Tomorrow night we're going to steal it."

There was a moment of silence, filled only by the whisper of air through the vents.

Roman folded Maijstral's trousers, the creases sharp as a knife. He put the trousers on a hanger.

"Very good, sir," he said. Which was Roman all over.

"With both of them in this small a place, what do you think of the possibility of a duel?"

"Miss Asperson, I hope they blow their brains out."

Paavo Kuusinen, pursuing the scent of mystery, followed Geoff Fu George and Vanessa Runciter to their suite. He walked past their door, stepped down a side corridor, and paused a moment, frowning. His cane tapped in time to his thoughts.

The period immediately following a theft by a registered burglar was the most dangerous for the thief: if he could hang onto his loot past midnight of the second day, it became his legal property; but in the interim he could be arrested for stealing. Furthermore, he had to keep the take in his possession, at his residence or on his person.

What would Fu George do with the pearl? Kuusinen wondered. Keep it in his room, or on his body?

A Cygnus Advanced Object, its black carapace reflecting each overhead spotlight as it glided down the hallway, lowered a covered tray before Fu George's door, politely knocked with its force fields, then moved on down the hall. Kuusinen ducked down his side corridor and sensed, rather than saw, the robot cross the corridor behind him. He heard Fu George's door open, then close.

Kuusinen hesitated, tapping his cane on the carpet. The robot had gone into a dead-end corridor, and he wondered why. Then he turned and retraced his steps.

He couldn't help himself. He was in the grip of a compulsion.

Paavo Kuusinen was the sort of man who was nagged at by irregularities. It wasn't that he disapproved of them, precisely: he didn't care whether or not things were irregular; he just wanted to know why. In this regard he was unlike, for example, Mr. Sun, who would in the same circumstances have done his best to make things regular again. But making discoveries was a compulsion for Kuusinen. Sometimes his compulsion aided him in his work; sometimes—as now— it was purely an interference.

He looked around the corner. An access panel was open in the wall of the dead-end corridor. The robot had obviously gone inside on some errand. Perhaps the access tunnel connected to another corridor somewhere.

Mystery solved. Kuusinen shrugged and began walking toward his own room. It was time to change for dinner.

It wasn't until he saw three uniformed security guards rushing up the corridor, each with hand on gun, that Kuusinen began to wonder.

Robot, he thought. Guards. Secret doors in the walls. Fu George and a covered tray.

Kuusinen sighed. He was beginning to get that nagging feeling again.

The soft sounds of a Snail concerto hung suspended from soft aural bands, filling the room. Another yellow light blinked on one of Gregor's boxes. He smirked. "Another Advanced Object in the walls," he said. This was the third light blinking on the box, the third in a row of twelve.

Roman was lacing Maijstral into a pair of trousers. The trousers were soft black; the laces were yellow. Roman's fingers moved deftly.

"I spoke briefly with Dolfuss," Maijstral said. He spoke Khosali Standard. "He's enjoying himself."

"I spent the voyage with him, in second class," Roman said, "and he never broke character once."

"I only hope no one recognizes him."

"It's been years since *Fin de Siecle*. He was a young man then; he's changed a great deal since. And the play toured only in the Empire."

"Until it was banned." Gregor, still bent over his equipment, spoke without looking up.

"Dolfuss shouldn't have been quite so ambiguous about the Emperor Principle. If the Empire had won the Rebellion, the play might have been taken as constructive social criticism. But the Empire was touchy about the defeat, and the play merely rubbed salt in the wound." Maijstral stretched a leg, tried a tentative dance step. "A little tight over the left hip, Roman," he said.

"Yes, sir." Roman began to rethread.

"Dolfuss has learned to make his points more subtly since, but still no one performs his work. A pity. I think this venture will enable him to mount his own production."

Maijstral looked up at the holographic waterfall. The liquid was unwaterlike, a quicksilver thing, falling like a slow, magic fantasy. "I wonder what Fu George is planning," he said.

Gregor, still wearing his goggles, seemed a particularly disreputable insect as he looked up. "He'll *have* to go for the Shard, won't he?'' he said. "I mean, Ralph Adverse *died* for it years ago, and so did Sinn Junior, and that made it priceless. And no one's stolen it for forty years. Fu George's name would live forever if he got it.''

"And survived,'' said Roman.

Maijstral watched insubstantial liquid tumbling over an insubstantial rim. "If it were me, I'd try for it,'' he said.

Gregor grinned. "It *is* you, boss.''

Maijstral's head tilted as he considered this. The waterfall spilled in slow accompaniment to the Snail. "So it is,'' he decided. He tested his trousers again. "Good. Thank you, Roman.''

Roman brought a jacket out. Maijstral put his arms in it. Roman began working with laces again.

Maijstral reached into the jacket pocket, took out a deck of cards with his right hand. He fanned them one-handed. The deuce of crowns jumped from the fan to his left hand. Then the throne of bells. Duchess of hearts.

"Vanessa Runciter is here,'' he said.

"So I understand, sir.''

"It's a small world.''

"Could you raise your left arm, please? I'm having trouble fitting the holster.''

Maijstral lifted his arm. Cards spilled upward from right hand to left, defying gravity.

"I wonder,'' he said, "if Zoot's jacket would be worth a try?''

"I think not, sir. Our own darksuits are doubtless more advanced.''

Maijstral sighed. "I suppose you're right. He'll probably be wearing it, anyway.''

Another display lit on Gregor's machine. Two blinked off. "Two burrowers,'' he reported, "still in their holes.''

* * *

"It was *awful*, Pearl. Just awful."

Pearl Woman gazed at a rotating hologram of herself. She had one of Advert's cloche hats pulled down over her ears, and the effect was hideous. She pulled the hat off and snarled.

"She asked me about the Diadem." Advert rattling on. "I don't know what I said. I just babbled on. I know I'm going to embarrass everyone."

"I'll have to plead illness for tonight," Pearl Woman said. "It's going to cause comment, but I'll have to do it."

"She asked me about your duel with Etienne. I didn't even *know* you then. But I did say I thought his eyeglass looked silly. And that the Diadem already had a duel that year, and that his timing lacked finesse." Advert laughed. "And *then* I said that Nichole's new play was unsuitable for her, that a Diadem role should have more grandeur. So maybe Asperson will quote me there. That would be lucky."

"I'll need you to go to the jewelry shops on Red Level," Pearl Woman said. "Find a substitute stone. It might fool them for a while. If I'm cornered, I can say the real one has been hidden, so it won't be stolen." She pounded a fist into her palm. "But then it would seem as if I were *afraid* of them."

"But I know I said something embarrassing about Rip and his friend—what's her name? Something about the way she laughs all the time."

"Are you listening, Advert?"

"Oh. Yes. I'm sorry. What did you want?"

Pearl Woman's eyes narrowed. "You should learn not to ask that sort of question, Advert. The answer might not be to your taste."

* * *

Another light glowed on Mr. Sun's console. Sun's nerves tautened. His blue heaven was beginning to smell of sweat and annoyance.

Sun touched an ideogram. "My lord," he said.

"Mr. Sun." Baron Silverside's anger translated very well to hologram. He was a compact, broad-shouldered man, a former amateur wrestler. Burnsides flared on either side of his face, a pale brown halo. One hand was visible, stroking the whiskers.

"What," the Baron demanded, "is the meaning of all these alerts? Have your people gone mad?"

Sun feigned surprise. "Sir?" he asked.

"They are running about the halls carrying guns while my guests are walking to dinner. I have been receiving complaints."

Both hands were stroking the whiskers now. Sun calmed his nerves. He was still the spider in its lair, ready to pounce. There had been a few problems: nothing he could not deal with. "Beg pardon, your lordship," Sun said. "We seem to have been receiving false alarms from the utility tunnels."

"You assured me," the Baron said, "the security system was infallible. And that your guards would be inconspicuous."

Sun could feel sweat prickling his forehead. "Sir," he said. "Begging your pardon, but I said *almost* . . ."

The Baron froze him with a look. He was twisting little lovelocks around his forefingers. "Sun," he said, "I will have no more of this. You have caught no burglars, and you have terrified my guests."

"My people are eager, of course," Sun said. "We have been drilling for a very long time. But I shall order them to be more . . . relaxed."

"Kyoko Asperson is here, Sun," the Baron said. "She

would dearly love to report that I have a fool for head of security." His eyes turned to fire. *"Do not give her that opportunity, Sun."*

"Yes, my lord."

"That's all."

"Yes, my lord."

The ideogram for "may I be of assistance?" replaced the Baron's features. Sun snarled and told his console to turn it off.

Another alarm cried out. Sun's finger hovered over the ideogram for "general announcement," hesitated, then stabbed down.

"Another alarm," he said. "Watsons, let's *walk* to this one, shall we?"

"Ah. Zoot. We were wondering if you were indisposed."

"Marquess. Marchioness."

The Marchioness Kotani was a young, dark-haired woman with wide, tilted eyes, a full, pouting lower lip, and a distinctive expression that was quite sullen yet in some inexpressible way attractive. Before her marriage, she'd been Lady Janetha Gorman, the daughter of an old and quite penniless Imperialist family; she had earned a living as a model and made periodic, if unsuccessful, forays into acting. Now that she was married, she had given up both modeling and acting. Even Kotani knew better than to use her in one of his plays.

"I expected to see you in your jacket," she said as she sniffed Zoot's ears. A choker of matched glowstones shone at her throat.

"Not for dinner, I think," Zoot said. He smiled, tongue lolling from his muzzle.

"One would have thought the Diadem would have insisted," said the Marchioness.

"There are still a few things," Zoot said stiffly, "in which I have a say."

"Bravo, Zoot," said the Marquess. His foot tapped the white carpet in brief applause. "Don't let 'em push you around. I speak from experience."

"I'm still disappointed," the Marchioness said. "You shall have to model the jacket for me."

Zoot inclined his head. "I should be most happy, milady."

Kotani cocked an eye in the direction of one of the entrances. "Here is Fu George. Take care with that necklace, my dear. I should hate to have to shoot the man over it. And I'd hate even more to have him shoot *me*."

Geoff Fu George gave everyone a bow, sniffs, two fingers. From Kotani and Zoot he received one finger apiece; from the Marchioness, three.

"My compliments, my lady," he said, concealing his surprise. "The glowstones suit your eyes perfectly."

"Thank you, sir. The compliment means all the more coming from someone of your undoubted expertise."

"Perhaps, sir," said Zoot, "you might enlighten us as to the alarms that seem to have sent the security people into an uproar."

Fu George's ears twitched in bafflement. "I am as surprised as you are, sir," he said. "It's nothing to do with me. Ah," he said, addressing a Cygnus. "Bring me a cold rink, please."

"Yes, sir."

"Possibly it's Maijstral tripping a few alarms," Fu George said. His voice turned dubious. "But even *he's* not quite *that* clumsy, surely." He smiled at the Marchioness.

"D'you know there's a Drawmiikh onstation?" Kotani said. "A Drawmii lord, no less."

"I believe," Zoot said, "that any Drawmii sufficiently

adventurous to leave its planet of origin and participate in the life of the Empire is almost always ennobled. It's a way of encouraging the others.''

Kotani smiled. ''Unsuccessful, I suppose.''

''I believe so, Marquess. There are only a handful at any time.''

The Marchioness turned her bored eyes on Zoot. ''I wonder if we'll see the creature at dinner.''

''I hope not, dearest,'' said Kotani. ''It created quite a sensation in the Casino a few hours ago. Its lordship was quite noisy and, I am given to understand, it stank.''

''The Drawmii have a very distinctive odor, or so I'm told,'' Zoot said. ''I gather it takes getting used to.''

''Media alert,'' Kotani said, seeing a pointed cap surrounded by floating silver balls. ''I've been through it already; I beg your leave. Dearest,'' offering his arm.

''Milord.''

Kyoko Asperson had changed for dinner: she wore baggy yellow trousers, a white shirt, a scarlet jacket, soft boots with gold tassels. If she weren't so short she could have been used as a beacon.

''Zoot. Mr. Fu George.'' Zoot, who like all Khosali had a very rigid spine, had to bend an uncomfortable distance to sniff her ears.

''I reckoned you would be wearing your jacket.''

Zoot's diaphragm pounded in annoyance. How often was he going to have to go through this? ''Madam,'' he said, ''surely not for dinner.''

''Meals, in some restaurants,'' said Fu George, ''may be considered unexplored territory. In that case, Zoot's jacket would be perfectly appropriate.''

Media globes rotated, pointed in Fu George's direction. ''I wonder,'' Kyoko said, ''if you were surprised to hear that Drake Maijstral would be here?''

Geoff Fu George smiled. "I don't believe I've given it much thought."

"You're both in the first rank of your profession."

Fu George's head tipped; his eyes sparkled. The message was clear, though unvoiced: *If you say so.*

"Do you anticipate a duel between the two of you?"

A laugh. "We are speaking of a metaphorical duel, I take it?"

"Whatever kind of duel you like."

The famous Fu George smile became a little forced. "I am here only for the view, and to see my friends. What Maijstral's plans may be, I cannot say."

"So you concede any contest to Maijstral."

The smile was back, and genuine. "My dear Miss Asperson," he said, "I concede nothing at all." He sniffed her. "Your servant."

Reasonably pleased with himself, Fu George moved away. A man in a green coat approached him. The man had a hand over one eye, and was blinking furiously with the other.

"Beg pardon, sir," the man said, "but may I borrow your handkerchief for a moment? I have something in my eye."

Fu George touched his breast pocket, felt the pearl still secure in the handkerchief, and hesitated. "My apologies, sir, I neglected to bring one."

"Sorry to bother you. I think the thing may be out, anyway." He stumbled away.

So, Paavo Kuusinen thought as he removed the hand from his eye. Fu George still has the pearl.

Interesting.

Maijstral could feel his deck of cards riding comfortably above his right hip in a pocket tailored just for them. The feeling was a pleasant one, far more pleasant than the gun under one arm, the knife up his sleeve, the other gun up the other sleeve. The cards were a reminder of pleasure; the hardware, of necessity.

A Cygnus approached. "Pardon me, robot," Maijstral said. "Can you direct me to the main lounge?"

The robot's voice was unusually resonant. Troxan engineering, Maijstral assumed as he reached into his pocket and palmed the programming needle.

"Pardon me," he said. "I think there is something on your carapace."

"Hullo, Maijstral." A familiar voice. "Nice of you to dust the robots."

Maijstral almost lost his grip on the needle. He straightened and returned it to his pocket.

"Hello, Vanessa."

Miss Runciter sniffed him, offered him three fingers. He gave her two in return. Her eyebrows rose.

"I thought we were old friends, Maijstral."

"I confess that I don't know what we are, Vanessa. I haven't seen you in almost three years. You left a bit suddenly, as I recall." He offered his arm, and then wondered how reluctant the offer was. "Going to dinner?"

"Yes. Thank you."

She was wearing a jet gown covered with dark red brocade that was shot with silver thread. She wore emerald earrings, a gold chain on one wrist. She looked very well indeed. "I keep thinking, Maijstral," she said, "we left some things unsaid."

"I doubt, Vanessa, that any of them need saying now."

She looked at him. "It's that way, is it?"

Smoothly. "I don't know what you mean."

"As you like." Her voice became reflective. "I don't like the way Laurence is playing you in the vids, Drake. Anaya was far smoother."

"I don't watch them."

"Still?"

"Still."

A brief silence, broken by Vanessa. "I lost a small fortune at markers this afternoon. I hope to win it back tonight."

"I lost at tiles."

"More than you could afford? Or is that still a problem?"

"It's not a problem," Maijstral said. "I've come into money recently. But it was more than I planned to lose."

"You should only play cards. If you lose you can start to cheat."

Maijstral smiled. "I could have cheated with the tiles. It's not as easy, but it can be done."

Her eyes were knowing. "But you wanted the Duchess to win. Do you think you can get closer to the Shard that way?"

"Perhaps," he said, "I merely wanted to get closer to the Duchess."

Vanessa was silent for a moment. Maijstral wondered at her peculiar vanity, that she was offended when men she had discarded were not faithful to her.

Ideograms announced the White Room. The orchestra was playing the same Snail concerto that Gregor had played in Maijstral's suite.

"I see Fu George. I'll see you later, Maijstral."

"Your servant."

They clasped hands, two fingers each. Maijstral repressed a shudder. He reflected that in a lifetime of dealing with thieves, fences, and other people little to be admired, Vanessa Runciter was the first and only sociopath he had ever met.

He watched her move away, then scanned the room and saw a man in a green coat walking toward him. He looked at the man in surprised recognition.

"Mr. Maijstral."

"Mr. Kuu—"

"Kuusinen, sir." Exchanging sniffs. "We met only briefly. I'm flattered you remember me."

"I have been meaning to thank you, sir," Maijstral said. "You were of some assistance, back on Peleng, to certain friends of mine."

Kuusinen smiled pleasantly. "That, sir? I was simply on hand at the right time. Think nothing of it."

"Nevertheless, sir, you are a keen observer."

"Yes, I confess that," Kuusinen said. "I have a . . . facility. My eyes are always detecting little puzzles for my brain to solve."

"That is a lucky talent."

"There seem to be puzzles here," Kuusinen said. "In this room."

"Has your mind solved them?"

Kuusinen's tone was light. "Possibly. We will know for certain if Pearl Woman fails to appear for dinner."

Maijstral looked at the other man.

"Have you heard that she won't?"

"No. But if she were not to appear, that would be a puzzle, would it not?"

Maijstral's heavy-lidded eyes narrowed. "Yes," he said softly. "It would."

"Mr. Fu George seems very conscious of something in his breast pocket. A small something, I think. He keeps putting his hand there, then withdrawing it. Another mystery. Perhaps the two are connected."

There was a tingling in Maijstral's nerves. He was not certain whether this was a warning or the voice of opportunity. "Have you observed any other puzzles, Mr. Kuusinen?" he asked.

Kuusinen was ordering a drink from a robot. When he

turned back to Maijstral, he smiled and said, "Something odd about the robots. I haven't decided what, just yet."

Maijstral's tingling turned cold. "No doubt the solution will come to you, sir."

"Or to my brain."

"Your brain. Yes." Maijstral's eyes, as if on cue, scanned the room again, fastened on Kotani and his wife. "I hope you will excuse me, Mr. Kuusinen," he said. "I see some old friends."

"Certainly, Mr. Maijstral."

"Your servant."

"Your very obedient."

Maijstral was very glad to get away. He felt Kuusinen's abnormally observant eyes on him all the way across the room.

"What do you think of the duel between Drake Maijstral and Geoff Fu George?"

Zoot gazed fixedly into the silver loupe over Kyoko Asperson's eye. "I don't think of it at all, I'm afraid."

"You don't follow the burglar standings?"

"It is not my preferred sport."

He was hoping, a bit wistfully, to lead the discussion toward portball; then he could lay down a smoke screen of chatter about portfires, snookerbacks, ridge plays, and the like. Kyoko Asperson refused to be distracted.

"Would you support the rumored action of the Constellation Practices Authority in trying to do away with Allowed Burglary altogether?"

"I am not familiar with that body's deliberations."

The journalist frowned for a moment. Zoot, for lack of anything else to do, continued gazing into her loupe.

"You are the only Khosali member of the Human Diadem," she said. Zoot readied himself: this was the prelude to the sorts of questions he got asked all the time. "Do you have any consciousness of being something of an experiment?"

"None," he said. "I am conscious primarily of the honor."

"Doesn't it handicap you? Don't you find your behavior constrained by your knowing that you are the only representative of your species in the Three Hundred?"

A palpable hit, but Zoot managed to avoid wincing. "Members of the Diadem excel at being themselves," he said. "Being myself is all I ever intended to do from the start."

"An admirable goal," Kyoko said. "If you can pull it off."

The Marquess Kotani cast a sympathetic glance in Zoot's direction. "Asperson will have to work damn hard to make that interview interesting," he said. "Zoot's share is slipping badly."

"I confess *I* don't find him interesting," said the Marchioness.

Kotani touched his mustache, then lifted his chin, gazing toward a nonexistent horizon and giving the Marchioness the benefit of his profile. "Men of action are so often dull in person, don't you think?" he said. "It's the ability to deal with things in a straightforward way. Admirable in its fashion, but hardly suitable for the Diadem."

"Here's Drake Maijstral." Her tilted eyes betrayed a glimmer of interest.

"My lord."

"Maijstral. Have you met my wife?"

"Honored, madam." Maijstral offered a finger in the handclasp and got three in return. He covered his surprise and smiled at Kotani.

"Mr. Maijstral," the Marchioness said. "We were just discussing men of action."

"I hope I am not included in their number," Maijstral said. "Being in essence a lazy man, I try to avoid action whenever possible."

"There," Kotani said. "My point exactly. And Maijstral's not dull."

"Surely not." The Marchioness looked at him through tilted eyes. "I'm pleased to find you taller than I thought, from seeing you only in video. I don't think Laurence's impersonation of you on vid does you justice, by the way."

"Is it an impersonation? Or is it just Laurence? I've never seen him, so I can't tell."

"Maijstral looks shorter because he's so compact," Kotani said. "He's very coordinated, moves well." He smiled at Maijstral. "It's a quality we share. People often think I appear shorter than my true height."

The Marchioness looked at Maijstral, then at her husband. "I don't think Maijstral's like you at all, Kotani."

"In that respect, dearest, he is."

"Not at all."

Kotani frowned minutely. "I think Asperson is heading this way. That woman is relentless." He held out his arm. "Shall we stroll toward the dining room?"

"If you like."

"Maijstral, we'll talk another time. When a certain person isn't eavesdropping."

"Sir. Madam."

Maijstral's heart sank. He was alone with Asperson, her next victim.

Zoot took three careful breaths and felt his tension begin to ebb. Asperson, apparently disappointed by his noncom-

mittal answers, had gone in search of someone more oblig-
ing, or at any rate scandal-ridden or controversial.

Zoot reached in a pocket, took out a cigaret, licked the
filter with his long, red tongue, and stuck the cigaret in his
muzzle. He didn't smoke often in public—he fancied himself an example to others, and didn't want to encourage bad
habits—but Asperson had him rattled.

Being himself, he had told Asperson, was all he ever
intended to do. That was all the Diadem had ever asked
of him. What he had never realized was that he would
have to do it in public, in a grand, theatrical fashion, and
to make it all seem natural and spontaneous and, worse,
interesting.

Back when Zoot was leading his team in the Pioneer
Corps, he hadn't had to worry about being interesting. The
perils he faced were all the interest he, or anyone else,
needed.

Zoot patted his pockets, looking for a cigaret lighter. He'd
left it in his other jacket, the famous one. He stepped toward
the nearest robot, intending to ask it for a light, but saw a
tall female Khosalikh standing beneath the giant diamond,
smoking a cigaret. He approached.

"Beg pardon, ma'am, but do you have a light?"

"Certainly." Her voice was clipped in a somewhat old-
fashioned way. She produced a lighter. "You are Zoot, are
you not?"

"Yes, madam."

"I am Lady Dosvidern."

They sniffed one another. Lady Dosvidern smelled of
soap and a strong perfume. There was no hand-clasping,
either, ridiculous unsanitary habit that it was.

"I am pleased," Lady Dosvidern said, "to see how you
look in proper clothes."

Zoot kept his mouth from dropping open only by a sheer act of will. He looked at her.

"You *are?*" he asked.

"Were you surprised to find Geoff Fu George onstation?"

Maijstral gazed down at Kyoko Asperson's malevolent silver loupe. "On reflection," he said, "no."

"So you were surprised at first, then?"

Maijstral considered this. "No," he said, "I don't believe I was."

"Fu George is rated in first place by the Imperial Sporting Commission. You are rated seventh—"

"Sixth. Marquess Hottinn has been slipping since his incarceration."

"Sixth." Her remaining eye was bright. "Then my question is even more relevant. With the two of you here onstation, do you anticipate a duel between the two of you?"

Maijstral gave a brief laugh. "I am here only for the view, and the company."

"Fu George said the same thing. In almost the same words."

Maijstral smiled thinly. "I don't believe I'm surprised at that, either."

"So you concede any contest to Fu George."

"I am not in Fu George's class, Miss Asperson. A contest, to be any fun at all, must be between equals." He looked over the heads of the crowd, saw the back of Fu George's unmistakable blond mane, and next to him, full-face, Vanessa Runciter. She was laughing and gesturing with a cigaret holder. Her emerald earrings winked at him across the room. His ears went back.

"It's been a mixed year for you, hasn't it, Maijstral?"

The question drew him back to the interview. "How so?" he asked.

"Professionally, you've done well. Though the videos haven't yet been released, the Sporting Commission has advanced your rating. Your book on card manipulation has been well reviewed. Yet you've had a tragedy in the family, and your personal life has suffered a certain well-publicized disappointment."

She fell silent. Maijstral gazed at her with noncommital green eyes. "Pardon me, Miss Asperson," he said. "Was that a question?"

A grim smile settled into her lips. "If you like, I'll ask a proper one. Nichole left you for a Lieutenant Navarre, and he is now her personal manager. Have you any comment on her subsequent career?"

"I wish Nichole every success," said Maijstral. "She deserves it."

"Have you seen her new play?"

"I have seen recordings. I think she's magnificent."

"That's very generous of you. Yet here on Silverside, you have encountered another old flame. With Miss Runciter here in the company of Fu George, and Nichole's success on everyone's lips, aren't there a few too many sad reminders present?"

"Nichole is a dear friend. And Miss Runciter is from a long time ago."

As he spoke he heard, from across the room, a woman's laugh. He looked up, saw Vanessa looking at him. Their eyes met, and she lifted her glass to him. He nodded to her, and reached a mental resolution.

Damn Kuusinen's eyes, he thought. And his other parts, too.

He'd do it.

"Lord Qlp is inactive now," Lady Dosvidern said. "The Drawmii have five brains, you know, each with one eye and one ear. They spend a lot of time not moving, just talking to themselves. Crosstalk, we call it.''

"I believe I'd heard something of the sort. That their interior life was somewhat complex.''

"It makes being Lord Qlp's companion a little easier. I should have dinnertime to myself, and most of the evening, before Lord Qlp grows restless again.''

"I should be honored, my lady, to take you in to dinner.''

She smiled, her tongue lolling. "Thank you, sir. It would be my pleasure.''

People talked without sound. The orchestra sawed away without any aural effect. Clear privacy screens, Maijstral reflected, are a wonderful device for creating inadvertent comedy.

"Gregor.''

"Yes, boss?''

"Is Roman there? I want you both in the White Room as soon as possible.''

"Something's up?''

"I'm going to do an unassisted crosstouch, and I want it recorded from two angles.'' Maijstral held the telephone with both hands, one cupped in front of his mouth, so as to inhibit lipreading.

The delight was palpable in Gregor's voice. "Unassisted? Right there in front of everybody? Terrific, boss. Ten points, for sure.''

"Hurry. I expect the trumpets at any moment.''

"Only too.'' Meaning, only too ready.

Maijstral put the phone down and told the privacy field to disperse. The sound of conversation returned, nearly drowning the orchestra. Maijstral glanced about and saw Advert huddling against the bar in an orange shell gown that clashed badly with her background, which was of bright closewood and mirrors. Deciding that Advert had failed to notice the clash and was therefore obviously very distraught, Maijstral concluded to rescue her. As he walked toward her, he saw something glitter against the hollow of her throat. Seeing him, she turned away and watched his approach through the mirrored Khanji relief behind the bar. Only when his arrival seemed inevitable did she turn to him. They exchanged two fingers and sniffed.

"My compliments on your choker, madam," Maijstral said. "The sapphire is wonderfully set off by the diamonds."

Advert raised a hand swiftly to her throat, as if to prevent him from snatching the choker then and there. Then she hesitated.

"Thank you." Through clenched teeth.

Maijstral glanced casually about the room. "Is not Pearl Woman here?" he asked. "There was something I particularly wanted to say to her."

"She isn't feeling well."

"I trust she will recover soon. Before the ball, I hope."

Sullenly. "I can't say."

"Perhaps my news will cheer her. I believe that she may have lost something, and I believe I know where it is."

Advert's eyes blazed. "So it *was* you."

Maijstral's lazy eyes widened in feigned surprise. "I said I knew where it was, Miss Advert. I did *not* say that I had it. I believe it was recovered by someone else, and I can probably get it."

Advert looked at him with suspicion. "What do you want?" she asked.

"May I escort you to your table? I think we may have a number of things to talk about."

She put her arm through his. Rings glittered against the dark material of his suit. "I'm not certain whether I should listen to this."

"You can always walk away."

She bit her lip. Maijstral guided her away from the clashing backdrop. She harmonized much better with white than with closewood and mirrors.

"I'll listen," she decided. "For now."

"Will you do me another favor, Miss Advert. Will you order a new deck of cards from one of the robots?"

Standing up amid the orchestra, trumpeters raised their instruments to their lips.

Trumpet calls rang from the giant diamond. A pair of leather-covered doors swung open. Couples began moving toward the dining room.

"The Waltz twins, definitely," Geoff Fu George said, wrapping Vanessa's arm in his. "Have you seen what they're wearing?"

"I've seen it," Vanessa said. They were barely moving their lips, wary of lip-readers hiding behind invisible cameras.

"They can't possibly wear those heavy pieces at the ball later."

"They may go in the hotel safe."

"In that case, we'll take them off the robot."

"Not as many points that way."

Fu George shrugged. "Risks of the game, Vanessa."

"I suppose. Look. There's Roman."

"Yes." Noncommittally.

"I always liked him. Perhaps I should say hello."

"Perhaps."

"He never approved of me, I always thought. He probably thought me a nouveau riche adventuress." She thought about this judgment for a brief moment. "He was perfectly right, of course."

"Oh." (A brush . . .)

"Ah." (. . . not a thud.)

Maijstral offered an excusatory smile. "My apologies. I must not have been looking where I was going."

Fu George looked at him and nodded. "Quite all right, Maijstral." He nodded. "Miss Advert."

"Mr. Fu George. Miss Runciter."

Maijstral stepped back. "Pray go on ahead of us."

Fu George was pleased. "Thank you, Maijstral."

The trumpets were still calling. In his formal dinner clothes, Roman watched, imperturbable, from his corner of the room. The trumpets were not, after all, calling for him.

"Another alert, Khamiss. Violet Corridor, Level Eight, Panel F22."

Sun's voice grated through Khamiss's skull. She drew her lips back in a snarl. She was getting tired of that particular voice and the inevitability of its announcements— Sun was fond of bone-conduction receivers, and this one was surgically implanted in the top of Khamiss's skull, where she couldn't get rid of it.

Khamiss turned back to her troopers. Her three uniformed subordinates were as weary as she, and she could see their stricken expressions, recognizing them as reflections of her own.

"Another one, ma'am?" asked one.

"Yes. Violet Corridor, Level Eight."

"We're not going to run all that distance, are we?"

Time, Khamiss realized, for a command decision. She knew, and her troops knew, that the alarm was false. Everyone but the guards were at dinner, and no one would be stealing now: their presence would be missed.

"We'll walk," Khamiss said. "At our own pace."

"Very good, ma'am."

Her upper stomach growled. Things were bad enough that she had to spend her day chasing up and down corridors; now she and her squad had to go without meals. She touched the microphone on her lapel.

"Mr. Sun," she said, "could you order a robot with some sandwiches to meet us in Violet Corridor? We're getting hungry."

"Certainly. I shall also send some bottles of rink."

Well, Khamiss thought. Things were looking up at least a bit. She began to feel a little more buoyant.

Her buoyancy fell considerably as she was informed that two more alarms had gone off before she and her weary troopers could quite respond to the first. She opened her bottle of rink with a move that could only be called desperate.

It was going to be a long night.

"If you will watch, madam." Maijstral fanned the cards on the perfect white of the tablecloth. This wasn't the deck Maijstral carried in his hidden pocket: this was a deck that Advert had just had delivered by one of the Cygnus robots.

"I'm watching, Maijstral." Advert, sitting in the dining room below the massive kaleidoscoping steel doors, was in a much better temper. She actually smiled at him.

He squared the deck. "Take your table knife and cut the deck at any point. Lift your card, look at the corner, then drop it."

"Very well." She did as he had asked. He squared the deck again (using a little finger break), shifted the deck from left hand to right (thumb holding the break), drank casually from his glass with the left. . . .

"Is this one in your book, Maijstral?"

"Actually, no." He put the glass down and moved the pack back to his left hand. (Maintaining the break, stepping the cards.) "My book is on advanced manipulations. This one's very elementary. I'm just doing it to warm up." (Glimpsing the card under the heel of the left hand: eight of crowns.) He squared the deck with his right hand, then offered it to Advert.

"Shuffle it, cut it. However many times you like." Riffling.

"I think the Pearl's going to be pleased."

"I daresay she'll be proud of you."

The lights of the dining room were darkening. Pale tablecloths glowed dimly. "Best hurry," said Maijstral.

"How do I know," casually, handing the pack to him, "you haven't hidden my card up your sleeve before you gave me the deck?"

He smiled. That was just the fear he intended to ease. "Let me run slowly through the deck. Take note that your card is there. Don't tell me when you see it, and I won't look at your face." (Spotting the eight of crowns, counting five cards above it. Breaking the deck there.)

"Did you see it?"

"Yes. It was in the deck." (A quick cut at the break.)

Maijstral put the deck down on the tabletop. "How many letters in your name?"

"Six."

"Turn over six cards."

The lights were almost entirely down. Advert had to squint at the deck. There was another trumpet cry.

"A-D-V-E-R-T. Oh." She laughed and held up the eight of crowns. Maijstral took it, took a pen from his pocket, signed the card, handed it back to her.

"Why don't you keep the deck as a souvenir?" Maijstral put the deck back in its box, wrapped it in a handkerchief, and signalled for a robot. "Have the robot take it to your room."

Advert smiled in admiration. "Yes," she said. "I believe I will."

"A great crosstouch. Better than any I've seen him do in practice."

"I believe," Roman said, "that the knowledge of his being on camera affects his performance for the better." He touched the micromedia globe in his pocket as a superstitious person would his Twalle amulet. "Mr. Maijstral always seems to work best under pressure." He looked up sharply. "Hush, now. Someone we know."

"Mr. Roman. Mr. Norman."

"Mr. Drexler. Mr. Chalice."

Roman and Gregor, walking toward the servants' dining room, sniffed and offered two comradely fingers to each of Geoff Fu George's principal assistants.

"Larmon and Hrang are not with you?" Roman inquired.

"No," Drexler said. "They would have loved to come, of course, but space is limited on this station, and Mr. Fu George won only two invitations in his card game with Lord Swann."

"Yes, I understand. I hope Miss Runciter's suite was not likewise restricted."

"She has her woman with her. Cooper."

"Miss Cooper isn't here?"

"She's getting Miss Runciter's ball gown ready. It's got a lot of special effects."

Roman gazed down his nose at Drexler. "Miss Cooper has my sympathy."

Drexler was a young male Khosalikh, not yet having reached first molt; he was a little shorter than average height but built broadly, as if for durability. He wore a gaudy stud in one ear, and Roman suspected it contained a small camera. He was Geoff Fu George's technician.

Mr. Chalice was another one of Fu George's associates: he was human, thirtyish, and rail-thin. His hair was red, and his gangly movements seemed strangely disconnected, like those of a puppet. Roman had always thought Chalice had missed his true avocation, which was that of clown.

Roman had considerably more respect for clowns than for thieves. Maijstral's life's work, alas, had not been chosen with Roman's consultation.

Roman was forty-six and had begun to despair of ever living a regular life.

"Shall we dine together, gentlemen?" Chalice asked.

"Certainly."

"Why not?"

A robot guided them to a table for four. (The servants' restaurant had only nonliving maitre d's.) When the next robot came by, they ordered a bottle of wine for the table.

Drexler looked at his guests, tongue lolling in a smile. His ears pricked forward. "I hope you weren't overly inconvenienced by the customs people here."

"They confiscated a case of equipment," Gregor said. "But I expect we'll survive."

"That's good." Chalice seemed buoyant. "We'd hate to be the only thieves operating on this rock. If they don't know which of us did what job, we'll be able to use the confusion to our advantage."

"There's one job I'm really interested in," said Drexler. He tapped his wine glass meditatively. "The Shard."

Roman carefully avoided exchanging a glance with Gregor. "It may not be here," he said.

"Personally," Drexler said, "I think it is. Why else would the station vid run a documentary of its history? It's too much to expect that sort of thing to be a coincidence."

"If it's here," Roman said, "her grace the Duchess will wear it. She won't have brought it all this way *not* to wear it."

"Her grace the Duchess," Drexler said, "has a very large staff. Including six people of no apparent function, who have not been seen since their arrival." He glanced around the room. "And who are not here."

"Perhaps they are readying her gown."

"All six of them?"

Chalice laughed. "Some gown."

"Perhaps," Drexler said, "a wager is in order." Roman's ears perked forward.

"How so?"

"Perhaps we should make a wager concerning who will hold the Shard in his hands first. Someone on your side of the table, or someone on ours."

"It's a bet." Gregor's reply was instant.

"It may not," Roman insisted, "be here."

"If it's not," Drexler said, "or if no one gets it at all—which I doubt—then the wager will be void."

Roman considered this. Gregor nudged him under the table. Roman's diaphragm throbbed. "Very well," he said. "Five novae?"

"Let's make it ten," offered Drexler.

"Five is sufficient."

"Ten," said Gregor quickly. "We'll bet ten."

Roman's ears went back. "Ten," he sighed, feigning reluctance. "Very well." Drexler grinned and raised his glass.

"Gentlemen," he said, "I give you success."

"Success," Roman echoed, and lapped his wine.

Next to him, Roman could hear Gregor's fingers tap, tap, tapping on his knees. *Success*, they seemed to be tapping. *Success, success.*

* * *

Baron Silverside, good will welling in his broad frame, entered the dining room with the Duchess of Benn on one arm and the Baroness on the other. Roberta was taller than both by several inches. The Baron showed Roberta to his table, then turned to his guests. The lights dimmed, the trumpets called. A few tables away, Maijstral finished his card trick and called for a robot. Baron Silverside, beneficence waxing in his veins, caressed his burnsides and waited for his moment. He could see a red light that meant he was being projected, in hologram form, into the servants' and the employees' dining rooms.

A bright light came on to his right, a back light behind him (which illuminated his whiskers splendidly), a fill light to his left—he was going to do this properly. A trumpet called again. The room burst into applause.

"My lords, ladies, and gentlemen," began the Baron. His words were buried beneath the torrent of applause. The Baron was surprised. He hadn't even unleashed the good stuff yet.

He shuffled. He turned crimson. He yanked on his whiskers. He was having the time of his life.

Geoff Fu George sipped his wine and enjoyed seeing, without really looking at him, the Baron go through his agonies of pleasure. His eyes were not directed toward the Baron, but beside him, toward where Roberta was illuminated in stray light from the Baron's spots. She was not wearing the Shard—in fact her jewelry was modest, possibly to contrast, later, with the Shard when she finally chose to wear it—but he watched her nonetheless.

He wasn't certain why he watched. Perhaps he was looking for clues. Perhaps he just wanted some idea of her character. Perhaps he was hoping for an indication why she would have a game of tiles with Maijstral—something like a covert glance, a secret signal. (He saw none.) Perhaps he simply enjoyed looking at her—with her deep green gown complementing her strong, pale shoulders and dark red hair, she was worth looking at.

The applause finally died away. The Baron essayed again. "My lords, ladies, and gentlemen," he said. "I am flattered by your reception. When I first conceived the idea of this resort, I knew that, if it were to be a success, every detail would have to be accounted for. . . ."

The Baron droned on, his burnsides flaring against the darkness. Behind him, fidgeting with her tableware, was his Baroness, a short, driven woman who Fu George knew was a middling-successful painter and owner of one of the most prestigious small collections in the Constellation. The Baroness was painfully shy, and almost never appeared in public—when seen, she usually wore an elaborate, pleated skirt of a type she'd introduced a decade ago, and which everyone else had long since ceased to wear. Roberta watched with apparent interest as the Baron wandered into minutiae concerning the process of selecting the absolutely *right* asteroid. Fu George watched Roberta and wondered why she had played tiles with Maijstral.

"Milords, ladies, gentlemen, I shall digress no longer . . ."

The pearl. Fu George smiled. His hand strayed to his breast pocket.

". . . may I present the *raison d'être* of Silverside Station . . ."

Fu George's smile froze on his face. His hand plunged into his pocket. There was nothing there.

". . . one of Creation's own wonders . . ."

Fu George remembered the brush with Maijstral, the man's uncommon civility. Vanessa perceived his agitation. She put a hand on his arm. "What's wrong, Geoff?"

"Rathbon's Star and its companion!"

Soundlessly, the steel doors irised back. The room was bathed in the light of one star devouring another.

There was no applause. The sight was too awesome.

Fu George glared across the room at Maijstral. He was sitting next to Advert, and both were smiling as they tilted their heads back to watch Rathbon's Star being eaten.

Maijstral, Fu George thought. *This means war.*

CHAPTER 3

The ball got under way two hours after dinner. The ballroom had no artificial light: the pulses and flares of Rathbon's Star provided both spectacle and illumination for the vast oval room. Maijstral shared the first dance with her grace the Duchess of Benn. Roberta's ball gown was blazing orange: eyes fixed on her as if she were a magnet. Baron Silverside and his lady, dancing just up the set, were eclipsed entirely.

Geoff Fu George, dancing a short distance away with Vanessa, couldn't keep his eyes off them. By those who make it their business to notice and remark upon such things, Fu George's intent gaze was noticed and remarked on.

Paavo Kuusinen had arrived late for the first dance, and so stood on the fringes of the ballroom, tapping his cane to the rhythm of the music, and watched the multitude. Because there was nothing to do, and because (being compulsive) he couldn't help himself, he glanced upward and numbered the media globes on the scene. There were eight, each controlled by Kyoko Asperson through her loupe.

At a Diadem event one could normally expect a great many more, but Baron Silverside had been firm in the number of globes he would allow onstation to harass his guests.

Kuusinen, his compulsion unsated, began to count the number of instruments in the orchestra.

* * *

Mr. Chalice attached the portable power source to his coat and smiled. He donned the coat, turned the collar up, and *thought* himself invisible.

He glanced at his reflection in the triple mirror placed in Fu George's suite and saw in place of himself a distorted smear of color. He knew that smear for himself, that his body was obscured by holographic camouflage tuned to the color scheme of his background.

Geoff Fu George had known that Silverside was going to feature unprecedented security measures, and even before he'd won his invitations at cards, he prepared for dealing with same. He'd thought his usual trunk of equipment would be confiscated, and he had been right. He and his assistants had solved the problem by having miniaturized versions of their equipment built into their evening clothes.

The advanced and unobtrusive design was expensive, but then Fu George could afford the best. The proximity wire in the collar enabled the suit to be given mental commands: it was powered by a micro-source available for a modest price in the station's Electronic Boutique and Gadget Faire; and the darksuit could be used as an evening jacket, permitting instant changes from social to burgling mode.

Chalice's jacket was the last readied: he'd prepared Fu George's first, then Drexler's. All three of them had assignments this evening.

He grinned. Maijstral wasn't going to know what hit him.

Gregor looked up from his watch and glanced carefully into the unique view afforded him by his smoked spectacles. As with Kyoko Asperson's loupe, one lens was arranged to show the view transmitted by media globes, in Gregor's case the superimposed view of two corridors, each broadcast by one of a pair of micromedia globes, which were acting as lookout. Taking a final glance to make sure he wouldn't be observed, Gregor took a tool from his pocket, inserted it in the wall, and swung an access panel out on its hinges. He stepped into the utility space, strolled as far as the door to the next suite, and then strolled back. He checked his spectacles again—no one present—and stepped out. He pushed the wall back into its place.

He walked twenty paces to an elevator and pressed the button. While he waited he took a hi-stick from his pocket and put it in his mouth.

He was going to the ball.

"Pearl Woman!" Delight shone from Kotani's features. He sniffed her ears and offered her three fingers.

"Marquess," said the Pearl.

"You look wonderful. I was given to understand you were ill."

"A brief indisposition. I am entirely recovered." Pearl Woman was flushed and laughing, dressed in an embroidered silk gown. A bandanna was wrapped around her leonine hair, its loose ends dangling above the trademark earring. She was truly radiant, the source of her radiance being relief. Her clothing had been thrown on at the last minute, but fortunately she had the sort of looks which were improved by a slight dishevelment. She'd been standing over a jeweler for most of the last two hours, badgering him while he reassembled the earring. It was now one link shorter, but no one could be expected to detect such an insignificant change.

Pearl Woman glanced over the ballroom. "Is Advert here?"

"Speaking to Janetha. There."

"Ah. You'll excuse me, Marquess?"

"Of course, Pearl."
"Your servant."
"Yours."

Drake Maijstral stepped into one of the private salons off the main ballroom. Gregor, a few moments later, followed, the hi-stick still in his mouth. An opaque privacy screen flickered into existence behind them.

A minute or so later, Gregor and his hi-stick were observed to leave.

Roman stepped around a corner and saw a group of tired, dispirited security guards led by the gangling figure of Kingston. Kingston, he saw, seemed to have forsaken his jester mode. Roman stepped back out of sight, waited until they'd gone on their way, then stepped into the corridor again.

A Cygnus robot passed by, carrying a tray with an empty wine bottle and empty glasses.

Roman glanced right and left, saw no one, took a tool from his pocket, and opened the wall. He closed the wall behind him, took a short stroll, opened the wall at another access point, and stepped into the corridor.

There was no one to see him.

Paavo Kuusinen, who had just noticed Gregor leave the ballroom, looked to his right and observed Fu George sliding out by another door. Smiling, he drifted toward the buffet and picked up a glass of rink.

Sipping, he perceived Kyoko Asperson, dressed in green and purple and with her loupe missing from over her eye, leaving by the same door as had Gregor. He looked up and saw her media globes still circling the assembly. Carefully, he counted them. There were six.

He frowned. Then he began to smile.

"Advert. Marchioness." Sniffing.

"Pearl Woman."

"Pearl!" Advert was delighted. "You look *splendid!*"

"Thank you, Advert. Enthusiasm becomes you, as always." She glanced at the Marchioness. "My lady, if you would excuse us? There was a small confusion regarding our bags, and I need to speak with Advert and sort things out."

"Certainly." Sniffs. "Your very obedient."

"And yours."

Pearl Woman took Advert's arm and pulled her aside, facing the wall. Advert wasn't practiced at speaking without moving her lips, and some important things needed to be said.

"Where were you when I got back from dinner?" Advert asked. "I dressed and you weren't there at all."

"I was hunting a jeweler."

"I wanted to tell you *everything*."

"You know, then, how it is that my pearl came to my room inside a deck of cards signed by Drake Maijstral, wrapped in a handkerchief with Fu George's monogram on it, and delivered by robot."

"Yes." Advert was laughing. "I arranged it. You see, Fu George was the one who stole your pearl. He had it wrapped in his handkerchief, and was carrying it in his pocket. And Maijstral agreed to take the pearl back for us. Wasn't that lucky?"

Pearl Woman gave her a look. "And the deck of cards?"

"Maijstral was doing a card trick, and he had to put the

pearl *somewhere* so that he could send it to you. You know, I think Maijstral is quite a nice man. He's very entertaining.''

''How much did you agree to pay him?''

Advert bit her lip. Pearl Woman's eyes narrowed.

''*How much*, Advert?''

''Sixty.''

Pearl Woman looked at the wall for a long moment. Her expression was calculating. ''Not as bad as it could have been.''

''Pearl, I've never done anything like this before. I didn't know how much to offer. And there wasn't any time to think. We only had a few minutes before Fu George went in to dinner.''

''What did that have to do with it?''

Pause. ''Oh.'' Another pause. ''It seemed important at the time.'' Advert's voice grew forlorn. ''I *did* talk him down from eighty.''

Pearl Woman tossed her head. The pearl danced at the end of its chain. ''Well. At least it's done.''

Advert's fingers fidgeted with her rings. ''You're not going to challenge Fu George, are you?''

Pearl Woman glanced over her shoulder at the other guests. ''I think not.''

Advert let out a breath. ''Good. I'm so relieved.''

Pearl Woman tossed her head again. It was becoming a habitual gesture, allowing her to assure herself the pearl was still there by the weight of it dancing against her neck.

Her voice was calculating. ''I *had* an encounter a little over a year ago, and I couldn't count on my points rising by that much if I had another. They might even go down.'' She frowned. ''And I still can't prove that Fu George did it.''

Advert's eyes widened. ''Whatever do you mean?''

"Maijstral might have had the pearl all along. He may have put it in one of Fu George's handkerchiefs to make you *think* Fu George had it."

Advert considered this for a moment. "Ah," she said.

"All this may have been an elaborate scheme to get me to challenge Fu George so that Maijstral could have the thieving here to himself."

Advert twisted her rings again and said nothing.

"That would be very like Maijstral," Pearl Woman went on "He's always been more subtle than was good for . . . well, for anyone around him."

"Oh." There was a long pause. "Pearl." Advert's voice was tentative. "You know, I've already paid Maijstral the money. He sent for one of those chips from the Casino."

Pearl Woman sighed. "I'm inclined to think he had the pearl all along. He certainly took advantage of the situation quickly enough." She turned and began walking toward the other dancers. Advert followed. "Where *is* Fu George, anyway?" Pearl Woman wondered. "I'd like to see the look on his face when I dangle the pearl in front of his eyes. If he *did* take it, he might not know I've got it back."

"The point is, Pearl," Advert said, "that sixty set me back a lot. When we consider how much it cost just to *stay* here . . ."

Pearl Woman gave her a casual glance. "You know I don't have that kind of money, Advert. After what I paid for the yacht, I'm completely skinned."

"But Pearl. You must have—"

"I'll get some royalties in a few months, of course. And if I win some races, well, things will get better." She gave Advert a sidelong look. "You know, Advert, one shouldn't become so dependent on the material aspects of existence."

"You're about to sign a contract with—"

"Until then"—Pearl Woman smiled at Advert—"I'm

entirely dependent on the goodwill of my friends.'' She put her arm in Advert's.

Advert let herself be drawn toward the ballroom floor. Her face was growing pale.

Pearl Woman glanced over the room, looking for Fu George. Inwardly, she was entirely satisfied.

If one was to have protegés, she thought, one ought at least to get some use out of them.

Roman, walking slowly down the corridor, observed an acquaintance walking in the opposite direction.

"Mr. Chalice." He nodded.

"Mr. Roman."

Ten novae, Roman thought, and smiled.

"Lady Dosvidern."

"Your grace."

"I wonder if you might walk with me."

"Happily, your grace." She took Roberta's arm and began to promenade.

"I'm afraid, my lady, that I have to confess to you my ignorance," Roberta said.

Lady Dosvidern's ears pricked toward her. "Is that so, your grace? I can't imagine your grace's ignorance including anything of importance."

"You're very kind. But no, I'm afraid I have a most embarrassing confession." She gave Lady Dosvidern a warm smile. "I must confess ignorance, my lady, as to the precise meaning of the honor, and the object, which Lord Qlp bestowed upon me this afternoon."

"Ah. That." Lady Dosvidern seemed bemused. "I'm afraid, your grace, my ignorance but only equals yours."

Roberta stopped. Her ears flattened in disbelief. "Truly?" she said.

"I know only that Lord Qlp insisted that it and your grace had to meet. I had no idea it was going to make you a gift, or what that gift was going to be."

"You have no notion of the significance of the object?"

"Not only have I no knowledge of its significance, your grace, I'm afraid I must confess I have never seen an object of that nature before."

Roberta frowned. "Drawmii do not . . . disgorge such objects regularly?"

"Not to my knowledge, your grace. And I have lived on Zynzlyp and in Lord Qlp's company for almost four years."

"How strange."

"Strange. That is Zynzlyp and the Drawmii in sum."

"My lady." Zoot bowed toward them. "Your grace."

"Zoot." Lady Dosvidern was smiling. "Such a pleasure to see you again. Please join us."

The two sniffed the newcomer, and linked arms, one on either side him.

"I was hoping, Lady Dosvidern, to ask for the honor of the next dance."

"Certainly, sir."

Roberta looked at the adventurer. "I enjoyed your last play, Zoot," she said.

"Thank you, your grace."

"I thought the critics were most unfair. The play didn't quite have the exotic appeal of the earlier series, but it seemed solidly done."

Zoot's nostrils flickered. "That seems to be the general opinion, your grace."

"I suspect the writers did not have as thorough a grasp of the material as on the earlier plays."

"I confess that's true, your grace. I have had some discussions with them on that matter. But it's difficult to find people who are at once writers and xenobiologists."

"I can imagine."

"I offered to advise them on Pioneer Corps procedure, but they were not receptive. They kept referring to their dramatic license. Unfortunately," he huffed, "I suspect their licenses had long expired."

A trumpet spoke, calling with perfect synchronicity at the precise moment of a particularly bright solar flare. Lady Dosvidern's eyes gleamed, briefly, red.

"Your grace," she said. "I hope you will excuse us. Our dance beckons."

"Certainly. My lady. Zoot."

"Your grace."

Roberta turned, looking for a partner, and smiled. Paavo Kuusinen was approaching.

"Marchioness Kotani?"

The Marchioness blinked. "Yes?"

"My name is Dolfuss, ma'am. I've always been an admirer of your husband. May I have the honor of this dance?"

The Marchioness looked left and right, seeking aid. There was none. She turned her eyes to Dolfuss and forced a smile.

"Certainly sir."

Grinning, Dolfuss offered an arm.

Consider the magic inherent even in modern life. One is at a resort hotel. One but touches ideograms on a service plate, and lights come on, breakfast is delivered, music floats on the air as if played by an invisible orchestra. Fresh water gushes from taps, robots appear to help you dress, the room is warmed or cooled at your command.

One might well picture a horde of bustling spirits dancing attendance, Ariels sweating manfully in service to their Prosperos. A first-class resort will strive to maintain this image: the omnipotence of their guests is a happy illusion shared, ideally, both by guests and management.

The reality, of course, is more prosaic, but the element of magic is not entirely absent. To demonstrate:

An artificial environment such as an asteroid resort inevitably poses unique problems in architecture. Water, power, air, and gravity must be created and delivered to where they are needed, and conduits for these resources, like the conduits for people, needs must be drilled through solid rock. And, should anything go wrong with the necessary deliveries, the conduits must be easy of access to persons charged with their repair.

One could create separate utility tunnels, but why bother? The utility tunnels would only be delivering their necessities to the same places to which the personnel tunnels would be delivering people. The creators of Silverside Station built their tunnels in parallel—one set for people, appropriately panelled and carpeted and papered in the finest taste. Marching alongside is another, secret set, built to carry the utility mains, and of immediate access behind false walls. Utilities can thus be maintained and repaired by people moving behind the walls, who can work without the distracting necessity of having to rip up floors or ceilings, disturbing people moving in the main tunnels, or (even worse) interfering with the residents' illusion that a host of Ariels is really at work, delivering all conveniences without human effort.

The utility tunnels are tall, narrow, and cramped. Movement is necessarily restricted.

But movement there is. Water, power, gravity, sewage . . . and other things.

Not Ariel or Caliban, not exactly. But something a bit more magical than anything the designers intended.

* * *

Drake Maijstral reached for a control on his belt and turned off the hologram that made him look like Gregor Norman. He took the hi-stick from his mouth and put it in his pocket—a nice touch, he'd thought, a magician's touch, insisting Gregor have a stick in his mouth when he entered the private salon. It made the illusion of the false Gregor all that much more convincing.

A micromedia globe hovered overhead, recording everything for posterity and Maijstral's eventual enrichment. Maijstral paused outside the Waltz twins' suite, took a tool from his pocket, and opened the wall. He donned a pair of goggles that would allow him to detect energy sources and see in the dark.

The utility tunnel smelled of fresh paint. Fingers moving nimbly, Maijstral disconnected the lock on the Waltz twins' door and then stepped out of the tunnel.

He had probably tripped at least one alarm in the tunnel, but it would be indistinguishable from the other alarms his reprogrammed robots were creating everywhere onstation. He could safely assume that the alarm would be ignored, or if answered, answered far too late.

Back in the main corridor, Maijstral stepped to the Waltz twins' door. It was already open.

Frowning, soundless, Maijstral pushed the door open. Moments before, he'd seen the elderly Waltz twins step onto the dance floor and engage in a dance far more vigorous than would seem safe for ladies of their age.

A pattern of energy displayed itself across Maijstral's goggles. The pattern of energy appeared to be dumping heavy, old-fashioned jewelry into a flat case.

"Sorry, Maijstral," said Geoff Fu George. "You're a little late."

"Didn't mean to interrupt," Maijstral said, and closed the door.

He glanced at his chronometer. Time, he thought, for Plan Two.

He retrieved his gear from the tunnel and, looking fore and aft to make certain he was unobserved, began to run. His low-heeled buskins made no sound.

Paavo Kuusinen turned the Duchess of Benn under his right arm. She spun to her place and smiled.

"You're a smooth dancer, Kuusinen," she said.

"I thank your grace." Properly.

Roberta looked at Kuusinen thoughtfully. "You have that secret look, Kuusinen."

"Do I?" His face disclosed a quiet smile as he danced a brief jig about her.

"What are you involved with?"

"I have engaged in a slight intrigue, my lady," he said. "Raising Maijstral's stock, as against that of Geoff Fu George."

"Very good, Kuusinen."

Kuusinen gave her a pensive look. "I'm having second thoughts, I'm afraid." Roberta danced in place, her heels flashing. "I'm afraid I've just heightened the rivalry."

"The better for us, then."

"Possibly, your grace. If it doesn't get out of control."

They touched hands, moved three vigorous, hopping steps to the right. Down the set, one of the Waltz twins gave a whoop.

Roberta retired a pace. Kuusinen made a flourishing bow. She smiled at him as they passed right, then left. "There's another mystery to which you might address your talents, if you're not feeling overstrained."

"Your grace?"

"The object that Lord Qlp gave me this afternoon."

"Ah. I heard about that."

"It looked at first like a wet lump. But now it's dried off, and it's looking more . . . interesting."

"How so, your grace?"

"There are . . . colors in it. Patterns. And the patterns change. It seems to have some form of internal life. I asked Lady Dosvidern about it, but she affects to be as baffled as I."

"Perhaps you ought to have it checked, your grace. It might be unhealthy in some way."

Roberta laughed. "The least of my worries, sir. But still, I'd like you to see the thing."

"Happily, your grace."

She regarded him carefully. "You still have that secret look, Kuusinen."

"Have I, your grace?" Touching hands again, and hopping to the left. Still holding hands (his left, her right), they turned up the set and began to perform an intricate series of steps while maintaining forward motion. Roberta sighed.

"Very well, Kuusinen. I won't insist. But I hope you'll let me know when something is about to happen."

"I will, your grace." He caught her eye and smiled. "You may depend on it."

Mr. Sun sat fidgeting in his cool blue heaven, possessed of a growing conviction that Lucifer had somehow got in amongst the angels and all PanDaemonium was going to break loose at any instant.

Alarms were still going off with dismal regularity. There were thirty lights on his board, and more appearing every minute. His people were an hour late in answering them.

Perhaps, he thought, something in the unique character of Silverside's Star had wildly increased the local rate of entropic decay. The security system on which Sun had labored for the better part of two years was falling apart at the first crisis, and Sun found himself helpless to cope with the shock.

He knew he had to deal with the situation somehow, take command. He had no idea how.

A light winked into existence on his console. He pressed an ideogram, said, "Yes."

"Khamiss, sir." Which Sun could see perfectly well, as a hologram of Khamiss's head had just appeared in the control room. Khamiss was looking weary about the eyes.

"Yes, Khamiss?"

"We've finished on Azure Corridor. No sign of anything out of the ordinary."

"Very well," said Mr. Sun. He reset the alarm on Azure Corridor. "Peach Division next, eighth deep."

"Sir." Speaking very carefully. "I think it's time for a command decision. My people are growing tired, and we haven't found a single intrusion."

Sun frowned. Entropic decay, it appeared, was beginning to spread to his minions. The Sin Balance was tilting in a ominous way. Sun needed to restore order to the universe, and do it immediately. "We cannot concede the battlefield to the enemy," he said. "If we do, we'll be allowing all manner of mischief to take place."

"With all respect, sir, we're not halting mischief now. We're doing precisely what our opponents want us to do— running ourselves ragged chasing false alarms."

Sun drew himself up. "Do you have any concrete suggestions, Khamiss?" he demanded. "Or are you just asking to be taken off the detail?"

"Perhaps we can have our computer experts review the alarm systems. Perhaps the programming has been interfered with."

"I've done that. They haven't found anything yet."

"In that case, sir, may I suggest that we make some attempt to categorize these alarms and respond only to those with high priority. I think we can safely ignore all alarms in remote parts of the station, or alarms that go off when our principal burglars are known to be somewhere else, and concentrate our forces on recent alarms that go off in the dead of night, or other prime thieving times."

Sun glared stonily at Khamiss's hologram. Khamiss's suggestions made perfect sense, but still it seemed to Sun that this constituted a challenge to his authority.

"I will consider the suggestion, Khamiss," he said. "In the meantime, you're due in Peach Division."

The weariness around Khamiss's eyes became more apparent. "Very well, sir."

Good, Sun thought. The incipient mutiny was quelled. Time for a bit of encouragement from the generalissimo. He would raise the level of morale and return to his troops their sharp combative edge.

"Keep fighting the good fight," Sun said. He broke into a rare smile. "You and your men are to be congratulated. You're doing very well."

"Thank you, sir."

"Lord bless you."

The hologram vanished.

The blue command center hummed on. Three more alarms went off in swift succession.

Very well, Sun thought. Prioritize. Everything fits into a category, and some of these alarms must seem more suspicious than others.

If this weren't someone else's idea, he'd implement it immediately.

Khamiss leaned wearily against the wall. Her crew echoed her posture. "Right," she said. "I hereby declare that the burglars have won."

One of her troopers, a young human, looked at her with an insubordinate grin. "Does this mean we fall on our swords, ma'am?"

"No. It means we go to the employees' lounge and get something to eat."

"Yes, ma'am."

"Ma'am." Another human, a blonde named Gretchen. "I have a bottle of hross in my room. It's only a few corridors down."

"By all means fetch it."

Khamiss smiled. For the first time in hours, her security division was moving with alacrity.

Leadership, she thought. There was nothing like it.

Geoff Fu George stepped back from the closet door and admired his handiwork. His blind looked exactly like the top of the closet, and no one could see the jewelry concealed above the false ceiling.

Moving in confident silence, Fu George let himself out of the Waltz twins' room and locked the door behind him. Mentally, using the proximity wire in his collar, he checked his darksuit's chronometers, turned off the holographic camouflage, and retrieved his hovering media globe, which he put in his pocket. He began moving briskly toward the ballroom.

Allowed Burglars are most vulnerable during the period immediately following their crime: the rules of their profession demand that they keep the swag in their residence, or on their person, until midnight following the day of the crime. Usually they accomplish this by renting another residence under a false name, simply hiding out for the day following the theft.

On Silverside Station, hiding out was impossible. Fu George knew for a certainty that his room would be searched if a theft was committed, and that his person would be at least scrutinized. He had therefore decided *not* to steal the Waltz twins' jewelry, at least not for the present—he merely made it appear that the jewels *had* been stolen, by hiding them above the false ceiling in the closet. He'd enter the room later and perform a genuine theft, but by that time the authorities would assume the one-day deadline had passed, and he'd be safe with the stuff in his rooms.

Idly, he wondered how Maijstral was coping with the problem.

Strains of music wafted up the corridor. It was the same dance he'd just ducked out of; his work was adhering to schedule.

Scheduling was important tonight: he planned to strike at least once more.

"The Colonial Service cannot be as dull as you say, madam," Zoot said. "After all, how dull can it be to engage in important Imperial business? Interact with subject species? Conduct important treaty negotiations?" He and Lady Dosvidern were walking to the buffet following the conclusion of the last dance.

Lady Dosvidern smiled, her tongue lolling. "On *Zynzlyp?* With the *Drawmii?*"

Zoot considered this. "Well, my lady," he said, "perhaps Zynzlyp is an exceptional case."

"The Drawmii are a bit more entertaining than the average subject, to be sure. Entertaining," she qualified, "by virtue of their unpredictability. But even that can grow tedious—and as for my posts previous to Zynzlyp, the most exciting treaty negotiation I can recall had to do with a last will and testament that divided an estate contrary to local custom, and which had taken two centuries to move through the Imperial courts to the point where someone in the Service had to deal with it."

"The details," stoutly, "must have been fascinating."

"*I* somehow avoided fascination. Thank you. The champagne, if you please." She lapped daintily in the wide glass, then looked up. "And while I was thus avoiding fascination, *you*, sir, were off making a hero of yourself in the Pioneer Corps, and have now gone on to greater celebrity in the Diadem. Your health, sir." She raised her glass.

"Life in the Diadem is not as you suppose," Zoot said.

"Please," she said, taking his arm again, "do not disillusion me. On a place as barren as Zynzlyp, I found the Diadem my only solace and recreation. Tell me, if you please, only the exciting parts."

"If you like, my lady."

Zoot was, after all, used to this by now.

"Fu George." Grinning. "Perhaps you'll give me this dance."

"Honored, Pearl Woman." Careful not to look at what dangled from her ear. "You look very stylish this evening."

"Thank you." Her grin broadened. "You look a bit out of sorts, yourself."

"Really? I can't think why."

He sniffed her carefully and offered her two fingers. She gave him three in return. No doubt his theft of her property had made them, in Pearl's estimation at least, intimates.

Fu George noticed that she tossed her head after the sniff,

to know whether the pearl was still present. Intrigued, he stepped onto the dance floor.

Perhaps, he thought, he could hold a substitute pearl under his tongue. Make the bite, and somehow switch pearls on her. She might not notice the absence of the real one for hours, even days. And he'd arrange for his own, substitute pearl to dissolve after a day or so, just so she'd know it was gone.

But how to make the switch? And how to fuse the new pearl to the old chain? And would this all require new dentistry?

Perhaps the long months he'd spent practicing this stunt weren't lost, after all.

Fu George began the dance, his mind abuzz with speculation.

Pearl Woman, for her part, was disappointed in his lack of reaction to the reappearance of her trademark. She'd hoped for at least a little jolt of surprise, perhaps even a double take. Instead, the only difference in his usual manner was that he seemed a little abstracted.

Oh well, at least she had her coup planned for the morrow.

That *was* going to be fun.

A cheeping noise began to sound somewhere in Lady Dosvidern's pocket. Her nostrils flickered, and she halted her dance in midcaper.

"You will excuse me, I hope," she said. "Lord Qlp has come out of his crosstalk, and my attendance is required."

Zoot offered his arm. "Will you allow me to take you to your suite?"

"That won't be necessary, but I thank you. You'd best keep our place in the set, otherwise our neighbors will be put out."

"I hope I shall see you again."

"I will be looking forward, sir. Your servant." She sniffed him and walked quickly toward the exit.

There was nothing to do but continue the dance. Zoot, feeling foolish, raised his arm and tried very hard to pretend Lady Dosvidern was turning under it. He was surprised when a hand took his, and he looked down to see a woman dressed in a patchwork motley of green and purple.

"I hope you don't mind," said Kyoko Asperson. "But I'm tired of standing on the sidelines and waiting for someone to do something exciting."

"The night is young, Miss Asperson. Excitement may yet manifest." He looked down at her. The loupe was off her eye: apparently she had put her media globes on autopilot.

"Only too." Meaning, only too right. She glanced at him and brightened. "I hope you and Lady Dosvidern haven't quarreled. She left in a hurry." She and Zoot circled the couple on their right in stately fashion.

"Not at all, Miss Asperson," Zoot said. "Her attendance was required on Lord Qlp."

"Odd, don't you think?"

"How so? It is her duty."

"Not that, Zoot. Just that a Drawmiikh is here at all."

"The Drawmii are not given to explaining themselves. I'm sure its lordship has a reason."

"I'm sure it does. I'd just like to know what it is."

"I suppose that will become clear later."

"Maybe."

He gave her a sharp glance. The word *maybe* was bad ton. *Perhaps* was far more suitable.

These humans, he thought. One never knew what they'd say next.

* * *

The orchestra was finishing the dance when Gregor Norman, hi-stick in his mouth, was observed to return to the ballroom. He stepped behind the screen that cut off the private salon from the main room and gave a cheery wave to the figure of Drake Maijstral that waited for him on a severe, straight-backed Louis Quinze chair.

The hologram of Maijstral dissolved and became Gregor. "You're late, boss," he said. "Run into any trouble?"

The hologram of Gregor dissolved and became Maijstral. "Geoff Fu George was already in the Waltz twins' room when I arrived," he said. "I went on to the next target."

Gregor looked dubious. "That was a risk. Roman wasn't covering you in that direction. You should have got at least one of us to help you carry the swag. There must have been a lot of it."

"There was. But I wanted to get to it before Fu George showed up, and I was able to hustle it down the corridor on a-grav."

"You've been gone for two dances. You'll have been missed."

"I'll stay for the rest of the ball and make up for it."

Maijstral pressed the proper ideograph on the service plate and asked the room to give him a holograph-mirror, and a perfect three-dimensional image of himself appeared in the middle of the salon. He removed the silver pins that held back his hair, let it fall to his shoulders, and straightened his jacket. Gregor rose from his chair and looked in his pocket for a hi-stick.

"So now we just have fun, eh, boss?"

Maijstral smiled. "We have good reason to feel pleased with ourselves." He told the room to remove the opaque screen. Sights and sounds of the dance filled the doorway.

Maijstral noticed one figure standing apart from the others and frowned.

"D'you see that man, Gregor?"

"You mean Kuusinen? He helped us out on Peleng."

"He spoke to me earlier. I found his converse alarming, in a quiet sort of way. I think he's some kind of policeman."

"Really?" Gregor looked interested. "Are you sure?"

"No, but let's not take chances. Be careful around him. Don't give anything away."

"Right, boss." Gregor peered past Maijstral toward the dancers. "I'll keep an eye out."

There was a moment of mutual embarrassment as Khamiss and her squad entered the employees' kitchen and encountered Kingston and his squad returning from the buffet with laden trays. But then grins and bottles broke out, and beneath the spectacle of one sun devouring another a spontaneous party began. Sore feet were elevated on cushions, groaning bellies were silenced by first-rate food, palates soothed by drink.

Every so often, Khamiss and Kingston would leave the party and report that they'd just scouted another corridor and found nothing out of the ordinary. Each time they did this, the false report seemed more and more hilarious. Sun, as was his wont, seemed not to notice anything amiss.

Khamiss raised her glass. "To leadership," she said.

"Leadership," Kingston echoed, and touched his rim to hers.

Another few hours and their shift would be over.

"My lord Silverside."

"Fu George. I hope you are finding your accommodations to your taste."

"The rooms and much else, my lord. I have been inconvenienced by one thing only."

Baron Silverside raised his brows. "Yes? Pray tell me, sir."

"Your security service, my lord. They seem . . . excessively zealous."

"They are zealous on my express instructions."

Fu George feigned shock. "I am dismayed, sir."

Silverside fluffed his burnsides. "This is *my* station, sir. I intend that it be run by *my* custom."

"No one disputes your right, my lord."

"I intend that my guests should be entirely at their ease, and the prospect of one's property vanishing can make one uneasy. I feel it my duty as host to relieve any source of perturbation."

"But, with all respect, my lord, my profession is sanctioned by High Custom and by both Imperial and Constellation law."

"They can sanction it all they wish, sir. There is nothing in law or custom, however, that says your profession must be made easy."

"Sir!"

"There are many professions difficult to practice on Silverside. Range-drover, say, or quellsider. Yours is simply among them."

"Come, sir. Can you compare a quellsider with a profession sanctioned by High Custom?"

Fu George, truth to tell, was enjoying this. He knew one fatuous nobleman who was going to pay for this, and soon.

Silverside fluffed his whiskers again and gazed self-importantly at the orchestra. "Merely an instance, Fu George. If you will pardon me for a moment . . . ?"

"Your servant, sir."

As Fu George stepped toward the buffet, Vanessa Runciter took his arm. "I've been watching Maijstral," he said. "I think he and Gregor pulled a Lugar switch."

"Yes, so I discovered. I encountered him a short while ago, in the Waltz twins' room. I got there first."

A pleased smile drifted across Vanessa's features. "Very good, Geoff."

"The least I can do to him, considering his behavior this afternoon."

She gave him a look. Vanessa had not been at all happy when Fu George informed her that she'd lost an earlobe for nothing.

"I've been thinking about that, Geoff. Where do you suppose he's going to hide his take?"

"I don't suppose he could have hit upon the same device we're using, do you?"

"It might be worthy of investigation. If we could preempt him everywhere . . ."

Geoff Fu George began to smile. "It would only be what he deserved."

She patted his arm. "My thoughts exactly."

"Hello. You're Gregor Norman, aren't you?"

"Yes. Your servant, Miss Asperson."

"Likewise. Had a good and profitable evening?"

Gregor grinned. "Had a nice dinner. I'm not much good at dancing, though."

"I think the next is a slow one. Silent Equations, according to my card. Will you join me?"

"Only too." Meaning, only too happy. "I hope you don't mind me stepping all over you."

"I'll look out for your feet, you look out for mine. Right?"

"Right." Gregor looked down at her. "Aren't you supposed to be on the job?"

"I've got all the globes dispersed and on autopilot. Nothing much exciting happens at grand balls, anyway."

Gregor, who could recall at least one hair-raising grand ball on Peleng, jauntily agreed.

"By the way," he said, looking at her costume. "I think green and purple suit you very well."

"Maijstral."

"Marchioness." Sniffs. "Will you join me for the Silent Equations?"

"Happily, my lady."

They clasped hands, faced one another, then turned their heads toward the orchestra, awaiting the first throb of music. They observed, standing by the orchestra, the Marquess speaking with Baron and Baroness Silverside. They seemed quite intent on their conversation.

"Kotani," said the Marchioness, "has a plan. He wants to do his next play here, and set its action on Silverside Station. He conceives that this will enhance the station's reputation as a place for society to meet, and will provide a perfect backdrop for his own work."

"The Silversides seem interested."

She glanced at Maijstral from the corners of her slanted eyes. "I think it will be a difficult sale. We've heard that Silverside has had other offers."

"Not from anyone of his lordship's stature, I'm sure."

"Very likely. But no doubt Silverside has been approached by people offering him a greater share of the profits. Kotani keeps his money close. I've always thought it his greatest failing as a lord."

Maijstral glanced at her ladyship's matched bracelets and choker: blue corundum, silver, and diamond, with tiny implanted glowstones hidden in the settings to make them gleam with a subtle inner light. She caught his look, and her sullen mouth turned upward in a smile.

"He is generous, yes, with some things, particularly if it might touch on his own reputation. He is not generous with his time, however. I daresay he'll be in conference with the Silversides all week."

"I hope your ladyship will not be too much alone."

She looked into his lidded eyes. "I share your hope, sir," she said, and then laughed. "But speaking of profits, I hope this evening has been profitable for *you.*"

Maijstral gave a lazy shrug. "I thought talk of business bored you, my lady."

"Most business, yes."

The orchestra began to play. The couples, holding hands and still maintaining their strict line fore-and-aft, began to revolve around mutual centers of gravity, moving in an unconscious imitation of the singularity above their heads, which, in its predatory orbit, circled the equator of its hapless primary every twelve minutes.

The dancers below, their appetites somewhat less all-embracing than that of the singularity, continued moving in their orbits.

All save one.

Geoff Fu George met with Drexler and Chalice in the corridor leading to Baron Silverside's private residence. Drexler's eyes were closed; he was communicating with the proximity wire in his collar and making mystic passes in the air with his hands. (His sleeves contained detectors.) "A rank of flaxes under the carpet," he concluded. "There are leapers set the door. Pulse alarms inside, and tremblors on the floor, ceiling, and walls. More leapers on the picture frames."

"Right," said Fu George. One could learn a lot by using the right detectors, and also by burglarizing the offices of Silverside's contractors. He buttoned his jacket tight and pulsed a mental command to his flight harness, which raised him several inches from the floor. With practiced ease, Fu George threaded his way through the net of flaxes, then paused by the door, scouting it carefully with his energy detectors before stopping to neutralize the leapers. His assistants followed him, as did a pair of micromedia globes. By the rules of Allowed Burglary, assistants were permitted only as far as the door: Fu George had to do the rest himself. Fu George opened the door and coasted inside.

He glanced over Baroness Silverside's famous art gallery, seeing barren picture frames and pedestals that held only empty air.

Maijstral, he thought. *You're going to pay for this.*

When the police made their unmistakable arrival, Maijstral was sitting cross-legged on his bed, massaging his feet and watching a video Western. *Rendezvous at Coffeyville* was one of his favorites. The Western featured Marcus Ruthven as Grat Dalton, and had been directed by the great Fastinn, whose training with the Imperial Theatre had, no doubt, contributed to the tangible, forbidding sense of inevitability that engulfed the main characters as they assembled, plotted, and began the raid that would result in their destruction.

The Daltons, wearing identical grey dusters and moving in line abreast on matched black chargers, trotted toward the twin banks that represented the summit of their criminal ambitions. The town was ominously quiet. Somewhere a dog was barking. Crouching in attics, citizens sighted over buffalo guns. Maijstral gnawed a thumbnail, his nerves humming with suspense.

Someone knocked on Maijstral's door. It was an authoritative knock: one could not mistake it, and Maijstral had heard it on many worlds, in many rented rooms. The police.

The knock brought Maijstral reluctantly back to the present. He uncrossed his legs and told the room to hold the Coffeyville massacre till later.

Roman entered. His ears turned back in disapproval as he observed the frozen figures of men wearing Stetsons: he was ever dismayed by Maijstral's low taste in entertainment. "Beg pardon, sir," he said, "but the police are here. Mr. Kingston is with them."

"Ah. Our comic." He rose from the bed, smoothed his dressing gown, and pushed his long hair back from his face. "Very well," he said. "I shall speak to the gentlemen."

Maijstral found Kingston in the front room, his troopers arrayed in a flying wedge behind him. Gregor surveyed them, his mien hostile.

"Just making sure they won't take anything, boss," he said.

"Beg pardon," Kingston said. His face was set in a fuddled smile. "Regrettably, sir, I must search your room. Some objects of value have been missed."

"Really?" Maijstral said. "Why search my room, of all rooms on the station?"

Kingston gave an elaborate bow. "Sir, your worship can guess why, I'm sure."

"It is my humor to hear you say it."

"Very well then, sir. I search your room because there has been stealing going on, and because you have been known to steal."

"This seems like persecution, Mr. Kingston. Has any witness connected me with the missing objects? I spent my entire evening in public. When were these nameless crimes committed?"

"I know nothing of your evening, sir, but searched

you and yours shall surely be." Kingston swayed as he spoke.

The man is drunk, Maijstral thought in surprise. "I take it, then," he said, "you have no confidence in your own handiwork. You took care—*very personal* care—to make certain I had no way to practice my profession on Silverside Station. If you really think I've been taking things I've no right to, it would seem you confess yourself incompetent."

Kingston's good humor snapped like a twig. "Search 'em," he growled, and his troopers spread out over the suite, deploying their detectors.

And found, of course, nothing.

Maijstral returned to his room and participated, while dressing, in the vicarious catharsis of the Coffeyville massacre. He then left his room and, after making certain he was not being followed, walked down deserted corridors to the room of Mr. Dolfuss, where he gave a knock.

Dolfuss opened in a few seconds. He was carrying an overnight bag. "Mr. Maijstral. I've been waiting up."

"The police took a little longer than expected. Perhaps they were a little behind in making their calls."

"Very good, sir. Sleep well."

"And you."

Dolfuss took himself and his bag down the corridor, where he would spend the night on Maijstral's mattress.

Maijstral, for his part, undressed and happily reposed himself on Dolfuss's bed, beneath which were elements of one of the finest private collections in the Human Constellation, that of the Baroness Silverside.

CHAPTER 4

Silver media globes orbited Baron Silverside like Indians in one of Maijstral's Westerns circling a beleaguered wagon train. The Baron looked at the globes through red-rimmed, weary eyes.

"Miss Asperson," he said.

"Baron," said Kyoko. This morning she was dressed in yellow with a silver-wire pattern. It stood out against the subdued decor of the White Room like an explosion in a paint factory. "My condolences on your loss."

"There is yet time. We may see the objects recovered."

"That's not likely, is it?" Kyoko Asperson's question appeared all innocence. "You haven't found the loot after the first few hours, and I wonder how you can expect to find it now that you've exhausted all the likely places to look. After all, an entire art collection can't be hidden very easily. You *built* this station, Baron—where is left to look? Where would you suggest the police go?"

The Baron looked away, found himself looking straight into a media globe, then looked up. He scowled. "I leave that to Mr. Sun, my head of security."

"Understandable, sir. It is his area of expertise." Kyoko smiled. "Would it be possible for me to speak to Mr. Sun?"

"He is very busy. You understand, I'm sure."

"Still, sir, it would be fascinating for my viewers to see such a man at his craft. His job must be an intricate one, and he is charged with considerable responsibility. After all, you must have spent a small fortune altering the design of the station so as to accommodate his security schemes. I'm sure my audience would like to discover whether it is well spent.''

Baron Silverside began to stroke his burnsides. "Matters of finance are of little importance beside the comfort of my guests, madam," he said. "But if you wish to see Mr. Sun at work, I will try to arrange it. I only trust you will not reveal any of his secrets to your public.''

"I will be discreet, my lord. Thank you.''

The media globes ceased their rotation and arranged themselves in formation above Kyoko's head. Bidding the Baron adieu, she felt entirely satisfied with the interview.

Kyoko wanted to see this policeman, this Mr. Sun. Events were beginning to form a pattern in her mind, and Mr. Sun was part of the pattern, an important one. She had begun to see him as one element of a triptych, Maijstral and Fu George and Sun, each orbiting Silverside Station as Rathbon's Star was being orbited by its devouring companion, each held in place by the tension of mutual antagonism.

Kyoko Asperson was not just an interviewer: she fancied herself a dramatist, a dramatist who worked with living, unknowing subjects. Seeing a pattern in life, and making it come to the fore fully realized, flowing before the enraptured eyes of her audience.

There were dramatic possibilities here. One had only to make certain the possibilities were realized.

A Cygnus robot hummed past Gregor as he reached for the lock with his left hand and performed a quick snap-off. Pleased with having done the job one-handed, Gregor opened the door and stepped into the ballroom.

The huge oval room was empty of people. Robots polished the floor, unimpressed by the awesome light of Rathbon's Star. Gregor smiled.

Reviewing wiring diagrams in his head, Gregor turned on his harness repellers and rose toward the ceiling. He'd spent the morning assembling devices patched together from harmless objects purchased in the Electronic Boutique and Gadget Faire, and now he intended to give them a field test.

"Pearl Woman. You're looking dashing."

"Kotani." She sniffed Kotani's ears and offered three fingers. "How are your schemes prospering?"

Kotani drew himself up. "Schemes?" He put a hand to his heart. "I, my dear? Schemes?"

She took his arm. "I observed you in consultation with Baron Silverside last night, Kotani. I know you wouldn't be devoting so much time to a self-important dullard unless you had something in mind."

Kotani gave a graceful smile. "Oh, very well," he said, "I have *projects*, certainly. But I would never *scheme*." He sniffed. "I'm not Drake Maijstral, after all."

Pearl Woman smiled. "How do your . . . projects . . . fare, then?"

"Things are going forward. Some details remain." He looked at her. "I missed you at luncheon."

"I had some fruit in my room. I'm racing this afternoon, remember."

"The Baron's oddsmakers are giving you five to three against."

"And the odds on the Duchess?"

"Even."

"Perhaps I should affect a limp. That would change the odds a bit." Pearl Woman stretched one leg behind her and massaged her thigh thoughtfully.

"You're planning on winning, then?"

"Of course. You know me, Kotani. I don't toss competitions. Besides," she gave a private smile, "I've just come back from the racetrack. I was doing a little practicing while everyone else was having lunch. I know a few tricks that her grace has probably not encountered in her amateur league." She started to walk again, limping slightly, then frowned. She adjusted the limp, making it a bit more subtle.

Kotani smiled at her performance. "My bets will be on you, of course."

"Thank you, Kotani. Your confidence bolsters me. You always had a good head for money."

"Baron Silverside."

The Baron's color rose at the sound of Maijstral's voice, and his burnsides seemed to prickle aloft like the nape hair of a growling animal. Maijstral did not offer him a handclasp, nor (so far as Maijstral could discern) did Baron Silverside take note of that fact.

"Maijstral," said the Baron.

"Baron, I really must complain about your police. I know they have their duty to perform, but their activities amount to nothing short of harassment."

"Maijstral," said the Baron again. His eyes were red, his voice rasping. Perhaps, Maijstral thought, he has been forsaking sleep in order to yell at subordinates.

"They rummaged through my bags and confiscated a large amount of my personal property on my arrival—"

"Maijstral." The Baron's color was rising through the purple end of the spectrum.

"—and last night a gang of them appeared in my rooms and disturbed me and my associates at our rest. As the officious Mr. Kingston had already deprived me of any means of practicing my profession, I consider their visit both a badgering and an impertinence. I'm certain this is not the reputation that Silverside Station wishes to acquire in relation to its guests. I wanted to bring this to your personal attention, Baron. Your reputation is such that I know you will want to see to the matter personally.''

"If it was you, Maijstral . . .''

Maijstral looked surprised. "It can't be me, Baron, not unless your police are incompetent or somehow corruptible, and I'm sure they're not. They're merely officious and heavy-handed.'' He smiled. "In any case, I'm sure your agents will be approached quite soon by someone who will offer a most reasonable price for your lady's collection. And you will have gained sensational publicity for your station that may, in the end, prove priceless. Good day to you, my lord.''

The Baron said nothing in reply. His voice appeared to have failed him. Maijstral sniffed his ears and went on his way.

Silverside wasn't feeling conversational today, anyway.

Roman sat in his room and busied himself with sewing. He normally depended on tailors and robots for this sort of thing, but he didn't wish to explain to a tailor just exactly what he would need this precise object *for*. Therefore Roman plied the needle, stitching the hem of a drawstring bag.

Before him, on a table, was another project. Roman was charting Drake Maijstral's genealogy.

Roman had always been bothered by the fact that he could trace his own lineage back over ten thousand years, connecting it to outposts of the Empire, conquests from the Khosali's very first leap into space, whereas Maijstral's ancestry could barely be traced past Earth's conquest.

Roman's sense of fitness was disturbed by this. It had not seemed *right*, somehow, that the servant should have a longer ancestry than the master.

Therefore he had commenced genealogical researches. Long ago he'd come across a dubious connection to Jean Parisot de la Valette; but that connection, via the wrong side of the blanket, seemed unsatisfactory for any number of reasons, less because of the element of bastardy than because Roman couldn't prove it. Roman dug deeper. He discovered, in another branch of Maijstral's family tree entirely, the name of Altan Khan, who if not as admirable a character as Valette seemed at least a bit more solidly within the family tree.

Roman kept persevering, but after years of searching, the Maijstral family tree proved barren of fruit. To Roman's unvoiced dismay, his employer looked to be merely the descendant of a ruthless, opportunistic Maltese nobody who managed, by dint of oppression of his own species, to worm himself into the Imperial favor and get himself a patent of nobility.

But now, it seemed, Roman's perseverence might have paid off. Was the Matilda, born in Karlskrona as the daughter of Rudolf von Steinberg, the same Matilda, daughter of Rudolphus the Dane, who after a brief visit to England contracted a morganatic marriage to the elderly fourth son of Edmund Beaufort I, Earl and Marquess of Dorset? Matilda daughter-of-Rudolf was a proven descendent of Henry the Lion, and was thus crossed with the Welfs, Frederick Barbarossa, and the Plantagenets. The Beauforts crossed both the Plantagenets and the Tudors, and through them to the ruling houses of all Europe.

Through all those ruling families, Roman could make use of their own family trees that traced their ancestry back any number of directions, usually ending up at either Noah or

Wotan. Neither of these two figures were as old as Roman's own confirmed ancestors, but Roman supposed they would have to do—it would be hard to trace genealogy back past the alleged creation of the Earth.

But still there was no confirmation. Were the two Matildas the same?

Roman had queried genealogical libraries on Earth. An answer had not yet come. He was in a fever of anticipation. He expected it at the arrival of each transmission of mail.

For the moment, however, he had naught to do but sew his drawstring bag.

A subtle shadow seemed to cross his perceptions. Roman's ears pricked forward. He suspected, without knowing how, that something was amiss in the front room. He rose from his seat, made certain his gun was loose in its holster, and glided silently forward.

In the front room the holographic waterfall splashed silently into its basin. Roman saw nothing else. He reached into a pocket, drew out a pair of goggles, pulled them over his eyes. Even with enhanced vision, he could see nothing.

His nose twitched. He could *smell* something wrong. Someone had been here, perceived Roman's presence, and left again.

The police, he thought, might be trying to gather intelligence. Or the intruder might be a rival.

He returned to his room, collected his sewing, and returned to the front room, where he settled on the couch with his gun in his lap. If anyone tried to break in, he'd be ready for them.

Behind him, the waterfall continued its silent descent.

"Roman was there, boss," Drexler said. "I barely got out in time."

"No sign of the art collection, I suppose?"

"Afraid not, boss."

Geoff Fu George shrugged. "I really didn't think Maijstral would stow the stuff in his suite, but it seemed worth a look."

"He's got to be living in a blind."

Fu George sighed. "I daresay. It'll be hard to find."

"Shall I follow him tonight?"

"We've got other things to do this evening. The Duchess's ball will prove perfect cover for any number of activities."

"In my spare time, I mean."

"If you can find any spare time, Drexler, you may use it to pursue Maijstral all you like."

"Only too."

Meaning, only too ready. Fu George gave a cold smile.

"I'm going to pursue him myself, Drexler," he said. "At the race, this afternoon. I know a few things about the Pearl, and I think tomorrow may find Maijstral a humbler man." His smile broadened. "Very much humbler, I suspect."

"Mr. Sun." At the sound of Baron Silverside's voice, Sun hastily buttoned up his tunic, brushed his hair out of his eyes, and leaned forward over his humming console. At least a dozen alarm lights winked at him.

The day, he concluded sadly, wasn't going to get any better.

After breakfast the Baron Silverside had finished his raving, and Mr. Sun entrusted the command center to a subordinate in order to collect a few hours' sleep, but now the pressure of his responsibilities had driven him back to the job. He had been appalled at the wholesale thievery that had gone on last night. All indulgence and license had, in the end, to be paid for, if not by the indulgees then by someone else. And now his security systems had failed utterly, his promises to the Baron were all naught, and for this his body and mind should atone.

He was not alone in his atonement. As of noon, all his crews were now working double shifts.

"Sir," he said, and touched an ideogram.

The Baron's burnsides were showing evidence of hard handling. "Sun," he said. "I trust you have made progress?"

"I am trying to prioritize the alarms, my lord," Sun said. "We will be responding only to—"

The Baron turned red. *"I meant progress in finding my wife's collection!"* he barked. His fists closed on his burnsides and made tearing movements.

Mr. Sun felt his scalp prickle with sweat. "Sir. We're hoping for clues."

The Baron's glare was that of a demon. Sun could almost see the flames of perdition behind the dark pupils, lapping from the Baron's mouth. "You designed the gallery, Sun, and its security system. You gave me certain guarantees . . ."

"No system is foolproof, sir. But—"

"This was not," acidly, "what you said at the time."

"Sir." Sun could feel hopeless despair welling up in him. Last night the Baron had shouted at him for *hours*—Sun's ears were still ringing. Now Silverside showed every sign of beginning again. "This is the first test of new equipment under field conditions. I think certain allowances should be made—"

"No allowances where my wife's collection is concerned! None!"

"No, sir. Of course not. But—"

"Find it, Sun." The Baron's lips drew back in a snarl.

"Find it, or you'll have the pleasure of explaining to Kyoko Asperson and billions of her interested viewers exactly what went wrong."

Horror crept coldly along the back of Sun's neck. "My lord!" he protested.

"Find it, Sun. Or else."

"Sir."

"And another thing, Sun." Abruptly. "Maijstral just came by to speak to me. He was gloating."

"I'm most sorry to hear that, sir."

"He as much said that he's bought someone in my police service. Is it *you* he's bought, Sun?"

Indignation gave Sun's chin an assertive tug upward. "Sir. He was lying, trying to lead us astray. I'll stake my reputation on it."

The Baron's look was cold. "That's precisely what you *are* doing, Sun."

The hologram disappeared, replaced by the service ideogram. Sun banished it and mopped sweat from his forehead.

Slowly, as he sat alone in his blue heaven, resolve began to fill him. Very well, he thought. If the Baron insists on *results*.

He touched the ideogram for general announcement. "Watsons," he said. "We are now at Degree Absolute!"

"Marchioness. Perhaps you would oblige me."

"Only too happily, Maijstral."

"Please sit on my left." Smiling, the Marchioness joined him on the white settee. He scooped up cards from the surface of the low table before him and squared the deck, then offered it to her. "Please glance through the deck and remove all the rovers."

Music and conversation vibrated from the diamond above their heads. The Marchioness was dressed in a light grey that complemented her coloring wonderfully. She took the pack and gave him a glance. "Your metaphors are appropriate, Maijstral."

"How so?"

Her fingers sorted nimbly through the deck. "The rovers are elusive cards, elusive as conjurers when they perform their tricks. Rovers are therefore my favorite. I suppose they are about to make me jump through hoops."

"Not unwillingly, I hope."

She laughed. "I have always found rovers irresistible, sir. Now what must I do?"

"Put the rovers on top, my lady."

"That will please them." Archly.

Maijstral took the deck from her hand and dealt the four top cards facedown onto the table.

"Now the rovers are on the table. Correct, my lady?"

"If you insist, Maijstral."

He dropped the deck to the table again. "Prove it if you like. Turn them over."

The Marchioness did so. "So. The rovers have been exposed." She looked at him. "Is that the trick, sir? I expected something a little more . . . intricate."

"The rovers have a few surprises left, my lady." The rovers were placed atop the deck again. Careful of his sight lines, Maijstral picked up the pack with his right hand. He dealt the top four cards down in one pile, turning the last over to assure her it was still a rover, then put the four cards on top and handed her the deck. He put his hand on hers. Her hand was warm.

"If you will allow me to guide you, my lady," he said. "Put the top rover here, then the others so." Making four cards arranged in a neat rectangle. "Now deal three cards on top of each."

"The rovers shall be resurrected, I hope."

"They shall roam, as is their nature." He guided her hand as she created four piles. He took the deck from her hand. "Indicate two of the piles, if you please." She pointed to two of the piles, the second and third, and he took them from the table and put them atop the deck. "Point to another pile." She pointed to the first. "That pile shall be spared," Maijstral said; he took the fourth and added it to the deck. He took her hand again, placed it on the remaining pile.

"Will you cover the rover, my lady?"

"It would give me nothing but satisfaction to do so, Maijstral."

He took his hand away. "We now have one rover buried under three other cards, all held prisoner beneath your hand."

"That seems to be the case."

"Firstly, I would like to remove the three other cards, so . . ." He made a swift movement of his left hand, which held the deck. With the sound of riffling, three cards appeared inside the crook of the Marchioness's elbow, held in Maijstral's right hand. She gave a laugh of surprise.

"A minor effect," Maijstral said. "I couldn't resist. But now, something a little more interesting. I intend to transfer the three rovers in the deck to the pile beneath your ladyship's hand."

Her pouting lips drew into a smile. "Rovers beneath my hand. My hand shall be envied."

Maijstral drew the deck down the inside of her forearm, moving gently but quite deliberately along the ulnar nerve. The Marchioness shivered.

"Look in the pile, madam," he said. She turned the cards over one by one, revealing the four rovers.

"Your rovers are thieves, Maijstral," she said. "They have stolen into my hand."

"You must be wary of rovers, my lady. They are liable to steal into any number of private places."

She looked at him. "Few but rovers are so bold."

There was an amused light in his hidden eyes as he drew the deck along her forearm again. "Not so. Look in your left sleeve pocket, and there you will find the three cards that were formerly under your hand."

The Marchioness looked, found them, and looked at him sternly. "Your commoner cards have been a little free with my person, Maijstral."

"Apologies, my lady. I seek only to amuse."

She laughed. "Fortunately your cards have a light touch." She tapped her foot on the floor in the pattern meant to applaud something surprising, yet delightful. A robot moved by, and the Marchioness signalled it and asked it to bring drinks. She leaned back in her chair.

"Another trick, my lady?"

"I think not." Feigning pique, she took the pack from his hands. "I'm confiscating the deck for its impertinence."

"The cards only strayed in sport, my lady."

She tilted her head, looked at him sidelong. "Perhaps you and your cards can stray later, Maijstral. But not now."

"I am at your service, madam."

"So one may hope."

The Marchioness looked up sharply at the shadow of media globes and saw Kyoko Asperson advancing toward them. Kyoko made a token bob toward them in lieu of bending over the table to sniff ears.

"Up to your old tricks, Maijstral?" she asked.

"Only exercising my hands, Miss Asperson."

"So I perceived. Will you do a trick for me?"

"I'm afraid my lady has forbidden me any further sleights." He glanced up at the hovering globes. "Besides, you'd record them and expose my manipulations."

"I'll turn the globes off if you like." Kyoko dropped into a seat near them. "Or record them from one angle only.

Whichever you prefer. I like magic tricks, and I don't think it's clever to spoil them.''

Maijstral bowed to her. "Thank you, madam. I wish all audiences preferred the delights of wonder to the inevitable disenchantment that comes with disclosure.''

"That being your attitude, I don't suppose you'd like to disclose who took the Waltz twins' jewels, or the choicest objets in the Baroness's collection, or Madame la Riviere's necklace.''

Maijstral's heavy-lidded eyes glowed with hidden amusement. "I'm afraid, once again, I prefer wonderment to disclosure,'' he said.

"I figured that.'' Kyoko leaned across the table, forcing an intimacy that compelled Maijstral to tilt back in his chair. She pursued her advantage. "How do you suppose the duel will end? Between Geoff Fu George and another thief who shall remain nameless?''

Maijstral smiled. "I would say, madam, that it's far too early to venture a guess.''

"Would you give me your thoughts on another contest? The race this afternoon.''

He steepled his fingers. "Difficult. I have not studied the field.''

"Be a sport, Maijstral. No one's going to shoot you for being wrong.''

Maijstral gave the matter some thought, then conceded. "Very well. I would venture to guess that the Duchess of Benn will be the victor.''

"Why so?''

"I don't believe there is anyone present who matches her in expertise or training.''

"Not Pearl Woman? She's raced professionally.''

"Her last race was a few years ago, I believe. Though of course she is a master tactician.''

The Marchioness fidgeted with the deck of cards. She made an impatient swipe at her hair, brushing it behind her ear, then stood. Maijstral, perceiving the movement, rose with her. "I ordered drinks a while ago," she said. "I'm going to go look for them."

"Marchioness. Your servant."

"Maijstral." She offered him three fingers as they parted. "Perhaps we shall meet again. At one or another sporting event, perhaps."

"Looking forward, my lady."

Maijstral returned to his seat. Kyoko was glancing left and right.

"Do you know where Gregor is?" she asked.

Maijstral was surprised. "I'm afraid not," he said. "He's off on his own somewhere."

Kyoko gave a shrug. "In that case, can you do a card trick?"

"Happily. We should signal a robot for a deck."

Kyoko did so. When the pack arrived, her eight media globes paused in their orbits, then dropped one by one to the white carpet. She took the cards from their pack.

"Right," she said, grinning. "What am I supposed to do?"

Khamiss was a mass of pain, from her head (too much hross in the lounge) to her feet (chasing down too many corridors). Her blistered feet had by now been cared for, decorated with semilife patches that promoted anaesthesia and healing; but regardless of what she did for the headache, it pounded on. The headache, in fact, had seemed to multiply its force the instant she was informed she'd be working a double shift, and multiply again since she'd been told about Degree Absolute.

At least on her current assignment she'd get to wear her

own footwear. She replaced the uniform boots with comfortable sneedskin pumps, threw off the uniform trousers and jacket, and called for a robot to lace her into correct lounging attire.

She called for a holograph-mirror and looked at it anxiously. Her dress was correct, but was it sublime enough to pass in this company? Khamiss turned left and right, patted the coat, the pockets. There was something *not right* about it, but she couldn't say what. Perhaps it was not a current cut. To make matters worse, there was an unsightly bulge over her gun, and no matter how she tugged the jacket, the bulge would not disappear. Perhaps she should go to Essenden's Armory on Level Nine and buy a smaller pistol.

The hell with it. If Sun wanted her to look more inconspicuous, let *him* buy the damn gun.

Her duties under Degree Absolute were to follow Drake Maijstral and never let him out of her sight. She was not optimistic about the outcome. Maijstral was intelligent—wouldn't he *notice* a strange Khosali female following him around the lonely corridors with a bulky service pistol jammed in her armpit?

Well. Hers was not to reason why. She dismissed the robot and stepped out of her quarters. She'd look for Maijstral in the Shadow Room and the main lounge.

As she approached the White Room, she heard music, the sounds projected along the carpeted corridors by the peculiar resonance of the giant diamond. A Khosalikh taller than she, wearing a peculiar jacket, appeared from a side corridor and almost walked into her. She looked at him in surprise and, just as she was about to step aside to let him pass, remembered that she was now a guest and not a functionary. She drew her ears back in assumed hauteur.

"Oh," said Zoot. "I beg your pardon."

"I beg yours."

"I am Zoot, madam."

"I am Khamiss." They exchanged sniffs.

Zoot was, she observed, wearing his famous jacket. She realized, a bit despondently, that it was very likely cut so as to hold any number of weapons.

Zoot offered his arm. "If I may escort you, madam."

Surprise washed over her. "Ah. Certainly, sir."

She took his arm and they began walking in the direction of the music. Pleasure warmed Khamiss at the thought of entering the White Room on the arm of the celebrated pioneer.

Undercover work, she realized, had a lot to recommend it.

"Maijstral." Kotani's ears pricked forward. "Fortuitous to meet you."

Maijstral sniffed him. "A pleasure to see you, sir, at any time. But why fortuitous?"

"I am seeking a wager."

"For the race, you mean? The house is accepting bets, is it not?"

Maijstral stepped onto the conveyer that was moving toward the station's racetrack. Kotani followed him and waved a languid hand.

"The house is accepting bets, yes. But there's no sport in that."

"Or good odds for your favorite?"

Kotani smiled and acknowledged the hit. "I don't think the house knows that Pearl Woman has pulled a muscle in her thigh. It would be foolish to back her at house odds."

Green amusement flickered in Maijstral's shuttered eyes. "Indeed? Why not bet on someone else, then?"

"Because I can't resist good odds, Maijstral. Offer me some!"

"Five to three, then. In favor of her grace the Duchess."

Kotani scowled. "Those are the odds the house has been offering. Give me three to one, at least."

"*I* don't know that the Pearl has injured herself."

"Look at her yourself, when you get the chance. It's plain to see, she's favoring one leg."

Maijstral gave a casual glance over his shoulder and observed, thirty feet behind, a female Khosalikh in a mass-produced lounge jacket. A bulky pistol was crammed in her armpit, straining the laces. He recognized her from the customs dock, turned back to Kotani, and smiled.

"The question is," he said, "has she really injured herself? Or is it sham? A sham injury would be quite like her, you know." Kotani rolled his eyes with impatience. Maijstral shrugged. "Very well, Kotani," he said. "I'll give you two to one, if you like."

"Damnation," said Kotani. He gnawed his lip. "Very well. Twenty novae?"

"To my forty, you mean?"

"Yes."

"Let's say my twenty, your ten."

Kotani looked at him. "You ain't as poverty-stricken as you pretend, Maijstral. You can afford a real wager."

"You're not as strapped as you pretend, either. But I've already made some bets: this one is just to oblige you."

Kotani gave a jerk of his head, indicating reluctant consent. "Very well, Maijstral. If it's all you can afford."

Laughter bubbled silently in Maijstral's mind. Kotani was subtle about everything but money—where cash was concerned, Kotani was a blunt instrument. His boyhood home had been noble, like Maijstral's own, but notoriously poor, also like Maijstral's. Through boyhood circumstance, Maijstral had learned fecklessness; but Kotani had learned parsimony.

He glanced ahead down the panelled corridor and thought about what Kotani's insistence on a bet might mean. Kotani thought Pearl Woman a certainty; and that meant the injury was feigned; and probably also meant that Pearl thought she was certain to win.

Maijstral stepped out of the conveyer and glanced over the gallery. The racecourse, looking like a simple hedge-maze tilted on edge, waited behind a glass wall. Spectator tables were stacked steeply before the course, some of them occupied. At the far end of the gallery, near the entrance that led to the starting gate, Maijstral saw Roberta standing amid a crowd of well-wishers. She was dressed in burnt-orange silks, and her helmet dangled from her hand.

"Maijstral. Pleased to see you."

Maijstral turned abruptly at the sound of Fu George's voice. "Fu George," he said, and exchanged sniffs. "Miss Runciter."

"Drake."

Vanessa was dressed in a chitin-gown studded with pearls. A matching cigaret holder, all complicated filters and laminated layers, was propped in her hand. In her other hand was a tote ticket. Maijstral observed she'd put a hundred on the Pearl to win.

"You're just the person I wanted to see," Fu George said.

Maijstral's green eyes seemed unusually intense. "You aren't by any chance looking for someone to give you odds on the Pearl?"

Vanessa cast Fu George a quick, disturbed glance, which was all Maijstral needed to know that, somehow, the fix was in.

"The Pearl's injured, you know," Fu George said. "She

was trying to hide it earlier, but she couldn't conceal it entirely. Still,'' he sighed heavily, ''I feel I ought to support her.''

''That's kind of you, Fu George. It's the least I can do to oblige such a devoted friend.'' Maijstral frowned as he considered. ''Two to one, Fu George? A quiller on her grace?''

Fu George seemed surprised. ''Uncommonly generous of you, Maijstral.'' Then he smiled. ''Still, after last night, I suppose you can afford it. I accept. Half a quiller on the Pearl against a quiller on the Duchess.'' They clasped hands, two fingers each. Maijstral was not surprised at the sudden elevation in his status: suckers are ever the friends of those who bilk them. Maijstral glanced over his shoulder at the Duchess.

''I should offer my best wishes to the woman on whose shoulders my quiller is riding,'' he said. ''I hope you will excuse me.''

''Certainly, Maijstral.'' They sniffed each other's ears. Maijstral turned to Vanessa.

''Congratulations on your performance last night, by the way,'' she said. ''That was fast work.''

''Thank you, Vanessa. Very kind.''

Maijstral sniffed her and moved away. As he passed in front of the gallery he saw Kingston, the policeman, sitting alone at one of the tables, his glance fixed unhappily on Geoff Fu George. Kingston was dressed in mufti and appeared to have something bulky under his left arm. Maijstral smiled and walked on.

The knot around the Duchess had thinned. Maijstral stepped toward her. He noticed that she was wearing the traditional stripes of bright paint on her cheeks: they were burnt orange, to match her silks. She looked up and saw him; she smiled.

''Maijstral. I'm pleased to see you here.''

"Your grace, I wouldn't have missed it. I was surprised not to see you earlier."

Roberta waved a hand. "All the preparations for the debut tonight. There's still so much to be seen to."

"I wouldn't be too concerned. These things have a habit of looking after themselves."

Roberta's answer was tart. "Not around me, they don't. I see to them myself, or they don't get done."

"Perhaps it's best you've been keeping busy, then."

She began strapping on her helmet. "Wish me luck, Maijstral."

"With all my heart, your grace. And my pocketbook."

Roberta seemed pleasantly surprised. "You can't have got good odds. All the betting seems to be on second or third place. Have you heard that Pearl Woman's been hurt?"

Maijstral looked at her. "I wouldn't have too much confidence in that, you grace. I seem to be finding a lot of takers for my bets."

She frowned and gazed at him for the space of half a moment. "Do you truly? Who, may I ask?"

"Kotani. Fu George. And Miss Runciter held a tote ticket for the Pearl."

Roberta's violet eyes glittered. "Interesting." She reached out a hand. "Thank you, Maijstral."

"Your obedient servant."

He kissed the hand and stepped away, and behind him there was a sudden loud murmuring, as of a crowd experiencing surprise. Maijstral turned and saw Lord Qlp undulating along the gallery toward him, its five eyes peering in his direction. Lady Dosvidern, demurely avoiding the slime trail, followed the Drawmiikh. Maijstral braced himself for the odor. When it arrived the smell almost knocked him down. The volume of conversation from the audience increased radically as a wave of the Drawmiikh's scent rolled over them. Khosali, with noses more sensitive than those of humans, seemed particularly affected.

Maijstral bowed, summoned his resolve, and made approximate sniffs toward Lord Qlp's head. To inhale at all required considerable willpower. The Drawmiikh ignored Maijstral and continued its motion, forcing Maijstral to move fast to keep from being knocked aside.

Lord Qlp halted in front of Roberta. "Lord Qlp," she said, and sniffed it. It reared back, its foremost eye looking directly in her face, and made a series of sucking sounds.

"Are not the Protocols correct?" Lady Dosvidern translated. "Is it not the Time of Exchange? Is not the Exchange correct in its commodity?"

Roberta gazed at the Drawmiikh for a long moment. It seemed to be expecting an answer. She looked at Lady Dosvidern for help. Lady Dosvidern's ears flicked back and forth, signalling her own bewilderment.

Roberta turned her eyes back to Lord Qlp. "I cannot say, my lord," she said.

Lord Qlp's reply was loud and violent. Its whole body trembled with the force of its ejaculation. "Interference!" Lady Dosvidern said. Her expression was bewildered, but her voice was calm and firm. "Your grace must guard the Protocols!"

Roberta considered this for half a second. "I have every intention," she said firmly, "of doing just that."

The answer seemed to please Lord Qlp. It bent its head and began to make gagging sounds. Many in the audience turned away or covered their eyes.

There was a thump. Lord Qlp had disgorged another object. There was a moment of silence.

"Thank you, my lord," said Roberta. Lord Qlp, after reversing its rearmost eye, began to undulate the way it had come without bothering to turn around.

"Allow me, your grace." Maijstral moved quickly. He unfolded his handkerchief and bent to retrieve the object. He wrapped the thing neatly in his handkerchief and rose. It was wet and implastic. Roberta had already signalled a robot.

Lord Qlp moved quickly to the exit and disappeared. Relieved, the audience began to chatter and wave handkerchiefs to disperse the stench.

"Thank you, Maijstral," Roberta said. Maijstral gave the object to the robot, and Roberta gave instructions for the thing to be delivered to her rooms.

"I wonder," Maijstral said, "how Lady Dosvidern deals with its lordship's odor."

"She's probably had surgery on her nasal centers."

"I should have thought of that." He looked at her. "Do you suppose that Lady Dosvidern could offer enlightenment on this . . . excrescence, your grace?"

"I've already asked. She's as puzzled as I." She looked over Maijstral's shoulder, and her face turned cold. "Here's that Asperson person," she said. "I suppose her media globes got an eyeful of what just happened."

"My condolences, your grace. I'm sure you'll handle any awkward questions."

"How can I answer questions when I don't know what just happened?" Her ears turned down in annoyance, and then she shrugged. "Well, I'll just have to pretend omniscience." She brightened a bit. "That could be fun, I suppose."

"Enjoy, your grace."

"Thanks for your assistance, Maijstral. I'll have the handkerchief returned." She began strapping on her helmet.

Maijstral turned, bowed toward Kyoko Asperson as the journalist advanced toward Roberta, and wondered where to sit. Kotani, the Marchioness, Fu George, and Vanessa were standing in a knot, and appeared to be taking care not to look in his direction. Maijstral saw Zoot talking to the armed female Khosalikh who had been his tail, and he considered for a moment the temptation to drop by Zoot's table and see how she handled it.

Pearl Woman, dressed in white silks, was poised by one entrance. An expression of annoyance was visible through the white stripes on her face, and Maijstral guessed she had made her grand entrance only to be upstaged by the arrival of Lord Qlp. Advert, looking uncertain, was fluttering by her elbow. Maijstral strolled toward them.

"Luck, Pearl," he offered, and sniffed her. "Good afternoon, Advert." He couldn't help but notice that if Pearl Woman was still wearing her pearl, it was hidden under her helmet strap.

"Thanks, Maijstral. I daresay I'll need it." She flexed one leg carefully. "I should warm up for a few moments. Pardon me."

"Certainly." She moved off. Maijstral admired the subtlety of her limp for a brief moment, then he turned to Advert.

"Will you join me at my table?"

"Yes. Thank you, Mr. Maijstral."

"My pleasure." He escorted her into the gallery. Advert bit her lip and clutched at something in her pocket.

"Are you anxious for Pearl Woman?" Maijstral asked. "She'll be all right, you know. That leg injury won't incapacitate her."

"She asked me to bet." She raised her hand from her pocket and mutely displayed two credit chips. Maijstral could clearly see the imprints of her nails on her palm.

"She gave you money to bet on her?"

She swallowed and gave a quick nod. "Fifty novae. I

don't know where she got it. She hasn't any money herself. Borrowed it from someone, I suppose."

"She wants you to bet her to win."

"Yes."

"And you don't think she'll come in first."

Advert shook her head, not trusting herself to speak.

"I see," said Maijstral. He signalled a waiter for drinks and considered the situation. He had known Pearl Woman long enough to be perfectly certain that the money was the Pearl's and that Pearl Woman's poverty was a pose. He knew that Advert had ransomed the Pearl's trademark with her own money, and that Pearl Woman had probably not covered the expense.

Maijstral also knew that he could not say so, particularly to Advert, without running a risk of Pearl Woman jamming one of her cutlasses between his ribs.

He wondered briefly why Pearl Woman hadn't let Advert know about her injury being feigned. Probably, he decided, the Pearl was afraid Advert would somehow give the trick away.

"I wanted to make a bet on my own," Advert said miserably. "Bet on her grace, but making a bet on someone else feels so . . . *disloyal.*"

Maijstral looked at her. "Miss Advert, I've had a bit more experience in these matters. Will you follow my advice?"

Advert thought for a moment, then gave a hesitant nod.

"Very well. You must bet Pearl Woman's money as she asked you. You are not the custodian of her pocketbook, and she may have had reasons for making the bet of which you are unaware."

Advert heaved a sigh. "I suppose so."

"But make your own bet," Maijstral went on, "accord-

ing to your own judgement. It's not disloyal of you to think
that the Duchess may win: she is clearly the favorite. Money
has no loyalty, and neither have wagers. Money is far too
serious a thing to owe sentimental allegiance to one person's
friendship or another's.''

Advert did not seem comforted. "Very well," she said.
She looked over the company. "Who shall I bet with, I
wonder?"

"Very little time remains. You'll have to bet on the tote,
I'm afraid, and you won't get as good odds as you might
on a private bet. I'll make the bets for you, if you like.''

''Yes. Thank you, Mr. Maijstral.''

Maijstral took the money and stepped to the tote, made
Advert's bets, made a bet on the Duchess for himself, and
returned to the table. The drinks had arrived in the meantime, and Advert had finished half of her own. Maijstral
handed her the coded betting tokens and sipped his drink.

Advert was looking at Roberta, who was going through
a careful warm-up after having finished her interview with
Kyoko Asperson. "I envy her," she said. "She's had so
many advantages.''

Maijstral gazed at the Duchess. "You find her an object
of envy? I do not.''

Advert was surprised. "Why? She's got money, talent,
looks, intelligence. A title. She's even got the Eltdown
Shard, for heaven's sake.'' She sighed. "And assurance,
too.''

Maijstral smiled. "And assurance. All that, yes.'' Maijstral steepled his fingertips and contemplated the Duchess.
''She is the head of an old and very regal Imperial family,
and they raise their heirs very carefully. From her earliest
days her grace has been strictly schooled in what was expected of her. The training is severe and uncompromising,
begun before she was even aware of being trained, not

entirely ending until the day of her death. She has been allowed no distractions and very few pleasures—the family will have seen to that. The training is intended to do one of three things: make her a duchess, break her, or force her into rebellion. She's too strong to be broken, and too responsible to rebel. She probably has a half-dozen brothers and sisters, and it was Roberta who was chosen as heir, not the others. Her grace is a successful product of a very difficult school, but that doesn't make her an object of envy." Maijstral twisted the diamond on his finger. "I'm sorry for her, I'm afraid."

Advert gazed at him in cool fascination. "You've got an old title, too, don't you?" she asked.

He nodded. "Yes, I do. But I escaped my fate. There was no money left, you see, and no property to speak of. Nothing to be responsible *to*." He gave a lazy shrug and smiled. "There are still restrictions, even in the Constellation. Certain occupations I cannot put my hand to, not if I expect to retain the regard of my peers. It's lucky I'm allowed to steal: otherwise I'd have to be a drunkard or a fortune hunter, and those alternatives would be," offering a slight smile, "tedious, as well as unsuited to my temperament. Any of those alternatives, however—" he nodded toward Roberta "—is preferable to what her grace will be compelled to undergo fairly shortly."

Advert's glance trailed toward Roberta. "How so?"

"I expect she'll be made to give up the racing. It's allowed here because it puts her name forward and makes for a splashier debut, but after this the racing will have no more practical use." He frowned, settling into his chair and his lecture. "The point of a debut, you see, is to advertise the fact that you're ready for marriage. In a year or two the family will arrange a husband for her, and then she'll spend the next ten years or so giving birth to a series of minor nobles, one of whom will, after going through the conditioning, doubtless make a suitable heir to the title and the fortune and the Shard and all the rest of it. Hers will be real pregnancies, too—artificial wombs aren't customary in the old families. So then she'll spend years supervising the children's education and such, and after they're all safely grown she can relax a bit. She'll be allowed to be a cynical old lady and make cutting remarks at parties. By then she'll be a family character, and her remarks won't matter. Some people in her situation drink or tyrannize their children, but I think her grace is probably too honest for that.''

Advert, gazing soberly at the Duchess, raised a hand to her throat. Light glittered from her many rings. ''You make it seem so sad,'' she said.

''I suppose it is. She'll never know what it is to choose her own course. She's not Pearl Woman, who runs her life exactly as she wants it.''

''But she's a duchess. She's got the money and so on in her own right. Can't she just break away from it all?''

''The path of rebellion. That's possible, of course,'' Maijstral conceded. ''That's where the training comes in, though. The chorus of Duty, Duty, Duty that she's been hearing since before she could remember. It's hard not to listen to that song, not when she's never listened to anything else. She *could* break away, I suppose. It takes a certain strength of will, and her grace has will in abundance.'' He gave Roberta a careful look. ''I don't think it's likely, though. The tendencies would have been visible before now.''

Advert looked at her lap. ''I'd no idea,'' she said.

''Why should you? You're lucky enough not to have been born to it. You're allowed to make choices.''

''Yes.'' She gave a brave grin. ''Like the bet, yes?''

''Yes. The bet. No matter how the race turns out, you have reason to rejoice. On your own behalf, or the Pearl's.''

Trumpets began to sound. The Priests of the Game appeared in their brocaded robes, incense rising from jewelled censers. The six racers, standing in their bright colors, assumed the Posture of Respect and Submission. Thankfully, the incense drowned Lord Qlp's remaining stench.

Maijstral leaned forward across the table, chin on his fist. The race was going to be very interesting: he wanted very much to know whether his judgement in this matter was sound.

His judgement of Roberta in particular.

CHAPTER 5

The scent of incense still stung Maijstral's nostrils. The Priests, having invoked the Active and Passive Virtues, finished their High Khosali chant and took their positions as referees. The race, its religious character now established, was ready to begin.

Three pairs of racers, each in their bright silks, crouched in the chute leading to the racecourse. Pearl Woman and Roberta, the favorites, formed the last pair of the three. Crowd sounds died away as the five-second gong sounded. The first pair of racers flexed their feet and ankles, making sure of their traction.

Floating holograms counted the seconds. Three. Two. One. Begin.

The first tone sounded. The first pair of racers flung themselves into the racecourse as the Priests moaned.

"Hello, Kyoko. Can I join you?"

"Gregor! Please sit down."

"I'm not interrupting your work, am I?"

"Not at all. I'm recording the race for later. I haven't seen you today."

Gregor touched his stomach. "A touch of the steggo—I think it was the roast fleth."

"Sorry to hear that. You're all right now, aren't you?"

"Right as Robbler." Grinning. "So who's going to win, then?"

Gravity channels had been cut off in the racecourse, and the racers flew like mapper charges on the first straight. Each tucked, rolled, came out feetfirst as they hit the initial turn.

The second tone sounded. The next pair of racers hurled themselves into weightlessness.

"Dear. Who's the one in red?"

Consulting the tote board. "Allekh."

"He's got a good turn. He won at least half a second on that first corner." Kotani leaned forward and smiled. "Pearl Woman will catch him, though, I'm certain."

"I've bet the Pearl for second. Her grace for first."

"You should follow my advice on betting matters, dear. I happen to know Pearl Women will win."

"Think you so?" The Marchioness was amused. "I disagree."

A sharp look. "Have you heard something?"

"No." A smile played about her sullen mouth. "Just an intuition that there's a wild card somewhere in this deck. A rover, perhaps."

"You're growing cryptic, my dear."

"Intuitions aren't supposed to be orderly, Kotani."

Marquess Kotani raised an eyebrow. "*Mine* are. And mine are betting on Pearl Woman."

Roberta's face was expressionless beneath the rim of her helmet, but there was something very intense about her eyes. Maijstral was reassured. Perhaps he had guessed correctly.

Roberta hadn't even spared Pearl Woman a glance as they waited in the chute; but Maijstral believed her concentration was such that she was perfectly aware of Pearl Woman's posture, the precise degree of tension in her legs, her back. . . . Maijstral suspected Roberta knew to the fraction of an inch where Pearl Woman was placed.

The third tone sounded. Roberta and Pearl Woman sprang from the chute to the sound of groaning Priests.

"There seems to be something in front of your face. Like a heat shimmer."

"Yes. My jacket. I built a magnifying field into it. Does it annoy you?"

"Not at all." Pause. "So you can watch the race close up."

"So I can see clearly at a distance, yes."

"Very handy."

"It seemed a sensible thing to have. I never realized how people would make a fuss."

"You sound as if you haven't enjoyed the attention you've been getting."

"Not exactly." Zoot's diaphragm throbbed in resignation. "It's just that—I don't know quite how to say this— the *quality* of it leaves something to be desired."

"Pearl's got ahead of her!" Excitedly.

"She's good on the long straights. Her grace is known to excel in the tight corners."

"She's ahead! She's ahead!"

Maijstral noticed that Advert's hands had become fists. Her nails were probably doing more damage to her palms.

He glanced about, saw his female Khosali shadow talking to Zoot, then saw, above them and almost in the last row, Mr. Paavo Kuusinen. Mr Kuusinen, he realized, was in a position from which he could watch the entire company. At this precise moment, however, Kuusinen was watching Maijstral.

Maijstral nodded, raised his drink in salute.

Kuusinen did likewise.

Maijstral turned back to the race and scowled. Something was wrong about that man.

There were barking noises from the Priests.

"A penalty. Who's in green?"

"Charusiri."

"She used her upper arms. The slut."

"It *is* an amateur event, Vanessa."

"A two-second penalty. They should disqualify her entirely."

Smiling. "Perhaps they should just dismember her and have it over."

"Maybe they should, Geoff." Vanessa's eyes blazed. "I *hate* that sort of thing."

The lead racer flung herself down a short straight, tucked, tumbled in air, touched on her lower back, and bounced to cut a corner on a forty-five-degree angle. Her body straightened as she kicked out, feet driving into the wall as she hurled herself on a new trajectory.

Just behind, Allekh caught his elbow on another's knee. The two tangled and thrashed, bouncing off walls. Penalty lights flashed.

"Are you expecting a crime at this event, ma'am?"

"Sir!" Khamiss looked at Zoot in astonishment. "What do you mean?"

"I first saw you in uniform at the entry port. Now I see you in civilian clothes with a pistol under your arm. I assume that since you're so conspicuously armed, you are therefore working. Am I not correct, ma'am?"

"Oh." Khamiss licked her nose disconsolately. "I'm

supposed to be watching Drake Maijstral. And Kingston over there is following Geoff Fu George.''

''Isn't that a little . . . unsubtle?'' A less tactful person would have said *obvious*. Khamiss appreciated the courtesy.

''I daresay. But Baroness Silverside's collection has been stolen, and the Baron's a bit upset.''

''I understand. Still, were I Maijstral, I'd complain. And if the complaints weren't listened to, I imagine Maijstral and Fu George between them could greatly reduce Silverside Station's popularity. Were I a prominent member of society, I would not want to attend a resort where guests were followed by armed employees.''

''My superiors doubtless feel that exceptions can be made in the case of known thieves. Besides,'' grinning, ''you are one, aren't you?''

Zoot was startled. ''Are what, ma'am?''

''A prominent member of society.''

''Oh. I suppose I am.''

''And an observant one. We didn't exchange a single word at the entry port, and you still remembered my face.''

''I've trained myself to remember things.''

''I envy you the talent. In my line of work, it would be very handy.''

''I've got a system for recalling faces. I'll teach it to you, if you like.''

''Would you? That's very kind.''

''Not at all. My pleasure.''

The racecourse was only slightly wider than two of the racers travelling shoulder-to-shoulder. It was possible to physically block someone trying to pass, and the rules allowed it, but blocking only invited a collision that could wreck both racers' times and might end in penalty assessment.

Pearl Woman, maintaining her half-second lead over

Roberta, had approached the racer immediately ahead of her, a Tanquer dressed in violet. Pearl Woman hung back through a series of short straights, then gathered her powerful legs beneath her and launched herself on a diverging pass. She squeezed between the Tanquer and the wall, touched the wall lightly, a graze on her stomach, and then rebounded gently into the other racer's path. The violet racer flailed in an attempt to avoid fouling her, but Pearl Woman had already tucked into a ball and was ready for the next corner.

The Pearl cast a glance over her shoulder. The flailing racer was squarely in Roberta's path.

Well, she thought. *That should hold her for a while*.

"Well done, Pearl Woman!" Vanessa tapped her foot in a congratulatory rhythm.

"Yes. Quite." Fu George's drink was covered in frost. He removed his numbed fingers and frowned. "Drexler and Chalice are mapping the route from the ballroom to the Duchess's suite."

"Good. You'll do the pick-off after the ball, then?"

"Yes. I don't want to give Maijstral too much time. He's already too friendly with her grace."

"What if her guards are with her?"

"We'll use dazzlers and smoke. Once we're inside, they won't be able to shoot without risking her grace. And we'll have the advantage of surprise." He chipped frost from his drink with his fingernail. "Once we have the Shard, we'll hide it in her grace's suite. Then remove it after the time has passed."

"The plan seems a little . . ."

"Over-direct? Violent?"

"Yes."

"I know." Frowning. "No points for style. Maijstral hasn't given me any time."

"This may sound a little odd, Fu George," hesitantly, "but have you considered simply approaching the Duchess?"

Pause. "I . . . *assumed* . . . she wouldn't make an arrangement about something as notorious as the Shard."

"Think about it, Fu George."

Fu George said nothing. He was already thinking very hard indeed.

Roberta passed the violet Tanquer on the next long straight. Concluding her first lap, Pearl Woman increased her lead over Roberta during the long, straight outer passages; but once she got into the twisting, shorter, inner passage, she lost time. Her massive upper body lacked flexibility: forbidden by the rules from using the power of her arms and shoulders, caught in a part of the course that demanded quick reverses and compact athleticism, Pearl Woman's rebounds were slow and slightly off-course. Roberta, who was surprisingly limber for a woman her height, began to shorten Pearl Woman's lead. By the time they reached the next long straight, she was only a fraction of a second behind.

Maijstral leaned forward. Now, he thought, he'd see it. The fix or whatever it was.

"Oh, yeah. I've been on my own since I was twelve."

"In this current line of business?"

"Or something like it. I mean, they won't give you a burglar's ticket till you're sixteen, right?"

"Right."

"So I got interested in the technical end of the business.

That way it wasn't me the police came looking for." There had been a few arrests to help him decide on that course, but Gregor saw no point in mentioning them.

"Hey." Kyoko's voice broke with excitement. "Hey. Did you see *that?*"

"Damnation!"
Smiling . "I told you, dear."

"Oh, *no!*" Biting a knuckle. "How did it *happen?*"
"Take comfort." Admiration rose in Maijstral's mind. "You've won your bet."

Pearl Woman's coup, Maijstral thought, had been perfectly timed and beautifully executed. Entering the first of the long back straights, her kickoff had seemed to go wrong. The pulled muscle had, to all appearances, taken its revenge. Pearl Woman had been propelled on a slightly wrong angle, drifting toward one of the walls. She tucked and prepared to carom off.

Roberta saw her chance and leaped for it. Her kickoff was flawless, her trajectory down the middle of the course perfectly timed to pass Pearl Woman just as the Pearl grazed the wall.

Roberta, in her tuck, had to reverse herself, touch the far wall with her feet, kick out and alter trajectory to fly down the next straight. She came out of her tuck, her legs cocked and ready.

Pearl Woman grazed on her helmet, came out of her tuck, prepared for her own change of course. She looked above her, left, and right, trying to find Roberta. She searched everywhere but where Roberta actually was, behind and below her. Pearl Woman was trying, Maijstral thought, to establish in the minds of the audience and Priests that she didn't know where Roberta was, and show that a foul was the last thing on her mind.

Roberta touched and kicked. Pearl Woman came down on top of her, her own legs lashing out.

Maijstral deduced that Pearl Woman intended to kick the Duchess on her thigh or knee as Roberta passed below her, crippling her for the rest of the race. But somehow Pearl Woman's driving feet passed through Roberta's legs without connecting—Roberta had twisted slightly in her trajectory change, and Pearl Woman flailed, bouncing into the corridor wall and missing her course alteration.

The proof of Pearl Woman's intent, Maijstral later concluded, was that loss of control. Had Pearl Woman *intended* to kick the wall, her course change should have gone off without a hitch. But since she *intended* to connect with Roberta, her timing was thrown off by her miss and she bounced hopelessly into the corner.

Maijstral settled back into his chair and smiled.

"What bad luck!" Advert cried.

"Yes," Maijstral said. "One might call it that."

Roberta passed the other racers to come in first, not simply in time-corrected listings but actually ahead of the others, even those who had started before her. She left the course to the enthusiastic, foot-tapping applause of the spectators, and the Priests of the Game, pouring incense, set up a hymn. Pearl Woman finished fifth.

"I think," Maijstral said, rising, "you should avoid mentioning your bets to the Pearl."

Advert nodded. "Yes. I'd already thought that."

"Please give her my condolences. It was a brave attempt."

"I'll do that. Thank you, Mr. Maijstral."

"Your servant, ma'am."

* * *

Khamiss sighed as she saw Maijstral rise from his place. "Duty calls, I'm afraid."

Zoot rose with her. The nebulous magnification field in front of his face vanished. "Please contact me when you're free. I'll tell you about my identification method."

"I'm working double shifts. But by midnight the Baroness's art collection will either be recovered or belong to the burglar forever, so perhaps I'll have more freedom tomorrow."

"Madam. Your very obedient."

"And yours."

"I'd never have got this far on my own. I'm learning a lot from him."

"Such as?"

"Ton and things. How to behave around people who are rich enough to have stuff I want to steal."

Kyoko laughed. "Ton and things," she repeated.

"I've got a bit to learn yet." With wounded dignity. "The point is, High Custom folk behave in different ways from the people I grew up with. I've got to learn how to use that, see?"

Kyoko looked at him. "Learning how to make use of the way people behave is different from turning yourself into an imitation aristocrat."

Gregor's ears flicked dismissal. "I didn't make the rules. It's their game. I've got to play it the way they want, or I don't play it at all."

"That isn't my point. My point is that you should make use of who you *are*."

"Of *course* I—"

Kyoko held up a hand. "How long have you been with Maijstral?"

"Four years."

"Yes. Four years to integrate yourself with High Custom. While everyone else here has been working at it their entire lives."

Gregor scowled. "I'm bright. I can learn."

Kyoko tipped her head to one side. "I'm sure you can, and have. My point is that you can't succeed *entirely*. The people on Silverside Station have had the same education, the same training, and moved in the same circles for years. They can spot a phony by his dress, his manners, his language—or just by the set of his ears."

Gregor threw up his hands. "So what am I supposed to do? Just resign myself to living as a servant for the rest of my life?"

"Of course not." Kyoko looked at him coolly. "I'm here, aren't I? Moving in the highest circles and behaving just the way I like. And I was brought up on the frontier, more than fifty light-years from the nearest noble house."

"You're a performer. That's different."

"Tell me how."

"You—you need to present a personality for your viewers. It doesn't matter as much what sort of personality that is."

"It's *access* that matters, Gregor," Kyoko said. "Once you're accepted in this crowd, you can do anything you want. Ask embarrassing questions, expose secrets, or steal. The trick is that first acceptance."

"So how did you get accepted, then?"

"I conducted Saxony Weil's first interview in twenty years. The first since the scandal."

"And how'd you manage that?"

Kyoko smiled thinly. "I was very young, and I pretended more naivete than I possessed. She wanted to get her version of events on the record, and thought she could use me. She assumed I'd be so awed that I wouldn't ask hard questions, and sufficiently inexperienced that I wouldn't check the record about what actually happened all those years ago. She spun a web of lies, and I called her down on each one."

"I sort of remember hearing about that that. Never saw the interview, though. Didn't know anything about Saxony What's-'er-name."

"One critic called it 'the definitive demolition.' I liked that." She frowned and sipped her drink. "She wanted to use me, and I used her instead, and now I'm famous and she's still in exile. All I did was know my job, and my audience, and be myself." She stood and put her loupe in her eye. "I've got to talk to Pearl Woman before she leaves. If she thinks she can race in front of *me* and get away with an attempt to break the Duchess's knees, she'd better think again. See you later, I hope."

Gregor grinned at her. "Only too."

"Bye." Gregor watched, his mind buzzing, as Kyoko's marshalled media globes began to arrow toward Pearl Woman like a squadron of warships stooping on a target.

The Marquess Kotani was strolling rather rapidly from the arena when Maijstral intercepted him. Kotani wasn't precisely running away: he was merely giving the Fates a chance to intervene between himself and his debt. Once caught, Kotani handed over the money with a flourish and congratulations, then made a much more leisurely exit. Maijstral collected his half-quiller from Fu George, who wrote his marker in an offhand way while conducting a conversation with the Marchioness Kotani and Vanessa Runciter, and who then offered Maijstral a single finger in his handclasp. Smiling for his own reasons, Maijstral put his winnings in his pocket and strolled toward the knot of well-wishers that surrounded Roberta.

"Great race," Mr. Dolfuss was remarking. "Never seen a better."

"Thank you, sir," Roberta said. She pulled off her helmet and shook her bobbed hair.

"But what were the Priests singing afterward?" Dolfuss asked. "I couldn't make it out." He was using his actor's voice that boomed loud in the enclosed space. Those nearby were falling silent, partly because they'd been outshouted and partly out of embarrassment for the man.

"They were thanking the Virtues and the Emperor for a race well run," Roberta said. Her voice was softer than usual: perhaps she was trying to lead by example.

"What's the Emperor got to do with it?" Dolfuss demanded. "We don't even *have* an Emperor any more. It doesn't make any sense."

"If you'll forgive my interruption, sir, it has never been a requirement of religion to make sense," Maijstral said.

"Of *course* it's supposed to make sense!" Dolfuss barked. "What's the point of a religion that don't explain things?" But Maijstral had turned to Roberta and offered her two fingers.

"Congratulations, your grace," he said. "You came close to mishap, but you avoided it splendidly."

There was a secret gleam in Maijstral's eyes, one answered in the eyes of the Duchess. "I had warning, sir. Perhaps I'm intuitive that way."

"That would explain it. It's lucky *I* was intuitive enough to bet on your success."

"I'm pleased to be the author of your good fortune."

Dolfuss, in the meantime, had spotted someone over the heads of the crowd. With roaring apologies, to which no one listened, he made his way toward Pearl Woman. Maijstral, pleased by his confederate's performance, smiled as he watched the actor leave, a smile entirely misunderstood by those present.

"You'll pardon me, I hope," Roberta said. "I have to make preparations for the ball."

"Your grace." Maijstral sniffed her and watched her leave. From somewhere he could hear Dolfuss's voice on high, offering his sympathy to Pearl Woman on her damned bad luck. Maijstral remembered he had a bet on the tote and walked toward the stair. Climbing, he passed by Khamiss, who, cursing under her breath, was compelled to jump aside to make way for him. Maijstral bowed and brushed past, nudging Khamiss's gun with his elbow. Khamiss's ears drew down in mortification, and she wearily reversed course and trudged up the stairs after Maijstral.

Standing by the cashier were the Marchioness and Mr. Paavo Kuusinen. The Marchioness smiled and waved. "Collecting your winnings, Maijstral?" she asked.

"I was lucky."

"My husband was not. Despite his other splendid qualities, he is simply not the sort of man who should gamble."

"How unfortunate."

She gave an easy laugh and brandished her winnings. "I always win by betting contrary to his instructions. I'm afraid it puts him in a temper."

Maijstral turned to Kuusinen. "Did you win yourself, sir?"

Kuusinen smiled politely. "I did indeed. I've seen her grace race before, and I was confident there was no one in this field she couldn't cope with."

"An astute observation," Maijstral said, wondering. *Cope*, he thought, was an odd word to choose. *Win against* might have been more obvious.

Kuusinen, therefore, had seen Pearl Woman's stratagem and recognized it for what it was. The man was disturbingly acute.

"Cash your marker, Maijstral," the Marchioness said gaily. "Then we can stroll to the White Room."

"I'd be honored, my lady," Maijstral said, and stepped to the cashier's desk.

As he deposited his winnings into his hotel account, he could feel Kuusinen's unsettling gaze on the back of his neck. The man sees too much, he thought, and whether he's police or not, this bodes ill.

"A moment, your grace, if you please."

Roberta cast a look over her shoulder at Geoff Fu George. "If you don't mind walking with me. I'm in something of a hurry."

"You're walking in my direction anyway." Smoothly. Fu George matched his stride to hers and offered his congratulations.

"It was noble of you," Roberta said, "to bet on Pearl Woman, despite her injury."

Fu George stiffened in surprise. "I wonder," he asked, "how your grace knew of my wager?"

Roberta shrugged. "Drake Maijstral mentioned you and he had made a wager."

"Indeed." His face darkened. Now he knew how he'd lost: Maijstral had put her on her guard somehow. Drake Maijstral, he thought, has a lot to answer for.

"Your debut tonight," he said, "is certain to be a success."

"Thank you. Success is something I'm counting on."

"Success becomes you well," Fu George said. "But I wonder if you have ever considered your debut being marked not only by success, but by sensation?"

She gave him a look. "Sensation? How so, sir?"

Fu George gave a deprecating laugh. "I don't mean anything vulgar. No arguments, no duels, no scandalous fashion . . ."

"Ah. I perceive your intent."

Fu George smiled. "Your grace is quick."

Roberta laughed. "I'm afraid the family would not approve of such a major sensation, Mr. Fu George. But perhaps a minor one could be arranged afterward. Why don't you speak to me after the ball?"

"I would be most happy."

"Here's my door. Your servant, sir."

"Yours, madam."

Geoff Fu George stood outside the door for a moment and gnawed his lip. Was Roberta just putting him off, or was she serious about the minor sensation? Should he proceed with the lift tonight, or not?

He'd go ahead, he decided. With Maijstral on station, he had no choice; he couldn't afford to give Maijstral a chance at the Shard.

Confident in his assessment, Fu George turned and stepped toward his room. He and his assistants would have to choreograph their movements perfectly, and that would require careful preparation and rehearsal.

He wasn't going to let Maijstral show him up again.

"Pleased to see you again. May I join you?"

Khamiss looked up and smiled. "Of course. You're very welcome."

Zoot drew the next chair closer, then dropped into it. "I see you're still keeping Maijstral in sight."

"And vice versa." Dourly. "He knows I'm here."

Zoot's magnifier appeared briefly in the air as he gazed across the White Room toward where Maijstral was seated with the Marchioness. The magnifier disappeared, and Zoot turned to Khamiss. "I thought you might be interested in a physiognomy lesson. I've nothing else planned for the afternoon."

Khamiss brightened. "I'd like nothing better."

"The theory is based on using geometry to divide the body and the head into zones, and then finding something in one of the zones that is unique and can compel recall. For instance, the human head can be divided evenly along a lateral line running left to right across the eyes. . . ."

Khamiss was surprised. "The eyes are in the horizontal centerline of the human head? I thought they were . . . rather lower down."

"That's an optical illusion. Because we're taller. Let me show you." Zoot took a notebook from his pocket and drew an oval on it with a pen. He bisected it, added eyes, a button nose, a mouth, and hair. A recognizable human, withal.

"I see."

"The upper attachment of the human's ears to the head are also on a line with the eyes. So . . ." Still drawing.

"Right. So if the ears are placed higher or lower than the corners of the eyes, then that's a distinguishing mark."

Zoot's tongue lolled in approval. "Quite. That's not a common one, however." He sketched idly. "I use a human head as an illustration because their ovoid shape makes for a simpler geometry. Khosali heads are formed along the lines of an oblate hexagon, the upper half larger than the lower."

Zoot continued adding lines to his pad. Khamiss watched and made comments, but her observations dwindled off after a few moments. Zoot's head, she noticed, was quite an admirable hexagon in its way.

"Damn!" Khamiss jumped up. Zoot glanced at her in alarm.

"Something wrong, miss?"

"Maijstral's leaving. I've got to run. Thank you."

"We can continue later."

"Thanks. Bye."

Heart pounding, Khamiss sped across the White Room as Maijstral sniffed the Marchioness's ears and moved toward an exit. She was aware of people looking at her.

She slowed, her ears turning down in embarrassment. Maijstral was waiting for her anyway, arms folded, standing in the doorway.

CHAPTER 6

Some objects have a way of becoming magic. They need not be the biggest or even the best of their type; yet somehow they gather romance unto themselves, and become legend. The Felkhorvinn Tapestry is one such object; and a sect of ascetic carpetmarkers on Pessch has even gone so far as to deify its architect, Pers the Younger. The Felkhorvinn is a little unusual to fit into the category of Magic Objects, in that it's very large: in fact it's so big that it's only been stolen once, by that romantic collector of objects-not-his-own, Ralph Adverse.

For usually it's theft that deifies an object, imbues it with the proper aura of romance. Would La Giaconda's smile seem quite so intriguing had it not been coveted, stolen, and cherished by so many? Would the Hope Diamond have shone quite so brilliantly had its origins not been so mysterious, and had all its owners, beginning with Louis XVI and Antoinette, died in such fateful, inexorable ways? Would Prince Orloff have paid quite so much for his blue-white stone had it not been pried from the eye of an Indian idol? Would the Zoot Torque have become the most celebrated piece of Imperial regalia had not Ralph Adverse managed to worm his way into the City of Seven Bright Rings and get his hands on it?

Most of the Magic Objects moving about the universe are, in fact, gems of one sort or another. The fact is that gems are portable and therefore more easily stolen; and when stolen in the right circumstance, by the right people, an object can be invested with the necessary aura of enchantment. Nothing could make it more romantic than the right theft, lest it be the right death. Blood, it seems, is more effective in creating romance than mere larceny.

Of the glowstones, those rare and lambent objects hurled at relativistic velocities from the cores of dying stars, none is more famous than the Eltdown Shard, which has seen more than its share of death and peculation. When the Countess Ankh was informed by her lover, the financier Collinen, that they must part, she saw no alternative but to disembowel the man and place his organs in cryogenic containers intended originally for selected parts of his pet Farq shepherds. She committed this crime not because she was sorry at losing Collinen, but rather because Collinen owned the Shard, and upon losing her lover she lost her access to its glorious fires, its cool and subtle majesty. (But perhaps she cared for Collinen after all: when the police finally blasted their way into Castle Sumador, they found the Shard in the same cryogenic container as the dead man's heart. Moved by this evidence of sentiment, the Emperor permitted his cousin her choice of deaths.)

Two Allowed Burglars later tried for the Shard and died; Ralph Adverse tried and succeeded, then later, when his lifestrand frayed at last, killed himself with the Shard clutched to his bosom, thus confirming his own legend and the Shard's. Other glowstones are larger, and others display the light of long-dead stars more beautifully; but none has as much romance as the Shard, none has its magic.

And none has its fatal attraction. Its relativistic flames have attracted many a moth, and few have escaped without burning. That's the problem with magic: it can exalt, or destroy, or do both at once; and few can honestly claim to predict which course a Magic Object will take once it has admirers in its spell.

The spell of the Shard had clearly been cast on the Silverside Ballroom. The air of expectancy was tangible: beneath the flares of Rathbon's Star the atmosphere was hushed, almost reverent. Costumes glittered; crystal goblets rang; people conversed; but still all this small world waited, knowing *something* was going to happen.

Drake Maijstral was perfectly recognizable through his domino mask. He was costumed as Grat Dalton, a six-gun on one hip and an elegant rapier on the other. Maijstral's brown hair had been darkened for the occasion, drawn back to a knot behind; glittering gemstones dangled from his ears. The red light of Rathbon's Star, reflecting from his white ruff, darkened his complexion to that of an outdoorsman gunslinger—the effect had been carefully calculated. He spun his six-shooter on his fingers as he padded through the ballroom.

People were talking about him. He gave no sign of knowing.

Baron Silverside's expression was stony. "You have instructed your people, Mr. Sun?"

"I have, my lord." Dutifully.

"Everyone is on alert?"

"Yes, my lord." Another alarm blinked on Sun's control board. He ignored it.

"Maijstral and Fu George will be followed wherever they go?"

"They will, my lord." Another alarm blinked. Against his will, a muscle in Sun's cheek twitched.

"Because they're sure to try something tonight, and if we can find out where they've been concealing the loot, we'll be able to find my lady's collection."

Sun chose his words carefully. "We have every reason to hope, my lord."

The Baron's reaction was icy. "*You* have every reason to *hope*, Sun. *Hope* that you find the collection, and *hope* that you toss these thieves in the calabozo. Because Kyoko Asperson is *hoping* to crucify you in an interview, and if we don't find the collection, I *hope* to hand her the nails and hammer."

More alarms winked. Sun swallowed hard. "I understand, my lord."

"I *hope* so, Mr. Sun. I *hope* so."

Khamiss was dressed as a waiter, in severe black with yellow collar tabs and cuffs. The waiter's uniform had been drawn from central supply and was not tailored for the service pistol that was still jammed in her armpit.

In something close to despair, she followed Maijstral through the crowd. People kept asking her for drinks, and she kept having to turn slightly away from them, concealing the bulge in her armpit, and then apologize for not being able to bring refreshments.

The night could only get worse.

"Mr. Maijstral?"

Kyoko Asperson was dressed as Ronnie Romper, a popular red-haired puppet whose visits to the Magic Planet of Adventure had entranced generations of children.

The last individual Maijstral encountered who dressed as Ronnie Romper had been a seven-foot-tall homicidal maniac who had tried to dissect Maijstral with a broadsword. The experience had been a particularly unhappy one, since the maniac, like a creature out of nightmare, had to be killed repeatedly before he finally snuffed the candle at last. The memory unsettled Maijstral's nerves.

Getting a grip on himself, he doffed his Stetson and sniffed this shorter Ronnie's ears, an act that took a certain effort. "Miss Asperson," he said.

"A fine costume, sir. Very appropriate."

"Thank you." The gleaming six-shooter spun as it marched down Maijstral's fingers. "Yours seems appropriately magical."

Kyoko sighed, a sound that seemed odd in a puppet. She gestured with her wand, scattering holographic fairy dust. "Tonight's magic belongs to the Shard, alas."

"If it's here."

The puppet cocked its head. "Do you really believe it isn't?"

Maijstral regarded the crowd. "If it isn't, there's been a criminal waste of anticipation."

"And preparation?"

Maijstral smiled. "On the part of *some* people, perhaps."

"Not yourself."

"Of course not." He glanced over his shoulder at Khamiss. "I'm being followed by armed police. I'd have to be mad to attempt anything here."

"So in the matter of your duel with Fu George . . ."

Maijstral's nerves, which he had been making a deliberate effort to soothe, promptly unstrung once again at the word *duel,* which reminded him of yet another unhappy experience in his past. He stiffened.

"I'm not in his class, as I believe I've said," Maijstral said. "To challenge Mr. Fu George to a duel, or to anything else, would be an act of presumption."

Kyoko lowered her voice. "I'll presume for you," she said confidentially. "I'm betting on you, Maijstral. The odds on the tote were too great to resist."

Maijstral wasn't entirely surprised by this. "They've posted odds in the Casino, then?"

"Yes. Two and a half to one in favor of Fu George."

Maijstral's eyes glittered in amusement. "Perhaps I'll lay a wager myself. The odds *do* seem a little excessive." He bowed and doffed the Stetson again. "Your servant, madam."

"The Casino odds are encouraging. They have every confidence in you. And," hand tightening on his arm, "so do I."

"Thank you, Vanessa dearest. But this situation *is* a bit unfair, you'll admit. If I outpoint Maijstral, it's only what's expected of me. If Maijstral's luck is in and he outpoints *me*, it's an upset and everyone starts speculating whether or not I'm slipping."

"This should put you on your mettle."

"My dear." An offended tone. "I'm never *off* it."

Vanessa's eyes glittered. "Personally, I'm quite excited by the competition."

"Should I believe the Duchess or not? That's the question."

"You were going to try for the Shard sooner or later anyway. You've always told me."

"Yes. But on grounds of my own choosing. *This* business . . . I'll be getting no points for style, that's certain."

"I think the costume will add points in that department, don't you?"

"I hope so." Approaching the door to the ballroom. "Well, here we go."

Geoff Fu George presented his pair of invitations. Seeing his name and coupling it with the costume, the majordomo's jaw dropped in a perfect attitude of astonishment.

Vanessa, who was dressed spectacularly in feathery orange, resigned herself to letting Fu George outshine her.

Roman strolled into the ballroom on the heels of Vanessa and Fu George. His invitation proclaimed him to be Lord Graves, who was, as it happens, a real person—a human in fact, a distant relative of Maijstral's who lived in the Empire. The door security, still goggling after Fu George's costume, passed him without a glance.

Roman was dressed as a Montiyy noble in the distinctive flounced overcoat and tall tapering hat. He carried a walking stick and wore a signet ring on one finger. From his considerable height, he peered down the length of his muzzle at the other guests and graciously inclined his head toward anyone who looked at him.

He *was* Lord Graves. No one who saw Roman doubted it for an instant. Even Maijstral, who had been looking for him, had to look twice to make sure.

Roman, Maijstral had to admit, was magnificent. His large, heavily muscled frame had somehow become suffused with nobility, elegance, courtesy. Noblesse oblige dripped like honey from his fingertips. People were warmed by his very presence.

If there were any justice, Maijstral thought, Roman would have been born a lord, and Maijstral something else. Roman was so *good* at it—he embodied the noble virtues and graces, and did so with an elegance that Maijstral knew perfectly well he himself did not possess. Maijstral knew how to act a lord; Roman knew how to *be* one.

Maijstral, standing across the room from the false Lord Graves, spared a few moments for the pure enjoyment of watching Roman live the life he deserved.

"A splendid costume. Countess Riefers, is it not?"

"Thank you, Zoot." Lady Dosvidern smiled. "Will you take my arm?"

"Gladly, my lady. Its lordship is in crosstalk?"

"Yes. It's been in a trance with itself since the, ah, incident this afternoon, and will be for many hours yet. I know the signs. The eyestalks have almost entirely withdrawn."

"Have you derived any notion of why its lordship is behaving this way?"

"Not yet, no. *Protocols? Time of Exchange?* The terms and context are new to me."

"But you have a clue?"

"No, not really. It's all very hard to sort out." Her diaphragm pulsed in despair. "Each of the Drawmiikh's brains has a different social function and personality, and when Drawmii meet one another each brain has its own say, and each has a different relationship with each of the *other* Drawmiikh's brains."

"A simple conversation must take a long time."

"There *is* no such thing as a simple conversation on Zynzlyp. The brains have their own quirks, and even with Qlp I have a hard time knowing who's talking at any one time. Sometimes I think even the Drawmii don't keep things straight. I know I can't." She looked up at Zoot and patted his arm. "Well," she said, "at least *now* I know whom I'm talking to."

"Pardon me, but can you bring us a pair of rink and sodas?"

"I'm afraid not, sir. I'm on an errand already."

* * *

"You'll forgive me, dear. I should speak to Silverside."

"He seems in something of a temper. Perhaps you shouldn't."

"Darling, you misunderstand my intention. I will catch him at a disadvantage. He may be inclined to make concessions."

Languidly. "If you insist, dearest." The Marchioness's eyes widened. "Good grief! Look at Fu George!"

Kotani gave a glance. His languor vanished at once. "Sink me! *That* should put the fat in the fire!"

Excitedly. "Is the Duchess here? Has she seen him?" Pause. "I can't believe he actually altered his hairstyle."

Spinning, winking silver . . .

"Casino? I was wondering what odds are offered on the score between Maijstral and Geoff Fu George."

"Three to one, sir. On Fu George. Three-point spread."

"The odds have changed."

"Yes. Have you seen Fu George's costume for the ball?"

"I understand." Spinning. "I would like to place a bet. Four quillers on Maijstral. Bill it to the Coronet Suite."

"Yes, sir."

The six-gun spun again, and dropped into its holster. Maijstral turned off the privacy screen, adjusted his hat, and returned to the ball.

"Perhaps," said Vanessa Runciter, "*I* should speak to her."

"We don't have time to arrange anything. Our plans are set."

"But still, Fu George . . ."

"I've got to beat Maijstral to this one. You know that."

"Yes."

"And here I am dressed as Ralph Adverse. I'm as good as shouting my intention to go after the Shard."

"Yes." Petulant by now. "Do what you wish, Geoff. I'm just trying to *help*."

"Imagine, Pearl. We may be witnesses to the crime of the century!"

"I am agog with anticipation," Pearl Woman said, her voice without enthusiasm. She was dressed as an Earth pirate in tall boots, headscarf, and eyepatch; her matched cutlasses gleamed. She had made an attempt to look authentic, not that anyone here would notice.

Advert was dressed as a dithermoon in bright silks, her swept-brim hat pinned at a jaunty angle. "Have you seen Fu George's costume?" she asked.

"Ralph Adverse. Yes. I've seen it." Pearl Woman winced at the pain in her thigh. Life had, unfortunately, imitated art: she had genuinely strained a leg muscle in a futile but heroic attempt to catch the Duchess in the last stages of the race.

"Fu George may steal the Shard right in front of our eyes!"

Pearl Woman winced again at the sight of someone approaching. "Just what I need. Kyoko Asperson."

"Who? Oh. The Ronnie Romper?"

"Yes. The Ronnie Romper with the media globes. Who else might he be?"

"I *love* Ronnie Romper. Being here is just like being on the Magic Planet of Adventure."

Pearl Woman smiled for the cameras. "You and Ronnie Romper have so much in common," she said, just in time for Kyoko to hear. "Empty heads, for one."

* * *

"My lady."

"Maijstral!" Happily. "I hope you have some diversion planned. Kotani has abandoned me again."

"That was callous of him." Sniffing her. "But do not despair. The evening promises excitement."

"I hope that means you're going to kidnap the Shard."

Maijstral smiled. "Ah. That, too."

Paavo Kuusinen, dressed as a red rover in hat, ruffles, and boots, walked observant among the crowd and counted media globes.

He couldn't help himself. He also was beginning to think it was important.

He counted, nodded, stepped to a telephone. Activating the privacy screen, he bet fifty novae on Drake Maijstral. He then made another bet on someone else.

"Yes, Kyoko. Advert's costume is lovely, isn't it? The dithermoon was my idea. The finger rings, of course, are Advert's own unmistakable contribution."

"Bring me some more brandy, will you?"

"I'm afraid I can't, ma'am."

"Why not?" Belligerently.

"I am already on an errand, ma'am."

"You're just *standing* there, staring at the cowboy. You're a waiter, aren't you?"

"Brandy. Right. Coming up."

"Get *on* with it."

Khamiss's mortification knew no bounds.

"You have no idea how relieved I am to be here, Zoot." Her fingers dug into his arm. "It's been so long since I was able to talk to anyone who wasn't—"

"Lord Qlp?"

"Lord Qlp. Yes. All five of it."

"Yes. The dithermoon *is* appropriate, isn't it. Dear Advert is in such a dither most of the time."

"Yes, Maijstral. I can give you the first dance. I can give you the last, as well. I only hope it's a slow one."

The entrance was timed perfectly, just as anticipation had built as far as possible. Right at the moment when people were about to forget they were in suspense and get on with enjoying themselves, the cymbals crashed, trumpets blared, and the Duchess of Benn made her entrance.

With the Eltdown Shard gleaming at her throat.

CHAPTER 7

The Eltdown Shard was still in the two-century-old Orkhor setting, which made the Shard the centerpiece of an elaborate necklace first worn by the Fourteenth Duchess. The setting featured twenty smaller glowstones. The dark Shard was teardropshaped, the narrow end downward, elaborately cut and faceted. Gleaming in the heart of the Shard, multiplied by the facets, a dying star was captured.

Her grace was dressed as the Countess Ankh, with a black-furred artificial Khosali head encompassing her own. Its brown eyes, made of dark glowstones, gleamed with a diabolical inner light. Her clothing was a dull red that, in the light of Rathbon's Star, brightened to the color of fresh blood. A thousand gemstones were sewn into the blouse and long coat; at her every gesture they flashed fire. Her loose trousers were tucked into ruby-heeled boots made of diresnake skin. At her waist she carried a curved sword identical to that with which the luckless Collinen had met his end.

Roberta stalked into the ballroom, her false ears cocked forward in defiance, the artificial muzzle set in a snarl of scorn. The costume was fully as sensational as the gem that pulsed in the dark hollow of her throat, and Roberta knew it.

Ralph Adverse walked toward her and bowed. "Your

grace," he said. "My fervent congratulations on your debut, and on your sensational costume. I'm sure the Countess Ankh herself never looked better."

"Thank you, Fu George." Roberta had to give the man credit—he was keeping his eyes on her face and off the Eltdown Shard. The gem's dark fires, however, shone in his eyes.

"Will you take my arm, milady?"

"Certainly, sir." They sniffed hello and began walking down the length of the ballroom. Guests parted before them, some with awe, but most because there was a general movement toward the telephones—people were placing bets.

"Now I can understand your disinclination to accept my offer of this afternoon," Fu George said. "Any sensation planned by me would pale beside your own."

"You do yourself injury, sir. Anyone arriving at a ball of mine dressed as Ralph Adverse cannot claim to be a stranger to sensation."

"I wonder, your grace, if you have given my idea any further thought."

"I have scarcely had time to think at all." Her costume head cocked an ear toward him. "But I will give your offer my best reflection, once I have a free moment. Tomorrow I should have several free moments—at least three or four."

"You do me honor to consider the proposal. I wonder if you would also give me the honor of a dance."

"The first I must give to Baron Silverside. The second I've already promised. Would the third suit? I believe it's the Pilgrimage."

"Appropriate, your grace. For a pilgrim I surely am, come to worship at your shrine."

* * *

Maijstral, hoping not to think of the figure from his past as an omen, was trying not to notice Ronnie Romper. He was about to commit the crime of the century, and he preferred not to have to think of anything at all.

He danced the first dance with the Marchioness Kotani, the second, as promised, with the Duchess. Roberta moved superbly in the heavy costume, her assured athlete's balance coping well with the weight of the jewels and head. Maijstral found himself admiring her, her self-reliance, her intelligence, her determination. Birth had given her advantages; but Roberta had made careful use of them—a calculated use, but Maijstral couldn't fault her there. In Roberta's social stratum, one either calculated or one drowned. There was no other choice.

The dance was a slow one, and the measured rhythms served to calm Maijstral's nerves. As the dance ended and Maijstral escorted Roberta to the buffet, he felt ready, his limbs tingling with anticipation, his touch sure. "I hope your grace will give me another dance," Maijstral said.

"I'm afraid not. As official hostess, I should circulate."

"I'm desolated, madam. Will your grace take champagne?"

"Just fruit juice, I think. The brightcrisp."

Maijstral handed the Duchess her drink, then took champagne for himself. He glanced over his shoulder to make sure that Roman was in position, standing near Baroness Silverside. He noticed Geoff Fu George moving through the crowd, heading toward Roberta.

The moment seemed ripe. The crime of the century, he thought. Readiness warmed his veins. He was faintly surprised that he didn't feel the least nervous.

"You will excuse me, your grace. I must congratulate Miss Advert on her costume."

"Certainly, Maijstral." She raised her glass. "We'll speak later."

Maijstral sniffed her, turned, and took four careful, measured paces. The champagne glass was three-quarters full in his left hand. The orchestra was tuning; the crowd was milling; the volume of conversation rose.

Maijstral's empty right hand dropped to his pocket and palmed two micromedia globes. Balancing the champagne glass carefully, Maijstral raised his left hand casually to his lapel and hooked the little finger over the loop of a drawstring bag that was folded carefully in an inner pocket of his coat. He seized mental control of the micromedia globes with the proximity wire in his Stetson, then his right hand emerged from his pocket, reached across his body to his rapier, and pressed a button on the hilt.

With a sudden crash of metal the room was plunged into total darkness. Someone screamed. Thanks to Gregor's tinkering in the ballroom that afternoon, Maijstral had been able to override the command circuits on the steel crash shutters, which were supposed to slam shut overhead in the event that Silverside Station was in danger of colliding with a runaway yacht or a careless meteor.

In one smooth gesture, Maijstral dropped the palmed micromedia globes, turned, and drew the hilt of his rapier —the hilt came away in his hand, revealing sonic cutters hidden in the swordblade.

The Eltdown Shard was the only source of light in the room, marking Maijstral's target. Countess Ankh's ghostly head, back to Maijstral, loomed above the precious glow. The micromedia globes rose to hover overhead, recording everything with ultrasensitive scanners. Maijstral took four measured steps toward the Duchess, cut the chain of the necklace, snagged it between his fingers, and dropped it into the drawstring bag that he had pulled from his jacket with the little finger of his left hand.

The orchestra, seeking to assuage panic, began a shaky rendition of "When the Moonlight is Mellow."

Maijstral turned again and took four measured paces to his starting point. Behind him he was aware of a disturbance. He pulled taut the drawstrings and flung the bag and the Shard high into the air. One micromedia globe followed it; the other dropped into his pocket. He slipped the sonic cutters back into the false blade of his rapier, an act that automatically sent out a signal that cancelled Gregor's interrupt signal on the emergency lighting.

When light first returned to the ballroom, Maijstral was observed standing where he had been when the lights went out, a puzzled expression on his face, a fizzing glass of champagne undisturbed in his hand. . . .

Four paces behind him, Geoff Fu George lay sprawled on the floor, rubbing his eye. The Duchess of Benn, reacting belatedly to the theft of her gem, had struck out blindly into the darkness and flattened him with a single punch.

"Seal the doors!" Baron Silverside's voice rose above the sudden turmoil. "Security to the doors!" And then, his finger pointing toward Fu George like the Hand of Doom, *"Seize that man!"*

The Shard, meanwhile, was closer to Baron Silverside than the latter suspected. The drawstring bag, containing an a-grav homing device and attracted by a transmitter planted in Roman's signet ring, had flown straight across the room and thunked solidly into Roman's hand. The micromedia globe following had been taken under command by the proximity wire in Roman's collar and dropped down the front of his carrick, whence it peeked out from beneath one of the capes and witnessed the next maneuver.

While the Baron shouted, Roman quietly approached the Baroness from behind. The drawstring bag, weightless with its a-grav repellers, was quickly attached by a small adhesive to the inside of one of the Baroness Silverside's elaborate, pleated skirts.

Smiling, Roman ordered the micromedia globe to roll into his pocket. Humming "When the Moonlight turns Mellow," Lord Graves quietly walked away into the crowd, his walking stick touching the floor at every third step, clearly someone too refined to have anything to do with thieves.

There was a palpable air of excitement in Sun's blue heaven. "Right. Watsons!" Sun barked. "Take Fu George behind a privacy screen and search him. Search any of his associates who may be present. Then search Maijstral and any of *his* assistants. And meanwhile *don't let anybody out of the ballroom!*"

"It looks as if Fu George may have beaten you to it," Kyoko Asperson remarked. Her media globes were circling the opaque privacy screen within which Fu George was being searched.

The privacy screen dropped and Fu George stepped into the crowd. His confident grin seemed a little strained. His eye was beginning to swell and turn purple.

Maijstral smiled. "It looks to me as if Fu George is the one that got beat," he said, and drained the last of his champagne.

* * *

"Search Vanessa Runciter!" Sun barked. "Then get Maijstral in there!"

"My condolences, your grace," Zoot offered. "I trust the stone will be recovered."

"One way or another," Roberta said. She was worried. She didn't know *who* had her necklace.

"I'm sure they'll get it back," Pearl Woman said. Unconsciously, she tilted her head to feel the reassuring weight of her pearl against her neck.

"I hope this won't delay the ball fatally," Roberta said. She managed a brave grin. "I realize they have to search people, but can't the rest of us go on dancing?"

Zoot's foot tapped the floor in an admiring pattern of applause. "Well said, your grace," he offered.

"Well, let's!" Roberta declared. She tried to signal the orchestra leader, but failed. "You'll pardon me," she said, and began to walk toward the floating gallery where the orchestra perched.

"May I have the honor of this dance, madam?" Zoot asked, turning to Pearl Woman.

"Certainly." Taking his arm.

"My compliments on your pirate costume, by the way. It looks very authentic."

Pearl Woman was surprised. "I didn't think anyone would notice."

"Old Earth costume is a hobby of mine. There's such a variety, you know."

"No, I didn't."

"Oh, yes. Why, in the age of piracy alone there was quite an amazing diversity of costume. Between the Barbary Corsairs and the Ladronese of Ms. Ching Yih there was a prodigious difference."

"Really? Tell me about it."

She could use this, Pearl Woman thought as Zoot launched into a lecture concerning Pierre le Grand and the dread Bartholemew Roberts. She'd have someone write her a play about Earth pirates—this Ms. Ching Yih sounded promising—with lots of costumes, action, sword fights, armed ships zooming about the atmosphere on scalloped wings . . .

It was time she appeared in a romance. It had been a few years.

"No luck, sir."

"Damnation." Sun scowled. Blinking alarm lights filled his console. "Very well. We'll search *everybody* as they leave the ball."

Khamiss looked startled. "Can we *do* that, sir?"

"Ask the Baron his permission, but I'm sure he'll give it. This is the Eltdown Shard we're talking about, not some damned chunk of asteroid."

"Mr. Sun!" The Baron's scowling visage appeared over Sun's console. Alarm lights shone through his holographic image. "Have you found the Shard?"

Sun touched an ideogram and ended the conversation with Khamiss. "I was just about to speak with you, my lord," he said. "We haven't turned up the Shard yet, but it's probably in the ballroom somewhere. If I could have your permission to search each guest upon leaving . . . ?"

The Baron seemed a little taken aback, but once he got used to the idea, he seemed to grow more cheerful. "Ye-es," he said, stroking his burnsides thoughtfully. "Yes, I believe that would be justified under the circumstances."

"And if by some mischance we fail to recover the stone, then my people can continue following the suspects. They may lead us to their treasure troves."

Baron Silverside brightened again at the thought of recovering his wife's collection. "Yes," he said again. "Good man, Sun. That's the ticket."

"Thank you, sir."

"Remember what's at stake, Sun." Somehow, with Baron Silverside looking pleased, the threat seemed all the worse. Sun commended his soul to the Eternal.

"I remember, sir."

"See that you do, Sun."

Another alarm blinked on.

"Yes, sir. I know very well."

The Baron disappeared. Sun looked sullenly at the control board and its winking lights. Finally his temper snapped.

"Cancel all alarms!" he roared.

The console obeyed. For a few minutes anyway, there was peace.

"Roman? Is that *you?*"

"Yes, Miss Runciter."

Vanessa looked at him in astonishment. She had just danced three figures with the Khosalikh in the carrick and tall hat, thinking only there was something familiar about him, and only now realized she had known him for years.

"Roman," she said, "you are an absolute treasure. You make a wonderful good Montiyy."

"Thank you, madam."

"Surprisingly good," she said, her eyes narrowing. Roman could read her like a book.

* * *

The Pilgrimage to the Cinnamon Temple was under way by the time Maijstral stepped from the privacy screen. He had been searched by a female Khosalikh in a waiter's uniform, the same who had been following him the last two days, and she had clearly been embarrassed by having to face him again: she wouldn't even look at his face. Were it not for the fact that a number of her confederates were watching, he could probably have kept the Shard on his person the entire time, moving it from pocket to pocket while she turned her eyes away and patted at him.

Maijstral decided not to join the dance. The urge to glibber and gambol, he reflected, might get the better of him. He refreshed his champagne glass and noticed a figure in layered silks standing by one of the barred doors. He approached her.

"Miss Advert."

Turning away. "Maijstral." He saw that she was weeping, her mouth rammed into a clenched fist. He reached into a pocket for a handkerchief.

"May I be of assistance?"

She took the handkerchief and said no. Maijstral waited for her to finish dabbing her eyes, then proffered his champagne. Advert returned his handkerchief, took the glass, gulped, returned the glass, took the handkerchief again.

"It's the Pearl, of course," Advert said.

"I thought so."

Her words were spaced by sobs and gasps for breath, but Maijstral was able to follow it. "She insulted me. (Gasp.) In front of Kyoko Asperson. (Gasp.) Several (gasp) times. Called me brainless (gasp). With Kyoko and her globes hearing (gasp) everything. She was so *cutting!* (Gasp.) Making witty jokes at my expense. *And I couldn't think of anything to do! I just stood there!"*

"I'm sorry," Maijstral said, as she exchanged handkerchief for champagne again.

"Why did she *do* it? I thought we were *friends!"* Advert tossed off the champagne and handed Maijstral the empty glass. He gave her his handkerchief again and Advert began wringing it.

"Pearl Woman is a member of the Diadem," Maijstral said. "There's that to consider."

"It puts her under pressure, of course, and perhaps she needs—"

"The Diadem do nothing in public without reason," Maijstral said. "That is another consideration."

Advert paused in surprise, handkerchief halfway to her eyes. "You think so? You think it was calculated?"

"Pearl Woman has had many protegés, Advert. She is very sophisticated and very talented, and because of who she is, she can trust very few people. Among the Three Hundred, people use other people, and often use them badly."

Advert looked at him. "You were offered Diadem membership, weren't you?"

"Not formally. But yes, I knew I'd be accepted."

"With Nichole sponsoring you. And you turned it down."

"Yes."

"Was it because you'd have to be . . . cruel?"

"No. I simply didn't want to live in the public eye for the rest of my life."

"Have you regretted your decision?"

"From time to time. But, to be honest, my regret is halfhearted, and never very serious. When I remember what it was like living with Nichole, with billions of people interested in my every move, I'm quite thankful I don't have to deal with those pressures.'' He gave a brief smile. ''Made it hard to earn my living, for one thing.''

Advert looked at her rings. Her voice was subdued. ''I thought Pearl Woman and I were special friends. I suppose that was silly of me.''

''I can't say. But I know that Pearl Woman doesn't adopt just anybody. She did see *something* in you, Advert.''

Advert swallowed hard. She gave a brave smile and handed Maijstral his handkerchief. ''She used me. Spent my money, let me support her. And I ransomed her pearl.''

''But she gave you access to the Diadem in return, let you live the kind of life you thought you wanted. Perhaps she considers this a fair exchange.''

''It's not.'' Her expression hardened. ''Not at all.''

''Perhaps this is her way of educating you. The Three Hundred use people, and in return are used by the institution of the Diadem. Not everyone is cut out for a life like that. It may be better that you know what it's really like.''

''Still.'' Advert's look was cold. ''She ought not to be allowed to get away with it entirely. Not in front of Kyoko and everybody.''

Maijstral thought about this for a moment. ''You don't want to call her out, of course.''

''No!'' Advert seemed shocked. Her expression, after consideration, turned calculating. ''No,'' she repeated. ''For a start, she'd win, and even though she'd be upset by being made to fight twice in a year, it wouldn't be worth it to me. I just think—maybe she should have a taste of her own medicine, that's all.''

''There's her pearl.'' Tentatively. ''She could . . . lose it again.''

Advert seemed surprised, then she thought for a moment. "And people could find out, this time," she said slowly. There was a certain enthusiasm in her look, but she frowned and shook her head. "I'll have to think about that, Mr. Maijstral."

"Call me Drake. And let me know what you decide."

"Certainly." Advert gave a tentative smile. "Thank you."

He sniffed her ears. The Pilgrimage was coming to an end, and he headed back to the buffet to refill his champagne glass before the dancers began to crowd around.

"Fu George." Slipping her arm through his.

"Yes?"

"You'll never guess who I just danced with."

"A big Khosalikh built like a pom boxer and wearing a funny overcoat."

Laughing. "Yes. He *is* a pom boxer, too. But the pom boxer is Roman."

Fu George's eyes widened. "Roman? Here?"

"He may well have the Shard on him."

Fu George looked at Roman and frowned. "I think this is worth a recce."

"I'd say so."

"If you'll excuse me, my dear . . . ?"

"Of course. But get some semilife patches on that eye soon, won't you? It's really starting to look ugly."

The Duchess of Benn stalked through the room, breathing fire. Maijstral was on his third glass of champagne, and in a sunny mood. "A setback, your grace?" Maijstral asked.

Beneath the Khosali head, Roberta's violet eyes flashed

anger. "Those fools are going to search everyone on leaving. *My guests!*"

Maijstral held his glass to the light, admiring the golden rise of bubbles. "Shocking."

She glared at him. "Treating my guests as if they were . . ."

"Thieves, my lady?"

Roberta froze for a moment, then laughed. "Thieves, yes." She looked at him. "I take it you are pleased with the results of the evening."

"I have no reason to be unhappy."

"And you've anticipated the searches, I suppose?"

Maijstral's heavy lids rose to reveal amused green eyes. "I have laid my plans."

Suddenly cheered, Roberta gave another laugh. "So all my guests are going to be searched for nothing."

"That seems likely. If the guards find any secrets, none will be mine."

She shook her head. "I didn't have time to think when the lights went out. I just reacted. Lucky I hit Fu George and not you."

"You wouldn't have caught me."

Roberta looked at him. "You're very sure of yourself."

"In some things. As sure as you are on a racecourse."

She thought about this, then turned to look at Baron Silverside. Anger entered her voice again. "That pompous idiot. I hope you get to *keep* his damned collection."

"I hope so, too."

She gave a laugh. "That *was* you? Interesting."

Maijstral's lazy eyes turned cautious. "Perhaps we should not speak any longer. You're supposed to be the one who's just lost your greatest treasure, and I'm supposed to be the one who may have taken it. People may hope for at least a small display of bad temper."

She nodded. "You're right. I forgot for a moment."

"Your grace." He sniffed her farewell. She stiffened, as if offended.

Both turned at the sound of a smack, and neither could help laughing once they did.

Roman had just felt Fu George's fingers in his pocket, and without thought had driven his elbow into Fu George's uninjured eye and knocked him to the floor.

CHAPTER 8

D rexler's ears were cocked at an indignant angle. His lips drew back from his muzzle in a snarl. "Roman *struck* you, sir?"

Geoff Fu George had changed from his Ralph Adverse costume into his evening jacket with the built-in darksuit. He applied a semilife patch to one of his blackened eyes. The little creature, happy in its purpose, awoke from its stasis and began to set its taproots into the swollen tissue.

"It was involuntary, I suspect," Fu George said. "He's a trained fighter, and I must have been more careless than usual. I triggered his reflexes." He sighed. "Anyway, he didn't have the Shard."

"With all respect, sir, Roman is also good enough to know when to use his reflexes and when not to. Perhaps," flexing his muscles, "I should have a chat with our Mr. Roman concerning this promiscuous use of 'reflexes.' "

Fu George looked at him sharply. "None of *that*, Drexler. Ten points for style, remember. Grudge matches aren't good ton."

Drexler snarled again, but didn't insist.

"What I need you to do, Drexler," Fu George said, "is follow him. Pick Roman up outside the ballroom and don't let him go. If we can find Maijstral's blind, we find the Eltdown Shard."

"And then what?"

Fu George looked at him in surprise. "I steal it, of course. If he can steal the Pearl's trinket from me, I can do it back to him."

"What about Gregor?"

"I've got Chalice waiting outside Maijstral's suite. If Gregor appears, Chalice will follow him."

"And Maijstral himself?"

Fu George trimmed a dormant semilife patch with a pair of pocket scissors. "Vanessa will do the shadowing there."

"And you, sir?"

"I'll be working. Have you noticed that the Marchioness changed her jewelry since this afternoon? I doubt she bothered to send her afternoon jewels to the hotel safe, do you?"

Drexler grinned. "I doubt it, sir."

The phone chimed once for attention. "Mr. Gregor Norman," it reported, "wishes to speak to Mr. Chalice or Mr. Drexler."

Interest flared in Fu George's wounded eyes. "Answer," he told Drexler. "Examine the background in the holo figure. Try and work out where he is."

Gregor's location was clear enough once his hologram appeared, obvious from the resonant quality of his voice, a quality that could only have arisen from his standing in the White Room, near the giant impact diamond.

"Mr. Drexler?" he said, grinning. "I think it's time you and Chalice began raising your ten novae."

"That's a little premature, don't you think?"

"The bet concerned who had his hands on it first, and that's already been decided. I won't show you the vids till tomorrow, of course, but I thought I'd give you a day's notice so you could start raising the money."

Drexler bit back the impulse to make a further bet concerning who would get to *keep* the stone—but that would give things away.

"Thank you, Gregor," he said. "I appreciate the consideration."

"Only too." Meaning, only too *very, very* pleased.

Fu George was on his feet the instant the hologram was replaced by the "at your service" ideogram. "Get to Chalice," Fu George said. "Tell him Gregor's in the White Room. I'll head to the White Room directly."

"Sir!"

Fu George took two fast steps toward the door, then hesitated. He returned, seized his box of semilife patches, and then ran like hell.

He met no one in the halls save a pair of robots and the security man Kingston, who had been following him all day. The both of them had been engaged in a daylong pretence that Fu George didn't know he was being followed, a pretence that was strained to the limits as Kingston was forced to sprint after his suspect. Fu George slowed as he entered the White Room, hearing as he walked the peculiar, resonant quality of the diamond as it reflected the orchestra and Kingston's hurried footsteps behind.

He straightened his jacket, shot his lace, and entered the room. Save for the bartender and a pair of serving robots, the orchestra was playing to an empty room.

Fu George turned and left frowning, passing Kingston once again, much to the latter's exasperation. Since the pearl business, all Fu George had done was to react to Maijstral—he had let Maijstral panic him into advancing his attempt to steal the Shard, and now all Fu George could do was follow Maijstral and his people in hopes of finding out something useful. Somehow Fu George had lost all initiative to Maijstral, and that was bad. He had to *do* something, he decided, something that might serve to define the situation and compel events to start moving his way once again.

He'd give Kingston the slip, he decided, then go out and steal something. At least it would make him feel better.

His tread was lighter as he stepped down the hallway. Pity he hadn't been able to intercept Gregor in the White Room.

The White Room. The place hung humming in his memory, resonating like the giant diamond. He realized that it hadn't occurred to him to wonder what Maijstral's chief technician was *doing* in the White Room.

He hesitated, then began to retrace his steps. As he crossed paths with Kingston again, he heard his tail mutter something about why didn't he make up his mind, for heaven's sake? Fu George walked to the bartender and ordered a brightcrisp.

"What time," he asked casually, "do you close tonight?"

The bartender told him. And there was his answer.

Mortification, it seemed, knew no end. Not only was Khamiss, still dressed as a waiter, following Maijstral again, it now appeared that someone was following *her*. She *thought* her tail was Vanessa Runciter, but the woman was still wearing her feathery orange ball costume and Khamiss couldn't be certain.

Maijstral, having been searched once more on leaving the Duchess's ball, was now walking, apparently at random, through the residential quarters of the station, twirling his gun as he moved. Maijstral was obviously up to *something*, but Khamiss couldn't believe the man didn't know he was being shadowed. She hadn't been able to believe in her role for some time, and she couldn't put any feeling into her skulking at all.

She craned around a corner, not bothering to just peek with one eye or try to hide, instead resignedly leaning out in plain view as she watched Maijstral walking up the soft carpet. Maijstral came to a four-way intersection, looked both ways, stepped to his right, hesitated, then abruptly jumped to his left.

Excitement burned in Khamiss. She swept around the corner and accelerated, moving at a run down the corridor, then stopped to peek around the next corner. Maijstral's figure dashed past another intersection, running flat out. Khamiss followed at a dead run.

The collision came too quickly for Khamiss to react. Without warning, a brilliantly costumed figure appeared in her path. The collision flung them to the floor in a tangle of flailing arms and thrashing legs. Khamiss's pistol spilled out of its holster and flew across the carpet.

Khamiss sat up, her head ringing, and looked up into the blazing eyes of Vanessa Runciter. "Idiot!" Vanessa spat. There was a bright scarlet abrasion on her pale cheek. "Can't you do a simple tail job right?"

Rage flared in Khamiss. "*I'm* not the one who's tailing someone while dressed like a big orange bird." Maijstral had *intended* this to happen, Khamiss realized: he'd seen his shadows from the start and doubled back to force them to collide. Khamiss and Vanessa had fallen into a trap.

Khamiss floundered after her pistol. "Didn't your nannybot ever tell you to look both ways?"

"I had a *live* nanny, you imbecile." Vanessa rose to her feet and flung her cape back over her shoulder. She hobbled after one of her shoes, which was lying near Khamiss's pistol.

"Even more reason to listen to her." Khamiss's hand closed on the pistol, and she rammed the bulky object back into her armpit. She picked up Vanessa's shoe and handed it to her.

"Thank you." Said without thought. Vanessa put a tentative hand to her cheek, came away with blood. "I could *kill* you for this," she said, enraged again.

"Just try it." Khamiss stood and drew herself to her full height, a head taller than the human. "Just try it," she repeated, rather liking the sound of the words.

Vanessa glared at her but said nothing. Did these High Custom people fight duels with waiters? Khamiss wondered. She decided to keep the initiative now that she seemed to have it.

"Why were you following Maijstral, anyway?" she said. And then, "Or was it *me* you were following?"

Vanessa decided on a belligerent response. "Who says I was following Maijstral? And who the hell would follow you?"

"*You* would. It was obvious. You were clumsy enough."

It was *wonderful*, Khamiss was finding, being belligerent to a guest. She should abuse her station more often.

Something caught Khamiss's attention, a movement out of the corner of her eye. She turned and saw a tiny black marble rolling along the ceiling, a little sphere that stayed in the shadows and tried to be inconspicuous.

With a practiced movement, Khamiss drew her service pistol. Vanessa gave a gasp and, assuming she was about to be turned to toasted cheese, clawed for the tiny chugger she carried under her cape. Khamiss lined up the micromedia globe over the sights and squeezed the trigger. Flame burst from the ceiling. The globe ran for cover. More fire leaped out, and the globe fell, rolled, and died.

Fire alarms wailed. Robot arms appeared from the service corridor and began spraying foam. Khamiss rather enjoyed the spectacle.

Being aggressive was so *satisfying*, she thought.

Vanessa finally got her gun out. She pointed it in at least three directions before she realized she was in no danger.

Khamiss ignored the foam that spattered her waiter's costume. She holstered her spitfire, and walked to the charred micromedia globe. She picked up the globe and let it roll in her hand. She turned to Vanessa.

"Yours?"

Vanessa, clutching her pistol, shook her head. Foam speckled her hair. She put her pistol back in its holster. She reached for her cigaret holder and a pack of Silvertips.

"Who was the operator trying to follow?" Khamiss wondered. "Maijstral? You? Me?"

"Who cares? *We've* lost him, that's the main point." Vanessa lit a Silvertip.

A robot fire fighter promptly covered her face with foam.

Five . . . Four . . . Three . . .

Baroness Silverside was growing larger in the view of Gregor's skulking micromedia marble.

Two . . . One . . . Now.

Gregor stepped briskly around the corner and walked deliberately into the Baroness.

"Beg pardon, madam."

The Baroness looked at him with irritation. "Be careful, young man," she said.

As Gregor walked away, he whistled his micromedia globe from the ceiling. He ordered it into his inside coat pocket, next to the glory that was the Eltdown Shard.

"It's after midnight, Sun."

"Yes, my lord."

"You have not recovered my wife's collection."

Sun gazed bleakly into a future that held no place for him. A sinner, he thought, in the hands of an angry god. Dangling over the candle flame like a spider, all for his own unperceived fault.

"Alas, my lord," he said.

Baron Silverside looked upon him with the face of the Angel of Judgement. "You will pay for this, Sun."

Sun acceded to the inevitable. "I know, my lord," he said. He suspected he would never cease paying.

The Duchess of Benn exchanged condolences with Baron Silverside, then let Kotani drag the Baron away for another conference. The orchestra members, instruments dangling from their hands, were making their way out by another entrance. Roberta looked at her last remaining guest, Paavo Kuusinen. He bowed over her hand as he clasped it: one finger, as was proper.

"Congratulations, your grace," he said. "You've achieved your object. A sensational debut."

"Thank you, Mr. Kuusinen. I couldn't have done it without your help."

"You are far too gracious." He glanced at the last of the musicians as they filed out to the waiting security watsons, who were frisking them in a final hope of locating the Shard. "I wonder how he got it out?" he asked.

"We'll have to wait for the videos to come out. Six months or so."

"Yes, your grace. I suppose we'll have to contain our curiosity till then." He frowned as he glanced up at Rathbon's Star, its astonishing display revealed once again now that Silverside personnel had removed Gregor's overrides.

"I hope the second part of your grace's plan goes as smoothly as the first," he said.

"Do you think it might not?"

"I suspect complications. There are . . . undercurrents."

Countess Ankh's artificial ears tilted forward in curiosity. "Do you think Geoff Fu George might interfere?"

"He might, particularly if he thought his position as top-ranked thief was in danger. He lost a number of style points when your grace knocked him down; that might even put his rating in danger.'' He glanced over the empty ballroom. ''But I think there's something else going on. I don't know whether it concerns us or not; but it would be well to be cautious.''

''You pique my curiosity, Kuusinen.''

''I would prefer not to speculate until I have further information.'' He glanced over the ballroom. ''Shall I escort you to your room?''

''That would be pleasant. Please take my arm.''

''Ever your servant, your grace.''

Drake Maijstral, still clothed as a bank robber, folded the Marchioness Kotani in his arms and kissed her. His pulse sped; his knees grew weak. His mind was racing.

Maijstral was trying to calculate his chances of getting killed. The Marquess, he knew, was a very good shot. But the Marchioness had assured him Kotani would be spending the night harassing Baron Silverside; in any case the two had separate rooms, and the chance of discovery was therefore slight.

It wasn't as if he hadn't earned this, after all. How often did one commit the crime of the century right in the middle of a public function and get away with it? Maybe, for a single night at least, one could get away with anything.

He decided to take the risk.

Still, it was not passion for the Marchioness that made his heart throb and turned his knees watery—rather, the thought of a pistol with Kotani at one end of it and himself at the other.

The kiss ended. The Marchioness gazed up at him with glowing eyes. ''I'll call a robot for you,'' she said, and brushed his cheek with the back of her hand. She touched the service plate and cast a look over her shoulder. "My rover," she said, and stepped into her dressing room. The dressing room door closed. The robot bustled out of a closet and unlaced Maijstral's jacket and trousers.

Maijstral dismissed the robot, sat on the bed, and pulled off his boots. "Fu George," he said, "I think this is your moment to leave."

An annoyed grunt came from beneath the bed.

"And kindly replace anything you stole," Maijstral went on. "Otherwise her ladyship will think I took it."

"Damn it, Maijstral," Fu George said as he rolled out of hiding. "You owe me something for this."

"Something, agreed," Maijstral said. "Not the Shard. The Shard is more than just something."

"Did I *ask* for the blasted Shard?"

Fu George's darksuit made his outlines uncertain, but the Marchioness's jewels, falling from the vagueness of Fu George's hand into the open jewel case, were clear. Maijstral rose from the bed to let Fu George out. Fu George turned.

"You're going to stay here for the night, are you?" he asked. "I wouldn't want to run into you again."

"I'm not planning on breaking into any rooms tonight, if that's what you want to know." Which was true to the letter, Maijstral reflected, if not quite to the spirit of Fu George's question.

"Your servant."

"Thank you, Fu George. You've been very decent. I hope you get style points out of this, at least."

"Your very obedient. And hasty." The shape rose on a-grav repellers and fled down the corridor.

Maijstral closed the door and stepped into the bedroom again just as the Marchioness entered from her dressing room. She wore a mothwing nightgown. Dark gemstones dangled from her ears and brushed against her neck. Her pouting mouth was drawn in a smile.

"Was someone here?" she asked.

"No one of consequence," Maijstral said, and dismissed Fu George, like her husband, from his mind.

"Thank you, Zoot. It's been the most delightful evening I've spent since . . ." Her ears fluttered helplessly. "Since I was condemned to Zynzlyp." She and Zoot stopped at her door.

"It has been entirely my pleasure, my lady. It's the greatest pity the evening must come to an end."

Lady Dosvidern looked at him with burning eyes. "It need not, you know," she said.

Zoot's heart boomed like a gong.

"Oh," he said. "Do you think so?"

"Yes. I think so," she confirmed, and lovingly closed her canines on one of his ears.

Eight silver media globes circled in a perfect halo over Kyoko Asperson's bed. Gregor kissed her and reached for his trousers.

"Time for bed check, lover," he said.

Kyoko sat up. "I didn't realize Maijstral ran such a tight ship."

"Sorry. Burglar's hours and all that. The boss might need me for something or other." Pulling on his pants.

"Can you come by later?"

"It would have to be *very* later."

She cocked her head. "I'll be here all morning. I can't sleep *too* late, because Baron Silverside gave me an interview with the head of security here—" She laughed at Gregor's sudden tigerish grin. "An interview about all the chaos you've been causing."

"What time is the interview?"

"Noonish. Why do you ask?"

A knowing smile. "Nothing."

"Come on." Coaxing.

"Forget I said anything."

"You can tell *me*."

"Not yet I can't. I'd like to see the man sweat, though."

"Speaking of *sweating* . . ." She reached to the bedside table for her loupe and stuck it in her eye. One of the media globes detached itself from its circuit and hovered in front of Gregor.

"Tell me, Mr. Norman," she said, "what's a noted burglar like yourself doing in this shocking state of undress, here in someone else's room?"

Gregor looked wide-eyed at the media globe and gasped in feigned surprise. "I'm afraid I've been the victim of a crime, Miss Asperson. A terrible crime."

"Yes?" Kyoko leaned forward intently. "And what might that be?"

Gregor leaned forward himself till their noses were almost touching. "Someone robbed me of my affections, that's what."

Kyoko grinned and kissed him. "G'night, sad victim that you are."

"Goodnight, thief."

He reached for his boots.

The White Room burned red in the nighttime, illuminated only by Rathbon's Star. Stark black shadows lay with precise knife edges on the soft blood-red carpet. Above, the impact diamond rang faintly with echoes of distant life.

Ghosts moved in the ruddy light. Nearly invisible, their shadows danced on the carpet, flickered on the walls, played tag with the rainbows cast by the giant diamond.

The ghost dance was witnessed by two people, each viewing the action via separate media globes set high in a place of vantage.

At the sight of the ghosts and their purposeful dance, the onlookers smiled.

Advert looked at the treasure in her hand and her fingers trembled as a wave of terror passed through her. Panic churned in her mind. Her fingers clamped shut. Moving as silently as she could, she stepped from Pearl Woman's bedroom into the front room of their suite.

Once in the front room she whispered for a spotlight and opened her hand. Her treasure seemed insignificant in her pink palm: a pearl, a length of minute chain, an ear-clasp.

She looked at the thing and experienced a wave of giddiness. She felt as she had when she was ten years old, and successfully evaded her nannybot to meet with her friends at midnight in the Haunted Pavilion.

She realized she was enjoying herself. She closed her fist around the treasure and performed a brief, giddy dance.

Serve her *right*, she thought.

"Did you really get the Eltdown Shard?"

"Perhaps." Maijstral reached for the bottle of champagne that a Cygnus robot had just delivered to the room.

"I'd like to see it."

"That might be possible. After tomorrow midnight, of course."

Her fingers lazily brushed the skin of her throat. Her tilted eyes challenged him. "I'd like to *wear* it."

He smiled as he poured the champagne. "I think it could be arranged. Assuming I've got it, of course."

"Of course." Crystal rang as the glasses touched. Maijstral raised his glass to his lips. A knock thundered on the door.

There was a practiced blur of motion. Moving swiftly and in perfect silence, Maijstral left the bed, scooped up his clothes, flung them through the open closet door, picked up his riding boots, sword, and gunbelt, and then loped for the closet, the champagne glass still in his hand. The Marchioness watched him through laughing eyes.

"Darling?" Kotani's voice, speaking Khosali Standard. "Why is your door locked?"

Maijstral turned in the closet, surveyed the room for signs of his presence, found none, and sotto voce told the closet door to shut as he glided backward, obscuring himself behind the Marchioness's clothing.

"I cannot close the door," the closet said, speaking Human Standard, as Maijstral had. "My sensors inform me there is a person inside."

The Marchioness glanced in apprehension at the closet, then at the door that was keeping her husband at bay. "What time is it, dear?" she called.

"I *am* the person inside," Maijstral explained, trying to keep his voice to a whisper. "Shut the door, please." His heart crashed in his ears as the closet's idiot brain considered the problem. Blackness ringed his vision, narrowing it. He appeared to be gazing at the world through the barrel of a gun. I am *not* going to faint, he told himself. He downed the champagne as a restorative.

"Five," said Kotani, "or thereabouts. Did I wake you?"

"I was dozing," said the Marchioness. She was looking more and more alarmed as she perceived the closet's stubbornness. She rose from the bed and donned her mothwing gown.

"Great news!" called Kotani. "Open the door. I want to tell you."

"Just a moment," said the Marchioness. She stepped into her changing room. Maijstral seized the closet door and tried to haul it shut.

"Do not attempt to close the doors manually," the closet said. "Damage to the mechanism may result."

"Then *shut the door*," Maijstral whispered. If he had his burglar's tools with him, this wouldn't have been a problem.

"There is a person inside the closet." Happy to get back on track again. "I cannot shut the door with a person inside. Please leave the closet."

Maijstral could feel beads of sweat gathering on his scalp. Terror yowled blindly in his brain. He gave the closet door a final despairing yank. The closet door yanked back. He thought about letting himself out the other door into the corridor, the exit used by Fu George, but decided against it. A man standing unclothed in the hallway might become subject to unfortunate amounts of attention. Not to mention derision.

"Do not close the door manually," the closet said again. "Damage to the mechanism may result."

"Why have you locked the door?" Kotani asked. His tone was growing suspicious.

The Marchioness reappeared, looking desperate. She had a spray bottle of scent in her hand, and she perfumed herself wildly as she searched her mind for an answer.

"I'm afraid of burglars," she said. "I have my jewelry here."

The door rattled from within as Kotani tried the knob. "I *told* you," condescendingly, "to keep your jewels in the station safe."

"I'm sorry, dear." Her eyes implored Maijstral to *do* something. Maijstral, in the last seconds before his vision faded away entirely, glanced desperately for another hiding place, recalled where he had found Fu George, and dived for the bed. As he rolled beneath it he heard the closet door slide triumphantly shut. The air was drenched with perfume. The Marchioness unlocked the door.

"Would you like some champagne?" she said, a bit breathlessly.

Kotani stepped in. "A nightcap would be pleasant," he said. "I've just struck a deal with Silverside."

"Congratulations, dearest. Would you fetch a glass from the other room?"

"A better deal than I expected, my only," Kotani crowed as Maijstral heard his footsteps leave the room. "In view of his problems with security here, the fact they'll be highly publicized, and the damage to his custom that could result, he conceded any percentage of gross revenues in hopes my play will contribute to restoring any of the station's lost ton. He's got a profit percentage only. I think the poor fellow was so down he was prepared to concede anything."

"Splendid, dear." Kotani's footsteps returned. Maijstral, over the demon pulse of his heart, heard champagne being poured, then the sound of a sneeze.

"Allergic to champagne, my dear?"

"Not at all, Janetha-my-dove. Your scent is exquisite, but you seem to have applied it a little generously this evening."

"I wanted to smell good for you."

"A charming and considerate thought, dearest. But it is a bit . . . overwhelming." He sneezed again.

"Shall we step into the other room? Perhaps a little fresh air might help."

"An excellent suggestion, my heart."

Good grief, thought Maijstral. Kotani's conversation in private was just like those in his plays. No wonder the Marchioness was getting restless. Who wants to live with someone who's a paragon of courtesy and sophistication even when sneezing?

The door closed behind them. Maijstral let a long breath out. Moving in trained silence, he rolled from under the bed and, in as low a voice as possible, asked the closet door to open. The moronic mechanism was happy to oblige. Maijstral drew his belongings into his arms and decided that he wasn't about to take a chance of Kotani walking in on him half-dressed. Therefore he rolled under the bed again and began dragging on his clothes. On his way to Dolfuss's room he'd be walking unlaced—no trained bots-of-the-wardrobe available in the corridor—but that would be far less conspicuous than wearing nothing at all.

There wasn't much clearance under the bed, but Maijstral was agile: he was performing the last operation, shrugging into his jacket, when the door to the front room opened again. Maijstral's heart leaped into his throat. He froze.

The door closed. Lady Janetha's plump, pretty feet appeared beside the bed. "Maijstral?" A whisper. "Are you still there?"

"My lady." He worked his way to the edge of the bed and stuck his head out.

"I wanted to say goodnight to you properly." She knelt and kissed him. Maijstral, almost smothered by her perfume, managed to give a convincing imitation of passion while keeping one eye cocked on the inner door.

"Don't forget," she said, "I'd like to feel the Shard against my skin."

"Tomorrow night," Maijstral promised. He could use Dolfuss's room for the assignation: no sense in taking ridiculous chances again.

"I wager you've done this sort of thing before. Your leap into the closet was a thing of beauty. You were hiding before I even had the chance to blink."

He appraised her. "I suspect you're not new to this, either. The trick with the perfume was a good one."

He rolled out from beneath the bed and hitched his trousers up. The Marchioness brushed her lips against his, took the champagne bottle, and stepped through the door with a careless laugh.

Maijstral knotted his trouser-laces, tugged his jacket close around him, and stepped out the other exit into the hallway. He yawned. There was one more thing he must do, and then sleep.

"Ah. He's making his move. You see?"

"Just like we thought, boss."

"Brilliant, my dear." The sound of a kiss. "We've got him where we want him."

Geoff Fu George smiled, brushed his lips over Vanessa Runciter's knuckles, and turned back to the video. The picture was blurred. It looked like a double exposure.

In the center was the giant impact diamond, picked out in the darkened White Room by spotlights. But right next to it was another, identical diamond, with straps around it and a blurring about its rim. The second diamond was moving, dropping downward.

"Follow that, Drexler," Fu George said.

"Yes, sir."

"Prepare to send the globe on its way. Don't get too close, now."

"Sir."

Fu George gave a cold, deliberate laugh. His eyes glowed as he looked at the screen. "A lovely decoy that Maijstral's made. With a holographic image of the diamond hanging there, no one will even know it's missing."

The diamond sailed to the floor in its a-grav harness, then

disappeared into a laundry cart. Sheets and blankets moved to cover it.

"He'll snap off the hologram at some suitably dramatic moment," Vanessa said. "With hundreds of people in the room, no doubt, to be fooled into thinking he somehow made the diamond vanish in front of their eyes."

"More style points that way."

"He thinks like a conjurer, boss," said Chalice.

"I'm moving the globe, sir," Drexler said. The point of view began to shift as the globe followed the cart, which was rolling, apparently under its own power, out of the room.

"Leading us right to the Shard," Chalice said. He gave a barking laugh. "This is great, boss. Almost worth losing ten novae for."

"Ten novae?" Fu George asked, distracted.

Vanessa's eyes glittered. She put her hands on Fu George's shoulders. "When will you take Maijstral's loot, dear?"

"Ah." Forgetting the ten novae. "That will depend, lover. We'll have to see if the room is guarded. It would be best to wait till the place is vacant."

"Pity you can't just turn Maijstral and his friends into stripped electrons."

Fu George patted her hand. "Now, now. No style points for violence."

Vanessa's mouth tightened. She touched the semilife patch on her cheek and eye, where Khamiss's elbow had bruised her. "More's the pity, Fu George," she said. "More's the pity."

As Maijstral, a mere blur in his darksuit, pushed the laundry cart down the corridor, Drexler's media globe followed cautiously behind. Drexler knew that Maijstral's darksuit contained detectors that might spot the motion of his globe: he kept his distance, and crept around corners with caution. He had no need to keep close, fortunately; the laundry cart was a large target. Drexler was entirely pleased with himself.

He might have been less pleased had he known that he, himself, was being followed.

Behind Drexler's globe came another, one that moved cautiously, keeping Drexler's dark sphere just in sight . . . following Drexler's globe, which was following Maijstral, who was moving at all deliberate speed to his hideout.

The second globe's operator was *very* pleased. And happily making plans for the morrow.

Dolfuss held open the door of his room as Maijstral pushed the laundry cart inside. As Dolfuss closed the door behind him, Maijstral turned off his holographic camouflage, stripped the darksuit's hood from his head, and shook out his long hair.

"Things went well, sir?" Dolfuss inquired.

"Very well indeed." Maijstral picked up the sixteen-foot impact diamond—in its harness, it was weightless. He frowned for a moment, then moved toward the closet.

"Full of art, I'm afraid," Dolfuss said.

"Well." Maijstral set the diamond down. "I suppose it will have to stand in the corner."

"Best not take any more bulky loot, sir."

Maijstral took off his signature ring, which he wore over his suit gloves, and began to peel off the darksuit. "I intend to take no more loot at all," he said. "A wise thief quits while he's ahead."

"I'd say you have reason enough to be pleased." Dolfuss reached for the Eltdown Shard, which had been tossed rather carelessly on the bureau top. The dark stone glowed softly in his hand.

"Pity I couldn't have watched you take it," he said. "But boors—even phony boors—don't get invited to the more exclusive parties. I spent the evening watching an old vid. *Prince of Tyre,* by Shaxberd. What a piece of rubbish."

"I like much of his other work." Maijstral cocked an eye at the actor. "The *Llyr* might suit you. You're old enough for the part."

"Too depressing. Satire's more my style."

"It dates rather more quickly than other sorts of comedy, however."

"True, sir. But while it lasts, it has more bite."

"I've subscribed to Aristide's translations. *Comedy of Errors* is the next."

"Farce. Even worse. It's so low."

"Taking the last few days into account, it does seem more true to life."

"Precisely my point, sir. If you take my meaning."

Maijstral reached for his dressing gown. "Literary debates later, I think. For now, I want only bath and bed."

"I'll get out of your way, then," said Dolfuss.

"Would you mind taking the cart with you, Mr. Dolfuss? Just leave it somewhere."

"As you like, sir." But he hesitated, frowning at the Shard in his hand. "Do you think, Mr. Maijstral, that the Shard is worth all the fuss? All the lives?"

Maijstral gave a self-satisfied laugh. "It's not worth *my* life, at any rate."

Dolfuss smiled. "As you say." He put the stone on the bureau and stepped toward the door. "Have a pleasant night, sir."

"I'm sure I will. And you."

"Your servant."

Dolfuss pushed the cart out of the room. Maijstral told the room lights to grow dimmer, and then told the room to ready his bath. The sound of running water came from the bathroom.

Maijstral looked at his Grat Dalton costume, now tossed on a chair, and smiled. Even the Dalton Brothers had never pulled off a string of robberies as glorious as this one.

Like Drexler, like Fu George, like the operator of the second globe, he was very pleased with himself.

Elsewhere in the night, unobserved by anyone, magic was happening. Wrapped in dark cloth, discarded in a corner of a room, a pair of objects were transforming themselves. Cold fire ran over their surfaces: burning red, cold violet, electric green . . . shimmering, iridescent, and wonderful.

Silent. Unseen. Entirely unanticipated.

CHAPTER 9

"Miss Asperson? Kyoko?" Gregor rapped on the door. There was no answer. Must be a sound sleeper, he thought. He reached into his pocket for a touchwire, snapped off the lock, then entered Kyoko's room.

"Kyoko?"

The room was empty. Six abandoned media globes circled the bed like moons bereft of their primary. The vidset was on.

The vidset was repeating, over and over, all known biographical data on Mr. Sun, Silverside's head of security. Gregor watched for a few minutes, learned nothing of any significance, and shrugged and left the room. Kyoko must have been studying for her interview. Poor Mr. Sun, Gregor thought, and grinned.

Too bad he'd lost his affections to such an early riser.

Sex and death have an unfortunate association in the Khosali mind. Every child of the Empire is brought up on tales of the disgraced Madame Phone and the spectacular suicide of her lover Baron Khale, whose internal organs were, as specified in his will, preserved and set up in a monument as a warning to future generations.

Studies by curious anthropologists have shown that the Khosali sex drive is at least as strong as the human; yet it remains a fact that adultery among Khosali is fairly rare, and though many Khosali do not marry till late in life, they manage to remain fairly chaste during bachelorhood. Adultery and fornication are often accompanied by elaborate displays of anguish and torment that must, in the words of Mad Julius (a human wit and debauchee), be at least as much fun as the act itself. (After making this remark poor Julius was banned from the City of Seven Bright Rings by an emperor who was himself a bit prickly on the subject of adultery, having been tormented throughout his life by a vain and perfectly chaste devotion to the wife of one of his ministers. Khosali emperors are only rarely known for appreciating jokes they suspect might be aimed at them.)

Human sexual attitudes and behaviors have continually proven a scandal (and a fascination) to the Khosali, and have contributed unfortunately to the frivolous stereotype with which the Khosali view humanity. If the humans can't be serious about sex, the Khosali wonder, what *can* they be serious about?

The fact remains, however, that only rarely does a human caught in adultery have the decency to slaughter himself in rightful atonement. For a Khosalikh caught in the wrong bed, a last regretful note (to be published afterward), a pistol, and a final cry of long life to the Emperor are often the only proper recourse. Retreating to the cloister, devoting a fortune to charity, or spontaneous enlistment in the Emperor's service are also popular. The point is that atonement should be seen to happen. One is not permitted the social luxury of private regret.

Flouting conventional Khosali taste is the Human Diadem, whose affaires are often broadcast before their audience of billions. That many of these billions consist of fascinated Khosali is, no doubt, a manifestation of Khosali, as well as human, perversity.

A Khosali in love is often a Khosali in torment, anguished and tortured, with High Custom gazing balefully over one shoulder and the Grim Reaper over the other. This is only decent. One cannot help but contrast the unfortunate behavior of Maijstral, who not only enjoyed himself with another's spouse but declined to feel sorry afterward; and who, if caught, wouldn't have slain himself, but would if possible have avoided death altogether (or at least made Kotani do it for him); and who (conclusive evidence of his froward nature) had the unmitigated gall to sleep soundly upon returning to his own room. His conscience should at least have made him thrash the mattress a little.

No wonder humanity proved ungovernable. One only wonders how they govern themselves.

A Cygnus robot scuttled into the hallway, its dignity upset by a kick that almost knocked it off its repellers. *"Where is it?"* Pearl Woman's tone mingled rage with incredulity. There were soft thuds as pillows and bedding hit the wall. Advert, her heart thumping, stepped from her dressing room and, with effort, gave Pearl Woman a soothing smile.

"Perhaps you left it in another room."

"I remember very distinctly where I left it." Pearl Woman's voice was edged with menace. She limped across the room—booting the robot had re-strained her leg muscle—and reached for one of her matched cutlasses. She drew it and the cutlass sliced air in accompaniment to her thoughts. "I can't *believe* Fu George or Maijstral went after it *again*," she said. Slice. "That would be so . . ." Slice. "Redundant."

"Perhaps it was a different one, this time. I mean the *other* one, the one who didn't take it last time. Possibly he did it to show up the other one. Whichever that was."

The Pearl's trademark was in one of Advert's inner pockets. She fancied she could feel it against her skin, a burning weight. Her excitement made her giggle.

Pearl Woman fixed her with a look. "What's so funny?"

Advert laughed again. "I was just thinking. Maybe I could hire the other one to get it back. Like last time."

The Pearl snarled. "I'll do it myself, thank you." The cutlass whirled over her head, cut air as it diced an imaginary enemy. "I'll do it *my* way." The cutlass flew through the air, sliced an innocent korni bloom above a rare matched Basil vase, and buried its point in the wall.

"But Pearl." Advert, to her rising pleasure, was finding this deception easier by the minute. "You can't leave the room, not without your trademark. Kyoko Asperson might notice it's gone."

A growl came from Pearl Woman's throat. The other cutlass snicked from the scabbard and flashed through the air like silver lightning. Pearl Woman lunged, then grimaced and clutched her thigh. The muscle had betrayed her again. She flung the cutlass across the room, and another innocent korni bud died. The second vase trembled but did not fall.

"Very well, Advert," she growled. "You're right, I can't risk it. Just go out and make yourself visible. Perhaps someone will approach you."

Advert's heart leaped. "You'll get your pearl back," she said, "if I have anything to say about it."

She turned and left the room, her feet so light she felt as if she were dancing.

Vanessa Runciter put her feet into her semilife boots and felt them roll up her ankles, calves, and thighs. She bent down, smoothed the dark proughskin with her hands, and asked the Cygnus for her matching jacket.

"Geoff," she said, "shall we find breakfast? We haven't tried Lebaron's yet."

Fu George appeared from the bathroom, still in his dressing gown. Gorged semilife patches surrounded his eyes. "I really don't feel like appearing in public, Vanessa," he said. "Let's have Lebaron's bring our breakfast here."

The robot began lacing Vanessa into her jacket. She reached for her cigaret holder—ebony with a matching proughskin band—and inserted a Silvertip. "If we're going to steal Maijstral's treasure trove," she said, "we shouldn't do it on an empty stomach."

Over the years Fu George had grown used to the gratuitous *we*. "There's no hurry. Maijstral won't be rising early. I doubt he'll make an appearance before sixteen."

Vanessa flicked her proughskin lighter. "Why sixteen, Geoff?"

"According to the station bulletin, that's when he's doing his magic act in the White Room."

The light hesitated halfway to the Silvertip. "Ah," she said.

"Quite so. His friends won't miss his performance, so his loot probably won't be guarded. That's when we do the job." He peered at her from between the swollen patches. "I'd like you to be in the lounge for the show. Advance lookout, if you like. I'm sure Maijstral's laid traps protecting his stash, so I'll need both Chalice and Drexler."

"Sixteen. So that's when we do the job?"

Nodding. "That's when we do it." That *we*, it appears, was catching.

Drake Maijstral, drowsing, rolled over and bunched the pillow under his head. His hand touched the alarmed box wherein he'd hidden the Eltdown Shard. Still half asleep, he smiled, and fell into a dream in which, a mysterious masked figure in black, he appeared before the Dalton Brothers as they rode into Coffeyville, and warned them away, telling them of a fabulous gem in the next town, ready for the picking.

"Miss Asperson. You're up early."

"I'm an early riser, Miss Advert. And I have an interview in a few minutes." Smiling. "You seem in high spirits. You're practically skipping down the hall."

"I'm on a secret mission."

"You don't say." The media globes performed a subtle change of position. "May I inquire as to its nature?"

"I doubt I can trust you with secrets." Advert's rings glittered as she wrung her hands in make-believe indecision. "Besides, it's not my secret. It's Pearl Woman's."

"Surely it can't be all that bad."

"But it is!" Glee bubbled in Advert like fine champagne. *Let* everyone think her scatterbrained—*she* knew better.

"Pearl Woman had her pearl stolen last night," Advert said. "She doesn't dare go out in public without it. I'm supposed to ransom it quietly and get it back before anyone notices."

Kyoko gave her a surprised look. "If this is such a secret, Miss Advert, why are you telling me?"

"Well, really, Kyoko—why should Pearl *care?* It's just an earring, after all."

Advert was beginning to realize how much fun people like Geoff Fu George and Drake Maijstral must have had, what with their opportunities to masquerade so often as someone they weren't.

"It's her Diadem trademark," Kyoko said. "She's never seen without it."

"*I've* seen her without it. Most of her friends have, I imagine. I think it's silly to invest so much meaning in a little trinket, don't you? Just because the public expects it?" She smiled. "That sort of thing can become a trap, can't it?"

"I suppose so."

"A trap," Advert repeated happily. A trap into which she'd just dropped Pearl Woman, and serve her right.

"One shouldn't become so dependent on the material aspect of existence," Advert said. "That's what Pearl Woman's always told *me*."

"Thanks for the chat, Miss Advert. I wish you luck on your mission."

"Thanks, Kyoko. I'm sure it'll go all right." *Right as Robbler*, she thought, and went skipping toward the White Room, wondering in whom else to confide.

Paavo Kuusinen had risen early. He hadn't slept much, as his mind, like a tongue unable to leave off prodding the site of a missing tooth, had been unable to cease working on a problem. He ate breakfast in his room and then set off on a private quest of his own. When last observed, he thought, she'd gone *this* way.

It took him some time, but he knew approximately what he was looking for, and with persistence he found it. A hammock, a cache, a disabled alarm.

Good, he thought as he stepped toward his quarters. Now maybe he could stop *worrying* about it.

Mr. Sun had neither eaten nor slept. He felt completely numb: he had been unable to summon the energy even to leave his control room, the azure, murmuring scene of his martyrdom. Transfixed by the awesome spectacle of his own downfall, he was unable even to rouse himself to Kyoko Asperson's first knock. He opened his door to her second rap.

"Mr. Sun. I hope you are well this morning." There was a brilliant smile on Kyoko Asperson's round face. Sun couldn't stop staring at it. She looked, he thought, like a daffle gazing at a prough, preparing herself to spring and rend it limb from limb. He couldn't remember having seen a more sinister expression in his life.

"Miss Asperson. Please come in."

He retreated deeper into his whispering blue heaven. Silver globes pursued him, diving gaily into the room's corners, swooping irreverently over the console like a flock of frivolous birds. Kyoko, her horrible smile still brightening her features, stepped into the control room and perched on the edge of the console.

The room was very quiet. Sun had disconnected the alarms: nothing would interrupt this inquisition.

He had been judged and found wanting.

His time of atonement was nigh.

Diamond studs winked at collar and jacket front. "I hope you can amuse yourself while I nail down my agreement with the Baron."

"I expect I'll visit the White Room and watch Maijstral's performance."

A sniff. "Trickery and illusion. One can do anything with holograms these days." Kotani's ears went back. "Still, dearest, one may attend such an event simply to be seen."

"I don't know, my love. From time to time, a little trickery can add spice to life."

Kotani gave her a look. "You really are turning cryptic, dearest."

"I assure you," putting her arm through his, "that in future I'll be very, very careful."

* * *

Zoot, pulling his costume about him, stepped from hiding in Lady Dosvidern's bathroom only after the Cygnus had left. He didn't want even the robot to know he'd spent the night here. Lady Dosvidern smiled at him from over a stack of waffles. "Honey?" she asked. "Or renbroke?"

"Renbroke. Thank you." He took his pistol from the table, put it in its holster, and seated himself at the breakfast table. The tablecloth was dark red, setting off the silver jugs filled with coffee, tea, and hot rink. His splendid breakfast lay on Brightring tableware. ("By appt. to His Serenity," etc.) He was eating as well as the Emperor, he reflected—or at least as well as the Emperor *had* eaten, before he'd lost the Rebellion, molted, and retired to his cold box. In which case, Zoot concluded, he was eating *better* than the Emperor—and in better company.

Lady Dosvidern reached across the table and took his hand. Adorably she licked honey from her nose. He cocked his ears forward and smiled at her. Sunshine filled his heart.

"Will you marry me?" he asked.

Her ears flickered in surprise. She stared at him. "Didn't you know, dearest?"

"Know what?"

"I'm already married." She licked a bit of waffle from her fork. "To Lord Qlp, in fact."

Zoot gazed at her blankly.

"It's not *much* of a marriage," Lady Dosvidern said, offhand. "Lord Qlp only has a masculine title for sake of convenience, since it's married to a female. I'm not sure what sex it is, truth to tell, and I doubt it realizes what marriage is, anyway. So I'm *almost* free. And the title comes with the arrangement, and a nice pension, so I don't mind, really."

Zoot reached for a cup of coffee, missed, tried again, and spilled half of it lifting the cup to his muzzle. Interspecies marriages were very rare, almost universally frowned upon, and generally based on motives either mercenary or . . . the last, Zoot decided firmly, did not bear thinking about.

"I'm . . . surprised," Zoot managed to say. Hot coffee burned his tongue.

"Travelling with *one* Drawmiikh, believe me, is far better than being stuck on a planet absolutely *teeming* with the creatures." She smiled. Her fingers caressed his arm. "Its lordship is usually very quiet, you know. It travels wherever I suggest. Perhaps you and I can arrange a mutual agenda."

"Perhaps." Zoot felt a bit feverish. He put down the coffee cup. Lady Dosvidern laughed.

"You look so *shocked*," she said. "And you a member of the Diadem!"

Zoot was seeking a reply to this when the inner door burst open. Zoot leaped to his feet. His nostrils were assaulted by an appalling stench as Lord Qlp entered. Its body convulsed in agitation. Lady Dosvidern ran for her translation stud.

"Alarm!" its lordship said, bubbling in barely understandable Khosali. "Astonishment!"

Zoot's soul wailed. "I believe I can explain, my lord," he said quickly. "It's all my fault."

Lord Qlp thrashed about as if in pain. Its eyestalks whipped in all directions, glaring. "Interference!" it howled.

"I see that you have reason to be upset, my lord," Zoot said. "But appearances can be deceiving, and I . . ."

Lord Qlp reared on its hindquarters, boomed loudly in its own language, then lowered itself to the floor and skated away with remarkable speed. Zoot took a hesitant step after it.

"My lord," he said. "I, ah . . ."

Lady Dosvidern gripped his wrist. "I've never seen it this upset. I've got to be with it."

An agony of distress clawed at Zoot's mind. He'd destroyed Lady Dosvidern's reputation, her marriage, her hopes of happiness. "I understand," he said. Lady Dosvidern ran for the closet and her clothes, shouting at the service plate to send her a wardrobe-bot.

Horrible, Zoot thought, horrible. However could he atone?

Khamiss slumbered on. Her feet, semilife patches decorating the blisters, were propped on pillows. Her gun hung from a peg in a closet.

Her waiter's jacket, the left armpit torn, lay on the floor. Degree Absolute had been cancelled. Khamiss was taking full advantage of it.

Maijstral, as the robot tightened his laces, watched with one eye a play on the station vid. An old-fashioned farce, the current scene featured milord's mistress, dressed as a maid, hiding behind the Montiyy screen in the corner, while milord's daughter and her suitor were beneath under the bed. Milady's current lover was in the closet, and the Marine captain who hoped to be her next was smothering in a trunk. A private detective swung madly in the chandelier, taking notes.

In a firm voice, Maijstral told the vid to turn itself off. It was one thing for one's life to threaten to turn into farce, he thought; it was quite another for an impertinent video play to remind one of the fact.

His head swimming, Zoot allowed Lady Dosvidern's robot to lace up his suit. He was feeling slightly ill. *Apprehended!* he thought. *Doomed!* Lord Qlp had rushed out without paying attention to his protestations, and Lady Dosvidern, as soon as she was decently clothed, had followed. Zoot had not only compromised a lady; he'd compromised a diplomatic mission. The consequences could be nothing short of hideous.

He lurched into the corridor. Something glanced off his forehead and he stumbled forward, almost knocking Kyoko Asperson to the floor. He reached out a hand to steady her while another careless media globe banged off his skull.

"I'm terribly sorry, Miss Asperson," he said. "I wasn't looking where I was going. Please forgive me."

Kyoko looked up at him while her media globes moved into assault formation. Her ears cocked forward. "You seem distracted, sir," she said.

"I'm truly sorry. An unforgivable lapse."

"Ah." Her silver loupe gazed at him like the blank eye of doom. "I forgive your lack of attention, Zoot. Lady Dosvidern is, no doubt, a distracting individual."

Zoot started, guilty memories flooding his brain. He drew himself up. "Lady Dosvidern?" he said. The words came out a yelp, and he cleared his throat and lowered his voice. "Whatever do you mean?"

Kyoko gave a disbelieving grin. "You're leaving her suite after noon, there's a breakfast cart set for two here in the corridor, and you're still dressed for last night's ball. Forgive me for making the assumption that she's been entertaining you for the last ten or twelve hours."

Horror crystallized in Zoot's mind. Everything was becoming *public*. He had to retrieve the situation somehow; he owed Lady Dosvidern that, at least. "Yes," he said, and forced a grin. "Lady Dosvidern's company, and that of her husband, was most stim—most *entertaining*. I confess I entirely lost track of the time."

"Lady Dosvidern's husband?" Kyoko's eyes barely concealed their rapture.

"Yes." He flicked his ears to indicate puzzlement. "You didn't know?" His facial muscles, he realized, were betraying him, producing odd tics and quiverings that he was finding impossible to squelch on command.

"I'm afraid that information escaped my researchers. She's married to Lord Qlp, then?"

"Happily. A devoted couple, so unusual and yet so . . ." He flailed for the next word. "Unusual," he repeated, and then he gave a frantic smile. "You must forgive me, Miss Asperson." He sniffed her. "I've got to be about my, ah, my breakfast. I mean business."

"Certainly, Zoot. It's been most . . . illuminating. I hope we can meet later, and then you can tell me what you and the Drawmiikh talked about till noon."

"Yes, yes." Zoot felt the fur between his ears rise in an involuntary attack posture. He swiped at it with the back of his hand. "Delightful. Later. Yes. Charmed."

Somehow he managed not to run. The effort cost him dearly, though; he kept lurching like Quasimodo at every other step.

One way out, he thought. He felt feverishly for his pistol. One way out.

The Duchess of Benn sat in her room, savoring her coffee and her triumph. A few minutes after midnight tonight, she thought, and she'd ransom the Shard. She wouldn't tell anybody, would keep it secret for months before she wore it again, and then the occasion would be a special event— Special Event, rather. She had begun thinking of it that way.

Roberta smiled and took another sip of coffee. The Special Event was going to be a surprise, perhaps even more sensational than this last.

There was a pounding at the front door of her suite, followed by a turmoil among her household staff. Annoyed at the interruption, she cocked an ear in that direction and continued sipping coffee. The commotion increased. Roberta frowned, and then her door burst open and Lord Qlp flung itself in. Roberta stood, wondering whether to be alarmed or affronted. Lord Qlp's ghastly odor, in the event, prevented either stance from gaining much ground. She raised a hand to her face, intending to cover her mouth and nose, and then remembered her manners and forced the hand to her side.

"Sorry, your grace." Her butler, Kovinn, hovering in the door, wrung her hands. "Its lordship just . . . insisted."

"Interference!" Lord Qlp thrashed in distress. "Alarms!"

Roberta steeled herself. "Very well, Kovinn. You may go." She looked at Lord Qlp. "Coffee, my lord?" she asked, denasal.

"Ah . . ." said Kovinn, but then another figure pushed past her. It was Lady Dosvidern, disheveled, tugging at the laces of her jacket.

"Beg pardon, your grace," she said breathlessly. "But I thought—"

"You and its lordship are welcome at any time," Roberta said, as if these things happened every day. The stench was making her glassy-eyed. "But have you any notion—?"

"Afraid not, your grace."

Lord Qlp continued thrashing. It belched out something in its own tongue. Roberta took a step back from the violence of its speech.

"Humiliation!" Lady Dosvidern said. Her tone was bewildered. "Has not the Time of Exchange passed?" More belching noises. "Has not the Commodity been sufficient?"

The sluglike body convulsed. Something flung itself across the room, thudded into a chair. It was, Roberta saw, another oval exudate similar to those which Lord Qlp had already spit up in her presence.

Lord Qlp roared in its bubbling tongue. Its eyes whipped wildly at the ends of their stalks. "The Commodity is thrice-offered! Discontinuation of existence is necessary if humiliation is increased! May one not be vouchsafed a glimpse of the Preciosity, the Eye at the Center of Existence, the Perfected Tear?"

"Tear?" Roberta said. Her own eyes were growing tearful at the continued olfactory onslaught. Lord Qlp's phrases gathered in her mind, and in a glorious wave of prescience she realized what Lord Qlp had been going on about all this time.

"The Eltdown Shard?" she said. "You wish to trade for it?"

"Yes! Yes! Yes!" Lord Qlp bounced high in eagerness. Its High Khosali was not quite grammatical—the sentences did not comment on one another in the preferred contextual mode—but its meaning was clear.

"I'd be happy to show you the Shard, your lordship," Roberta said, "but I'm afraid the Shard has been stolen."

Lord Qlp's response filled Roberta with alarm. It moaned as if in pain. It fell heavily on its side and thrashed, knocking a chair halfway across the room. It boomed painfully, and Roberta held her hands over her ears.

"Woe, woe!" Lady Dosvidern translated. "Your Existenceship promised to guarantee the Exchange!"

"I did?" Roberta searched her memory. "I suppose I did, then," she said, recalling her conversation with its lordship just prior to the race.

"The Condition is altered. Discontinuation of existence is necessary for assuagement."

A chill crept into Roberta's heart as she thought she understood what Lord Qlp meant. "No!" Roberta said. "You don't have to kill yourself. It's not your fault!" She thought frantically. "Can't you just take the . . . objects . . . back?"

Lady Dosvidern's expression was frantic as she translated the bubbling sounds. "Exchange has already commenced. Blamings are impertinent. Zynzlyp awaits the Object of Desire. All meaning is now invested in the Perfected Creation. Pointlessness of existence is alternative! Planetary discontinuation will soon be necessary!"

Alarms clattered in Roberta's mind. Was Lord Qlp talking about the suicide of his entire *species?* She shook her head frantically, tried to think. She had to *do* something.

"I will locate the Shard!" Roberta declared. "I will bring it to you!"

Lord Qlp wrenched itself upright and began undulating out of the room. "Crosstalk necessary before further action. Must consider method of regaining Center of Meaning."

Roberta's mind swam with relief. It didn't sound as if Lord Qlp was planning on murdering itself anytime soon. She'd have a while, at least, to get the Eltdown Shard from Maijstral and bring it to its lordship.

Lady Dosvidern was following Lord Qlp from the chamber. She looked terrified. Roberta snatched at her sleeve. Wild-eyed, Lady Dosvidern spun, her arm trembling in Roberta's grasp.

"Wait!" Roberta said. "I'll try to get the Shard from—from whoever has it. Don't let its lordship do anything hasty in the meantime."

"Yes, your grace." Lady Dosvidern ran after Lord Qlp. Roberta stepped to the service plate and touched the ideogram for "telephone."

"This is the Duchess of Benn," she said. "Call Drake Maijstral's room. Inform him this is an emergency."

Just below the service plate, Roberta saw the two objects that Lord Qlp had previously offered her, each wrapped in a dinner napkin. While the phone rang endlessly, Roberta bent to unwrap them. She gasped in surprise.

Enchantment dazzled her eyes. The objects of exchange had transformed, become something magic and beautiful.

Colors spun bright webs at Roberta's feet. Iridescence shimmered, altered, became substantial. The telephone rang on and on.

CHAPTER 10

"**M**iss Asperson."

"Miss Runciter. Are you here for the magic show?"

"I'm here by chance, but if Maijstral's putting on a show, I daresay I'll sit through it. Even though I know his tricks."

"Perhaps he's learned some new ones." A beat's pause. "You seem to have met with some injury. I hope you are well."

Vanessa touched her cheek. The semilife patches had happily sopped up most of the swelling before expiring in gorged bliss, but faint bruising was still visible even through her cosmetic. "An accident, unfortunately."

"A pity. Bad luck seems to be making the rounds. First Mr. Fu George, then yourself."

"Luck has a way of turning."

"Looking at the both of you, one might almost think Fu George and yourself had been in a brawl."

"Neither of us would ever condescend to brawl, Miss Asperson." A cold smile. "Good afternoon."

"Your servant."

"Miss Advert."

"Marchioness. Will you sit by me?"

"Gladly. It's very kind of you to share." Settling into her seat. "You've got a very good view of the stage."

"From here I can watch Maijstral. It's very important that I do so. I'm on a secret mission for Pearl Woman."

"Really?"

"Yes. I'm afraid she's just too desolate to appear in public right now." Smiling. "She's lost something very important to her."

Roberta's holographic head and shoulders floated in Lady Dosvidern's video display. Lady Dosvidern observed that the Duchess had changed into a one-piece racing suit, probably in case she had to get somewhere in a hurry.

"I haven't been able to find Mai—to find the person who took the Shard. I've told his suite to give him my message when he arrives, and I've sent my household staff looking."

Lady Dosvidern tried to conceal her nervousness. She ceased her pacing and faced the holo cameras. "I looked in on its lordship a few minutes ago. It was still in deep crosstalk. Eyes and ears totally withdrawn."

Roberta gave a relieved sigh. "So Lord Qlp isn't likely to kill itself in the next few minutes."

"I'm not sure what it would kill itself *with*. Neither of us carries guns. It doesn't have wrists to slice. There isn't anyplace high to throw itself from."

"There are airlocks."

Lady Dosvidern's ears turned down. "Oh. I hadn't thought about that."

Roberta's violet eyes glittered as she considered possibilities. "Unfortunately there's no way to stop someone from killing itself. The right to self-annihilation is supported by High Custom. I assume we can't prove it's insane?"

"By what standards?" she asked. "Its lordship is perfectly mad by the standards of the Khosali or humanity, but it's entirely normal for a Drawmiikh, I think." Helplessness filled Lady Dosvidern. Was she responsible for this? What if Lord Qlp really *was* angry about Zoot? Standards, Lady Dosvidern wondered. Did Drawmii standards include sexual jealousy? She hadn't thought so.

"Its lordship is normal," Roberta repeated, "except that it travels."

"Yes. Of course."

Roberta gazed into the holo camera. "*Why*, Lady Dosvidern, does it travel?"

"Your grace?" Surprised.

"Why does it travel, and how long has it done so?"

A moment's thought. "Four years now. It approached the Imperial Protector and requested permission to leave Zynzlyp. The Lady Protector promptly gave it a pension, a title, and . . . ah . . . made other arrangements."

"Did it say *why* it wanted to travel?"

"It didn't need to. The Lady Protector was so delighted to have one of the Drawmii take an interest in anything outside of Zynzlyp that she didn't inquire."

"Didn't *you* ask its lordship? You've been travelling with Lord Qlp for . . . how long now?"

"Since the beginning. And no, I never asked—one doesn't ask a Drawmiikh *why* it does anything. If one gets any response at all, one gets an incomprehensible recitation of the latest debate between its five brains, with annotations and second thoughts by each of the brains in turn. Anything a Drawmiikh does is by consensus." She thought a moment further. "But its lordship never decided the schedule. It always let me choose the itinerary."

"Silverside Station was your idea, my lady?"

"Of course, your grace. I didn't want to miss the opening of such an exclusive resort, not when I had the means to attend."

"So its lordship didn't come here on purpose to trade for the Eltdown Shard?"

"No. I didn't even realize it *knew* about the Shard."

"There was a history of the Shard on the station vid. Did its lordship by any chance catch sight of it?"

Lady Dosvidern froze. "Yes. It did. I was watching it off the station feed while waiting for the *Viscount Cheng* to dock. We were sharing quarters at the time and . . ." She frowned. "I remember its lordship was very restless. I assumed it just wanted to leave the ship."

"So that was when its lordship conceived the notion that the Eltdown Shard was the foundation of reality."

Lady Dosvidern's ears flickered. "Is that what it did? I didn't understand that part."

"That's what it seemed to imply. That the Shard was Perfected Creation, that the alternative to its possession was the pointlessness of existence and planetary . . . was *discontinuation* the word, my lady?"

"Good grief." Private relief rose in Lady Dosvidern. She and Zoot hadn't anything to do with this after all.

"Lord Qlp came here on a search for meaning, and apparently it found what it was looking for. Unfortunately someone stole the Perfected Creation, and now it's upset." Roberta considered this notion for a moment. "For which I can't blame its lordship, I suppose. If someone stole *my* species' meaning, I daresay I'd be annoyed."

"Yes." Abstractedly.

"My lady, if I may make a suggestion, perhaps you should speak to Lord Qlp again and assure it that meaning shall be restored within a few minutes if we're lucky, and at the very latest a few minutes after midnight."

"It's hard to talk to when it's in crosstalk."

"Perhaps you should try, my lady."

Lady Dosvidern's diaphragm throbbed. "Yes," she said. "I suppose you're right. Thank you for the suggestion, your grace."

"I'll wait."

In case Lord Qlp attempted something drastic, Lady Dosvidern had left ajar the door between Lord Qlp's room and the front room of the suite. She stepped to the door and saw, through the crack, that the vidset was on, set to a schematic of Silverside Station's power system. Curious, Lady Dosvidern thought, but at least its lordship is at home.

But its lordship wasn't. When she pushed open the door, she saw that the door between the private room and the hallway was ajar, and that Lord Qlp was gone.

"Miss Runciter, is it?"

"Yes." Lighting a Silvertip, looking at him with one eyebrow raised. "Who're you?"

"My name's Dolfuss. I'd just like to say that I've seen you on vid often, and I admire your sense of style. All that leather, now—that's the way I think a woman of your type should dress." He gave a booming laugh. "You're my favorite, next to Nichole. I can see why Geoff Fu George keeps you around."

Vanessa smiled. "Thank you, Mr. Dolfuss." To Dolfuss's surprise, she put her arm through his. "Would you join me for Maijstral's program? I have some seats reserved, right up close."

Astonished laughter boomed out. "If my friends could see me now! They'd be jealous as anything."

"Your friends have taste, I see. Like yourself. Good afternoon, Mr. Kuusinen."

"Your servant, madam. Mr. Dolfuss."

"I saw that orange number you wore last night," Dolfuss said. "Made you look like a big pismire bird. You ever seen one of those?"

"I'm afraid not. You'll have to tell me all about it."

* * *

"I think the woodwinds were a little *off* just now, don't you?"

"Not now, dear. Maijstral's started."

"They just didn't sound as *full* as they did yesterday."

Paavo Kuusinen listened to his neighbors' conversation with only a fragment of his attention. He was concentrating on working out how Drake Maijstral did the Disappearing Bartender. Here the bartender was, plainly the Khosalikh on duty and not a plant, tugged from behind the bar and asked to mix a road agent while standing inside a roomy felt-covered box. To the sound of the shaking mixer, the box was closed, knocked to pieces with hammers wielded by Roman and Gregor, reassembled twenty feet away, and opened. To enthusiastic foot-tapping applause, the bartender appeared and a road agent was poured from the mixer into a glass held by Drake Maijstral. Maijstral smiled, tossed off the drink, and pronounced it excellent. The bartender was sent back to his duty.

Kuusinen frowned. How the hell was it done? The White Room had no stage, therefore no trapdoors. The box had been literally taken apart. The sound of the shaker had continued throughout.

Damnation. Kuusinen had been up all night working on one puzzle, and now here was another, come to torment him.

The shaker was the key. There had to be a *reason* why the sound had continued. But what was it?

But now another illusion commenced. Kuusinen soon figured out how it was done—that wasn't Maijstral's hand holding up the screen by its corner; that hand was a clever fake, complete with trademark diamond ring. Maijstral's real hand was elsewhere, manipulating things. And when Roman walked onstage to give Maijstral a prop that could have been on Maijstral's table all along, Kuusinen realized that Roman had passed Maijstral something he had concealed beneath his coat.

Having lost interest for the present, Kuusinen glanced over the audience. Why, he wondered, had Vanessa Runciter claimed that insufferable oaf Dolfuss? Normally she ate such people for breakfast. Doubtless, Kuusinen considered, this was part of a scheme. Kuusinen craned his neck, looked for Geoff Fu George or his assistants, and failed to see any of them. It seemed likely that Dolfuss was getting his room ransacked right now, with Miss Runciter on hand to alert the thieves should Dolfuss tire of the magic act and decide to stroll back to his suite.

Pleased with his feat of deduction, Kuusinen turned back to the program.

One of Kyoko Asperson's media globes hovered closer, taking a first-row seat for the climax of the illusion. Kuusinen looked approvingly at the arrangement of media globes—in order that the tricks wouldn't be given away unfairly, the globes had been arranged with careful regard for Maijstral's sight lines.

The trick, the one Kuusinen had figured out, was building to a satisfactory conclusion. Kuusinen, because he couldn't help himself, started counting the media globes again, and received a mild surprise.

Khamiss, her feet up, watched the magic show on station vid, broadcast live by Kyoko Asperson's globes. Not having noticed the phony hand, she wriggled her toes in silent, delighted applause at the production of the live clacklo, wondering how it was done.

Her phone rang. Feeling too lazy to reach the service plate, she told the room to record the performance and put the caller on vid.

Appearing on her vid unit was an elderly Tanquer that Khamiss recognized as a female who worked at the front desk. The Tanquer's eyes bulged and her whiskers trembled; she looked on the verge of hysteria.

Tanquers, Khamiss knew, suffered from an unfortunate fact of evolution. In their early history they were prey to a large carnivore that would stalk and kill anything that moved, but which would leave a motionless victim alone. Tanquers, in a crisis, were therefore subject to a Darwinian tendency to wring their hands, dither, and become subject to the vapors. As compensation they were masters of orderly procedure; but they tended to unravel in an emergency.

"You're with security, aren't you? I need your help!"

Khamiss smiled: she was off-duty. "Call security central," she said. "I can't—"

"I've tried!" Desperately. "I've been trying to reach Mr. Sun, but I can't get an answer!" The Tanquer made a strangled noise.

"That's strange. Perhaps someone's interfering with communications." Khamiss perked her ears forward. "What's the problem, then, ma'am?"

The Tanquer's tall, bushy tail swished frantically behind her head. "Someone's just stolen the hotel safe!"

"Oh." Khamiss sat bolt upright. "The *entire* safe?" she asked.

"Ye-es!" A wail of perfect despair.

"Continue your attempts to contact Mr. Sun. I'll be there as soon as I can."

While she flung on her uniform, Khamiss told her phone to contact as many members of her security detail as possible. She sent some to lurk outside Fu George's room— she assumed Maijstral, whatever his talents as a magician, hadn't been doing a live performance and robbing the safe simultaneously—and Khamiss told others to meet her at the location of the hotel safe. Once dressed, she ran flat out for Sun's headquarters.

The scent of smoke and the sight of flying robots told Khamiss what had happened before she saw the headquarters door. She was forced to slow to a walk—firefighting robots crowded the hallways, and there was retardant foam on the mothwing carpets. Mr. Sun, purple of feature, lay propped against the wall, wheezing into a handkerchief as bright red smoke poured from the door that led into his blue heaven.

Moving carefully so as not to slide on foam, Khamiss approached her boss.

"Are you all right, sir?"

Sun waved his hand feebly. Bronchial spasms reduced him to monosyllables. "Smoke bombs. In the console. Planted." He rallied enough to make a furious Holmesian declaration. *"Game's afoot!"*

"Someone's stolen the entire hotel safe."

Mr. Sun's purple tones darkened. His eyes popped. He clutched at his throat, unable to speak.

"Shall I handle it, sir?" Tactfully.

Sun gave a frantic nod. Khamiss raced away.

"And now—" removing the ring from his hand "—the Disappearing Diamond."

"Your grace. Have you heard from your people?"

"I'm afraid not, my lady. I don't know when I'll be able to retrieve the Shard. Have you located its lordship?"

"Its mucous trail led to one of the central elevators, but I lost it there. It had been looking at plans for the station power plant, so I ran there, but its lordship never appeared."

"Grief."

"I don't know what to do. Do you suppose I should alert station security?"

"I've been trying that, my lady. They don't answer."

Heavy beam cutters, Khamiss recognized at once. The thief had started in a storage locker, cut a hole in the wall, then cut the entire safe from its cradle. At least a dozen alarms must have been triggered, but Mr. Sun's headquarters had been filled with smoke and the alarms had been ignored. She picked up a telephone.

"Contact Mr. Kingston," she said. "Tell him to search Geoff Fu George's room at once."

The diamond ring, placed in an envelope sealed with red wax, rose slowly in the air, swooping upward in slow, graceful arcs in response to gentle waves of Maijstral's hand. The envelope, flaring redly in the light of Rathbon's Star, rose higher, higher, hovering at last in front of the giant impact diamond.

There was a startling bang, a gush of red smoke, and bits of the envelope fell in slow charred droplets toward the floor. There were shouts from Maijstral's audience as they began to realize it wasn't just the diamond ring that had disappeared.

Overtaken by sensation at the vanished giant diamond, few of the audience observed the ring that glittered on Maijstral's finger as he took his bow. Overshadowed by the large effect, Maijstral thought, the reappearance of the smaller diamond proved somewhat anticlimactic. He wouldn't use it as a finale again.

Kuusinen realized, as he stood and tapped his foot in the applause-pattern for "joyous surprise," why the woodwinds' sound had been off. The resonance provided by the diamond was missing, which meant of course the diamond had been missing for quite some time, and replaced by an illusion. Maijstral hadn't stolen it just now: it had been gone at least since morning.

Pleased with his acuity, Kuusinen turned from the performance to see Roberta's butler Kovinn walk into the room and do a perfect double take at the sight of Maijstral speaking to a gathering of his admirers. Kovinn fairly leaped for one of the telephones and slammed down an opaque privacy screen.

Kuusinen's nerves began to tingle. His walking stick tapping the floor, he moved so as to place himself between Kovinn and Maijstral. Another mystery, he thought resignedly, was clearly at hand. And here he'd planned to have luncheon undisturbed.

Khamiss appropriated the station's central switchboard as a poor substitute for Sun's console, but her hunt hadn't got very far. The hulk of the safe had been found in a service elevator, neatly peeled, all its contents gone. Fu George's room had been searched, but nothing had been found, and neither Fu George nor his assistants had been seen.

What now? Khamiss, marshalling her watsons, was beginning to appreciate what Sun had been going through the last few days. The desk Tanquer's whiskers were becoming sadly disordered as a result of the unexpected interruption in her routine, and her tail, following its evolutionary imperative, kept wrapping itself around her neck and tightening. Khamiss was beginning to be irritated by the constant sounds of strangulation.

"Don't you have a guest to take care of?" she asked.

More choking noises. "No. I'm just here in case someone needs to send a message offstation. What's that?"

"What's what?"

The Tanquer pointed to a light that had just started blinking. "That. An incoming radio transmission from somewhere in the system. We're not expecting any ships for three more days."

"Let's listen."

Khamiss turned on the audio. Incomprehensible bellowing filled the air.

"Yes, your grace. Maijstral was in public all this time."

"You mean all any of us had to do was look at the station bulletin board and see that his performance was listed all along?"

"I'm afraid so, your grace."

"Hold him there. I'm on my way."

"My rover."

"Lady Janetha." Maijstral took her hand and sniffed her ears, observing to his satisfaction that she wore the emerald earrings he'd saved from Fu George the previous night. "I hope you slept well."

"I found the ball and its aftermath so stimulating that I collapsed straightaway into the land of dreams. Yourself?"

"I slept very well. In fact I haven't had breakfast yet."

"Poor rover, creating a sensation on an empty stomach."

"I thought to try Lebaron's. Would you join me?"

"Gladly." She took his arm. "Though breakfasting *à deux* in your rooms might prove an interesting alternative."

"Unfortunately the local watsons are due to sack my suite at any moment. I'm afraid intimate meals might be fraught with inconvenience."

Her ears flickered in disappointment. "Lebaron's, then."

"Perhaps we can arrange a dinner later. After the security people have found someone else to harass."

"I hope so, Maijstral." She brightened. "I've just heard the most interesting news about Pearl Woman. Perhaps you had something to do with it."

Vanessa Runciter finished her polite applause and reached for a cigaret. Dolfuss looked at her. "I thought I'd take a look at the Casino," he said. "I haven't been there yet. Would you like to join me?"

Vanessa smiled smoothly. "Of course, Mr. Dolfuss. I was heading there myself."

Alarms clanged vaguely in Dolfuss's nerves. Why was Vanessa Runciter being so friendly?

"Great!" he said. "I'm happy as anything."

She lit the Silvertip in its ebony holder. "You *do* play tiles, don't you?" It might be fun, she realized, to pauperize this geck in retaliation for having to sit next to him through Maijstral's performance.

Dolfuss frowned. "Tiles? I'm afraid not."

"Or pasters?"

Dolfuss shrugged hopelessly. "Sorry. I play cheeseup from time to time, but I always lose."

Vanessa brightened. She put her arm through Dolfuss's. "Cheeseup, then. We'll have a jolly time."

"I'm not certain I can afford the stakes."

Vanessa looked at him in mock-indignation. "Mr. Dolfuss, I'm surprised! I thought *everyone* could afford a nova a point."

"A nova a point?" Dolfuss strove to master his shock. "Well, I suppose . . ."

"Settled then," Vanessa said, and smiled.

Ah, Dolfuss thought, and cancelled his internal alarm. She just wanted to fleece him. Reason enough to be friendly.

Bellowing still echoed from the receiver. The Tanquer's fingers danced over her keyboard. "Wait a minute. That signal's coming from the *Viscount Cheng*."

"I thought she was waiting in the dock."

"She is. I think."

"Then why doesn't whoever's making that awful noise use the telephone? *Cheng*'s got communication through the station coupling."

"Oh, no." The Tanquer's tail began to make self-throttling gestures again.

"Stop strangling yourself," Khamiss said edgily, her patience frayed entirely, "and tell me what just happened."

The voice was a burbling whisper. "*Viscount Cheng*. It isn't in dock."

Khamiss looked at the Tanquer in shock. "You mean someone's just stolen a *passenger liner?*"

The Tanquer's eyes were bulging with self-inflicted oxygen deprivation. Still she managed to give an affirmative blink.

Khamiss looked at the Tanquer, then at the board. There had to be a proper response to this.

If only she knew what it was.

Paavo Kuusinen was poised and ready when Kovinn finished her phone call and dropped her privacy screen. She goggled when she saw that Maijstral was gone. Kuusinen approached.

"May I be of service, Kovinn?"

"Yes. Have you seen Drake Maijstral?"

"I believe he and the Marchioness Kotani were walking in that direction. Please allow me to accompany you."

"Thank you, Mr. Kuusinen. If I lost Maijstral again, I don't know what kind of trouble might result."

"Perhaps," lightly, "if I knew the nature of the crisis, I might be able to assist."

"I'm afraid I don't really know, except that it has to do with Lord Qlp. It burst in on her grace this morning, and —there's Maijstral. Sir! Sir!"

Kuusinen watched as Kovinn broke into a run. The mystery, it seemed, was deepening.

Cheng's captain was a short Khosali female who was clearly annoyed at being roused out of bed. Khamiss suspected, from the way she kept looking over her shoulder, that she was not alone. Khamiss also couldn't help but notice that the captain's annoyance increased a chance resemblance to the crusty-but-loyal Cap'n Bob, one of the fixtures on the Ronnie Romper program.

"Well, no," the captain said as she fingered the collar of her dressing gown. "There was no one aboard *Cheng* except the maintenance robots. We all have four days' station leave."

"So anyone could have got onto the ship."

"The airlock was sealed, and only the ship's officers had the codes, but I suppose the lock could have been broken. . . ." The captain's ears suddenly pricked forward in alarm. "What's happened aboard my *Cheng*?"

"It appears someone's stolen your ship."

"The whole thing?"

Given time and thought, Khamiss might have found the captain's response curious and asked if the captain were more accustomed to having her ship stolen one piece at a time. Under the pressure of the emergency, however, Khamiss could only reply in the affirmative.

"The whole thing, ma'am. Sorry."

The captain sat down suddenly. The phone camera, with a jolt, tracked her collapse. The resemblance to Cap'n Bob became even more pronounced.

"I don't suppose," she said, "there's any way this could be kept quiet."

"Advert. What news?" Pearl Woman's holographic face, broadcast against the opalescence of one of the White Room's privacy screens, showed taut signs of strain. Her fingers twined in her leonine hair, drawing it down over her ear. The duelling scar gave her anxiety a sinister cast.

Advert, trying to remember not to giggle with joy, nodded and gave what she hoped was an encouraging smile. "I know who's got the pearl," she said.

Pearl Woman's eyes gleamed with a tigerish light. "Good. Give me the name."

"The name was given me in confidence. I'm sorry, but in return for the information I had to promise not to tell."

"Come now, Advert. You can tell me. After all, I—"

"The price is ninety." Firmly.

Baffled rage entered Pearl Woman's face. "That's outrageous! Last time he only asked sixty."

"Apparently the stakes in the contest between Fu George and Maijstral have risen. The price is firm, but at least it includes media rights. No one will ever know the pearl was taken."

"Drat." Pearl Woman chewed her lower lip. "Very well," she said. "If you'd be so kind as to advance me the money, I'll—"

"Pearl!" Advert widened her eyes in feigned surprise. "I don't have anything *like* ninety novae. I spent everything paying for the pearl last time. Now that you've gone and lost it again, I'm afraid you'll have to raise the money yourself."

With visible care, Pearl Woman mastered her indignation.

"Are you certain you can't give me ten or twenty? Perhaps you can get an advance on your allowance."

"Sorry, Pearl." Advert struggled to contain her inward delight and simulate proper regret. "I'm really broke. Possibly you can get a loan from the Marquess Kotani. Or an advance from the Diadem."

Pearl Woman's eyes narrowed. "I don't know if it's worth ninety, Advert. Can't you negotiate?"

"I wouldn't know how. Besides, as I said, the price is really firm."

"Let me think about it."

"I don't know how much longer the offer will hold. The price may go up."

"I said I'll think about it." The Pearl's face was hard.

"Very well. But one shouldn't become so dependent on the material aspects of existence. You've told me that often enough."

Pearl Woman's face vanished before Advert had quite finished, replaced by the "at your service" ideogram. Advert gave a short, delighted laugh, then composed her features carefully and dropped the privacy screen. The White Room leaped into existence around her. Kotani was passing by, walking stick dangling from his fingers. It was time, Advert thought, to increase the pressure.

"Ah," she said. "Marquess Kotani. I'm afraid the Pearl is in an unpleasant situation, and I was wondering if I might ask your advice."

"Thank you so much for waiting. I know her grace will be eternally thankful."

"If it is, as you say, an emergency, then how could I refuse? It's cost me nothing but a late breakfast."

"No doubt," observed the Marchioness tautly, as the others moved away, "her grace has her own reasons for

interrupting Maijstral's breakfast. Whatever they may be.''
The sullen quality of her beauty had increased.

Paavo Kuusinen followed Maijstral's party in companionable silence. He was thinking about the Disappearing Bartender.

Kyoko Asperson told her telephone to record, then rang Pearl Woman's suite. She smiled as she saw that Pearl Woman only answered on audio.

"I apologize, Miss Asperson, but I just stepped out of bed and I'm not presentable.''

"I understand. I'm sure you must be prostrate.''

"Oh?'' Badly disguised suspicion.

"I gather you've lost some property.''

Pearl Woman's voice turned cool. "Might I ask where you obtained this information?''

"Sorry, Pearl Woman, but you know that I can't say. I have to protect the confidentiality of my sources.''

"It was just that I wondered who might be spreading this story about me. It's quite inaccurate, you know.''

"Really? I'll have to question my source further.''

There was a moment's suspicious pause. "I'll see you later this afternoon,'' she said, "and we'll straighten out the entire misunderstanding.''

"I'll be looking forward. Thank you.''

"At your service, Miss Asperson.''

Kyoko rang off. Smiling, she sent one of her media globes to hover outside Singh's Jewelers on the main commercial level, just in case Pearl Woman decided to purchase a substitute.

"You know, I keep thinking I've heard that voice somewhere before.''

"That bellowing sound?'' The Tanquer shrugged delicately. "How dreadful. It sounds like a large and very wild beast."

"Wait a moment." Recollection rose in Khamiss, then clarified. Her nostrils slammed shut at the memory. She touched an ideogram on the console.

"Get me Lord Qlp's suite," she said, denasal. "I'd like to speak to Lady Dosvidern."

"An interspecies emergency?" Maijstral gave the situation a moment of thought. "Do you truly think Lord Qlp might do away with itself?"

Roberta gave an exasperated wave of her hands. "I think Lord Qlp's *species* might do away with itself." She glanced above and made certain no hovering media globes were recording their conversation. "I'll pay you the amount we agreed upon, and I'll pay it right now. You won't be involved any further in the matter of Lord Qlp."

Maijstral frowned and twisted his diamond ring. Roberta's appeal *might*, of course, be part of an elaborate trap, an attempt catch him red-handed with the Eltdown Shard before it was legally his. On the other hand, the situation seemed too implausibly bizarre to constitute a trap—if Roberta were involved in an attempt to snare him, Maijstral suspected the excuse offered him might be more conventional: a family crisis, say, that required her instant departure from Silverside and the immediate ransoming of the Shard.

"Give me a moment," he said. "I must offer my apologies to the Marchioness."

"Of course."

Maijstral stepped toward where the Marchioness waited out of earshot and leaned toward her, speaking in her ear. "I'm afraid this is a matter of some urgency, my lady."

The Marchioness drew herself up. "If it's quite *that* important, Maijstral . . ."

"There may be lives at stake. I still trust we may sup together, perhaps tonight."

She looked at him suspiciously, then relaxed her famous pout. "Perhaps," she said. "I'll have to see what Kotani has planned."

"Till later, then." He sniffed her and turned, seeing Roman and Gregor moving some of his equipment to their suite. He caught Roman's eye. Roman nodded, then glided across the room toward him.

"I require a tail track to Dolfuss's room," Maijstral said. "I need to run a very important errand, and her grace and I may be followed."

Roman's eyes glittered. "Shall I tell Gregor, sir?"

"Yes. The more eyes and detectors, the better. Have robots take the stage equipment back to the Coronet Suite."

"At once, sir."

Roberta was speaking with Paavo Kuusinen. Suspicion awakened in Maijstral, and he gave the man a cautious nod. "Shall we go, your grace?"

"Yes." She hesitated. "May Mr. Kuusinen accompany us?"

"With respect, I'd rather he didn't. My apologies, Mr. Kuusinen, but this is private business."

Kuusinen bowed stiffly. "No offence taken, sir."

"Your grace?"

"Yes." Roberta moved at once for the exit. "Let's hurry, if we may."

"Yes," Lady Dosvidern said. "That's its lordship's voice. You've found Lord Qlp, then?"

"In a manner of speaking, my lady," Khamiss said. "It appears that its lordship has stolen the *Viscount Cheng*."

Lady Dosvidern's muzzle gaped in surprise.

"My lady," Khamiss went on, "could you come to our communications room? I think we may need a translator."

"Excuse me, Vanessa," Dolfuss said. He looked at his cards with a puzzled expression. "Could you remind me of the sequence from secundus onward?"

Vanessa looked at him from over her cards and smiled. "Of course, Mr. Dolfuss. Secundus, response, octet, and cheeseup."

"Ah." Dolfuss frowned over his cards for another moment, his brows knit, then he put his hand on the table.

"That's octet," he said. "Isn't it?"

"Yes," she said. "Congratulations, Mr. Dolfuss." She folded her hand and dropped her cards atop the discard pile.

"And with the Emperor in Elevation, isn't that something else?"

"Camembert." Stonily.

Dolfuss grinned. "So that gives me forty-one, right? My luck is in this afternoon."

"It seems so."

Dolfuss's laugh boomed across the Casino. Heads turned. "I *thought* that's what it was!" he roared. "*Camembert!*" Heads turned away.

Vanessa reached for the cards and began to shuffle. "I hope you will consent to another game, Mr. Dolfuss," she said.

"For you, lady," Dolfuss said, "anything. Anything at all."

Zoot gazed at the contents of his closet in bleak despair. How to dress for one's suicide? he wondered. Did this count as a formal event, or was he allowed to dress casually?

Formal, he decided. Go with dignity.

He reached for his evening clothes, then hesitated. The jacket he'd invented might be more appropriate: it was his trademark, after all. If the back of his head was blown off, he thought morbidly, at least he'd be recognizable.

He stood away from the closet. Perhaps he should just write the note first. Traditionally this was done in High Khosali, in which the parsing of each sentence commented on the sentence before, the whole unrolling, ideally anyway, in as precise and rigorous terms as a mathematical statement. Zoot spoke High Khosali fairly well, but minor mistakes were easy to make; and he had to be careful as possible. Nobody wanted to be known for bungling his last words, and Zoot would need to produce two sets of them. A public apology, suitably phrased, to be found in his breast pocket, along with a private note to Lady Dosvidern to be hand delivered by a discreet member of the Very Private Letter service, apologizing for destroying her reputation. There were certain delicacies to be observed as well: in the public statement, he had to make his reasons for killing himself clear, publicly exonerate the lady of all suspicion, and yet in so doing never mention her by name.

It was ironic, Zoot thought, that the cause of all this was just the sort of thing that members of the Diadem were *supposed* to do. He was *expected* to have affaires and scrapes and then have them broadcast throughout the Constellation and Empire by the Diadem's own exclusive news service. But Diadem members weren't supposed to botch things, weren't supposed to babble and stare when subjected to pointed interviews, to blurt out obvious untruths and cause potential Colonial Service incidents between opaque aliens and their wives.

There was only one way for a gentleman to behave once he'd wrecked things to *that* degree.

Zoot stepped to the closet again, hesitated once more.

It was a practical issue that finally decided him. After he'd blown his brains out, the famous jacket would be a lot easier to clean than would formal evening clothes.

He still had to write his note.

Suicides, he realized in growing despair, were much more complicated than they seemed.

Maijstral hastened down the corridor with her grace of Benn at his side. Roman and Gregor followed behind, hovering at the edge of Maijstral's awareness, their detectors deployed. Roberta had a stylus and one of the credit chips from the Casino: carefully she rearranged molecules as she walked, wrote an amount, signed and thumbprinted it. She handed it to Maijstral.

"There. Your losses at tiles multiplied by a large factor."

Maijstral came to Dolfuss's door. He reached for the lock, hesitated, drew his hand back. Electricity crackled through his nerves.

"What's wrong?" asked Roberta.

Maijstral did not quite trust himself to speak; instead his hand went to the small of his back and drew out a pistol. His other hand took Roberta's shoulder; he gently guided her away from the line of fire. Turning toward Roman and Gregor, he gestured significantly with the pistol. Weapons drawn, detectors screening their eyes, the pair moved silently down the corridor. Roman reached into a pocket and handed Maijstral a pair of detector goggles: he drew them on with his free hand. A pair of media globes rose out of Roman's pocket and hovered in the air.

Maijstral paused for a moment of consideration. Roman and Gregor waited.

Roberta, violet eyes alight, bent and drew a small, elegant

Nana-Coulville Elite spitfire from an ankle holster. Roman and Gregor observed this with a certain amount of admiration.

Maijstral, with careful consideration for the state of his nerves, concluded that he was not going to be the first person into the room. With gestures, Maijstral told Roman to dive through the door: he and Gregor would provide cover fire and support.

Roman bowed; he flexed his muscles, set his pistol to "lethal," opened the door lock with a touch of his hand, and charged.

Through the haze of his fear, Maijstral experienced a moment of admiration for the absolute grace of Roman's movement, for the elegance of Roman's execution, his total silence.

Roman entered low and dove to his right out of the line of fire. A media globe swooped over his head. Maijstral and Gregor followed, guns thrust forward.

The giant impact diamond was propped in a corner. No person was visible. The bed was unmade—Maijstral hadn't permitted maid service since he'd begun stowing his loot in the room.

Roman, Gregor, and Maijstral fanned over the room. Maijstral's heart thundered in his breast. He dropped by the bed—into convenient cover—and kept his arms locked rigid in a firing position, thereby feigning an inspection of anything beneath the mattress. There was, he discovered, nothing—none of the rolled paintings or compact sculptures that had once belonged to the Baroness Silverside and that, as of midnight, had become his personal property. Anger growled in his nerves. He stood, flipped over his pillow. The box with the Eltdown Shard was gone.

Roberta glided into the room, pistol ready in her hand, her eyes questioning.

Maijstral stepped to the closet and pointed his pistol at the closed door. "Fu George," he said, "come out, please."

There was a moment's pause, then the closet door came open. Geoff Fu George, elegantly attired in an evening jacket that made an unfortunate contrast to the bruising around his eyes, smiled ruefully. A pair of media globes orbited his head as he stepped into the room. Apparently, with his equipment, he'd managed to overcome the closet's reluctance to close.

"Gentlemen," he said, and bowed. "Your grace."

Fu George, Maijstral realized, had four pistols pointed at him. Maijstral's nervousness eased; he seemed to be in control of the situation.

"The Shard, if you please," Maijstral said.

Fu George spread in hands in a helpless gesture.

"Sorry, Maijstral," he said. "I'd be perfectly happy to oblige you, but as it happens I don't have it."

"Its lordship is threatening the station?" Khamiss stared at Lady Dosvidern in surprise.

Lord Qlp's voice boomed from the speakers. "It says," Lady Dosvidern said, her voice trembling, "that if it doesn't get the Perfected Tear, it's going to ram the *Viscount Cheng* into the antimatter bottle in the surface power plant and blow everything up."

Khamiss ignored strangling sounds from the Tanquer and considered the situation, wondering primarily if it was still possible to throw up her hands and turn the situation over to Mr. Sun.

Mr. Sun's choked, purple face rose in her mind. Probably not, she decided.

"Can its lordship *do* that?" Lady Dosvidern said. "Is there really antimatter onstation?" Her eyes were hopeless.

"Isn't that old-fashioned? I thought everyone used sidestep systems these days."

"Silverside Station's in an unstable orbit around an unstable star system," Khamiss said. "There's tremendous gravitational stress, and we need to adjust our position and gravity from one second to the next. Energy expenditure is enormous, and a matter-antimatter reaction was the most efficient way to provide it. The power plant got put on the surface so that if there was a problem with the magnetic containment bottle, the antimatter would boil off into space instead of blowing up Silverside." Her ears flickered uncertainly. "That was the hope, at any rate."

"There's nothing protecting the bottle?"

"Cold fields to keep out the odd meteor strike. But I doubt they're strong enough to keep out anything with the size and mass of the *Viscount Cheng*."

There was a thud. Khamiss glanced over her shoulder and observed that the Tanquer had passed out from lack of oxygen.

"Good," she said. "She was making me nervous."

Advert smiled as she entered Pearl Woman's suite. "I'm so glad you changed your mind," she said. "I really think it's for the best."

Pearl Woman looked at her without joy. "I really wish you'd tell me," she said.

"Pearl! You know I promised."

"I'm not entirely happy about the way the price went up."

"I'm sorry, Pearl, but you really shouldn't have delayed."

Pearl Woman handed Advert a credit chip. "Here," she said. "A hundred."

Advert looked at the chip and smiled. "I'll be right back. Wait here." She paused in the doorway. "You're doing the right thing. I'm sure of it."

"I'm afraid the place was gutted before I arrived," Geoff Fu George said. "The only thing of value remaining was the big diamond—I suppose it was too awkward to transport." His ears fluttered in an offhand way. "Sorry, Maijstral. Say, can I lower my hands?"

Maijstral stared at Fu George over the sights of his pistol. Anger tugged at his nerves, his mind, his trigger finger.

"I can't accept that, Fu George," he said. "My swag's stolen, and you're in my closet. These are facts difficult to ignore."

"About my hands, Maijstral."

"I need the Eltdown Shard. I need it *now*."

"The boss is telling the truth."

Startled, Maijstral swung his pistol to cover the new voice, his heart hammering anew. Chalice had appeared in the doorway—also, strangely, in evening dress. Observing that Roberta and Gregor had Chalice covered, Maijstral swung back to Fu George.

"Shut the door, Roman," he said. "Let's keep this gathering private, shall we?"

"It took us a long time to get through your traps and alarms." Chalice stepped into the room while Roman stepped behind him to close the door. "Once we got through, Mr. Fu George entered and found your room plundered. I was running black boxes outside. I heard you coming and hid around the corner. It was too late for the boss to get away."

Maijstral kept his pistol aimed four inches below Fu George's famous hairline. Probably Fu George's evening jacket/darksuit contained defenses; but since his encounters with the Ronnie Romper creature on Peleng, Maijstral had been carrying the most powerful Trilby 8 spitfire available, and he was reasonably certain of blasting through Fu George's shields. This certainty served to elevate his confidence.

"I might point out," he said, "that we've caught you red-handed in an act of burglary. We've got *recordings*. I don't know what Baron Silverside intends for anyone caught stealing on his station, but he's a sovereign lord here and he's got a very simple and very medieval court system in which he plays both judge and advocate; and I assume that there would be little problem for him in sentencing you to ten or twelve years of breaking rocks on Gosat. I suggest therefore that returning my property would seem by far the most convenient alternative."

"Love to oblige, old man," Fu George said. "Unfortunately, it ain't in the cards. Look, can I put my hands down?"

"You may *not*," Maijstral snarled at him, happy to vent his anger. "I *like* you with your hands in the air. I think it suits you. Perhaps you'll be *buried* that way."

"I prefer cremation, old man. Incidentally, I wouldn't put too much trust in those recordings. They also record the presence of this big diamond, which I suspect is not yet your legal property."

Maijstral hesitated, then smiled. "This isn't my room. The diamond has nothing to do with me."

"If this isn't your room, then what are you doing in it?"

"Making an arrest, looks like."

"Mr. Fu George," Roberta said. "There are lives at stake here."

Fu George offered her a graceful inclination of his head. "No one regrets that more than I, your grace. Except possibly for Chalice."

"That isn't what I meant." Quickly, her pistol trained

unerringly on Chalice's right ear, Roberta explained Lord Qlp's behavior and its threat of planetary discontinuation.

"Very strange, your grace," Fu George said. "Were the Shard in my possession, I'd be happy to arrange its ransom. However, as I have no idea where the Shard might be—"

Maijstral's exasperation boiled over. "Oh, shut up," he said. "I don't believe you."

Fu George raised an eyebrow. "Are you calling me a liar, Maijstral?"

"Damn right I am," Maijstral snarled. *"Old man."* He glanced over his shoulder at the Duchess. "I'm going to have Roman and Gregor hold Fu George here while I take a look in his suite. The Shard may be there."

While Maijstral spoke, Fu George glided forward with absolute, professional silence; Maijstral turned back at the motion and saw a slight smile on Fu George's face in the instant before the man's right fist filled the vision of his left eye.

The fist drove full-force into the detector goggles, which in turn drove into Maijstral's eye. Caught by surprise, Maijstral sat down on the bed. In purest reflex, he jabbed his pistol into Fu George's midsection: Fu George folded backward into the closet, cracking his head on the back wall. One of Dolfuss's loud jackets dropped silently on his head.

"Are you injured, sir?" the closet said. "I can summon medical assistance if necessary."

"I will ask the Marquess Kotani to act for me," Fu George said, his voice muffled. "And thanks anyway, closet, but I don't need your help."

Horror glibbered in Maijstral's mind at the realization of his own invidious carelessness. He had called Fu George a liar, which was a killing offence, and he'd done it in front of witnesses; he could have got away with an apology save that Fu George had then gone and hit him, which was *another* killing offence, and this meant he couldn't possibly escape the inevitable violence. Maijstral was possessed by a desperate need to shriek and dive under the bed, but his body seemed paralyzed, so instead he simply sat where he was, pistol braced, while he gazed at Fu George's plaid-draped form and contemplated his own speechless terror.

Training, in the end, loosened his voice. The Nnoivarl Academy had drilled its students well, or at any rate well enough to be able to speak formulae while terrified witless.

"Your grace," Maijstral said while his mind cringed at what his mouth actually had the audacity to say, "will you do me the inestimable favor of acting for me in this matter?"

"I would be honored, Maijstral." She paused for a moment's thought. "So what do we do now? Are you still going to search Fu George's suite?" Maijstral felt the Trilby begin to quake in his hands, and he lowered the pistol while he contemplated his situation. His stolen loot, the Eltdown Shard, and even planetary discontinuation had begun to assume an air of insignificance.

"There wouldn't be a lot of point," Chalice interrupted. "Drexler was with us, helping with the black boxes. He's run back to guard the suite."

"Fu George," Maijstral said. "Take that stupid thing off your head and leave."

"Your servant," replied Fu George's muffled voice. "Old man." Fu George removed Dolfuss's jacket, rose from the closet, and brushed at his clothing. "Come, Chalice."

"Good work, sir," Chalice said.

"Mr. Chalice," Roman said, as he showed the others the door. "I believe you still owe Gregor and me ten novae."

Fu George looked at his assistant. "Ten novae?"

Maijstral stared down at the pistol in his hands and wondered if it was too late to shoot the pair of them. Perhaps he could arrive at a plausible reason for it later.

No. There were too many witnesses.

The words took up a dull refrain in his head. Too many witnesses. Too many witnesses. Too many witnesses.

The door closed shut behind Chalice and Fu George. Maijstral put his gun on the bed and stretched out with his head on the pillow. He looked up at Dolfuss's empty ceiling. There was a moment's silence.

"I don't see what else we could have done," Roberta said.

"I'm sorry, sir," Roman said. "It's my fault. Once I closed the door, I should have returned to help you cover Fu George."

"If it's *your* fault," Maijstral almost said, "*you* fight the man," but he bit the words back. No purpose would be served by getting his servant and chief henchman angry at him.

"Don't blame yourself," he said. He felt mild surprise at how well he was articulating. "I let things get out of control."

"You handled that real cool, boss." Gregor's tones were admiring. Another savage comment came to Maijstral's mind, and again Maijstral squelched it.

Roberta bent to return her pistol to its holster. When she straightened, there was a serious light in her eyes. "What weapons?" she asked.

Maijstral's mind curdled as it raced through the appalling possibilities. The inventory of classical Khosali duelling weapons, developed over millennia, was impressive. There were weapons for cutting, weapons for hacking, weapons that shot flame or explosive bolts. There were strangling cords and bludgeons and sophisticated devices for picking apart the opponent's mind and leaving him a pain-riven vegetable all the rest of his days. The weapons had one thing in common: Maijstral had no confidence in his ability to damage Fu George with any of them.

Why, he asked the ceiling, had he been born in a society that countenanced mutual slaughter, but only so long as the slaughter was done on what purported to be a fair basis? Why was *fairness* the criterion? Why not *cleverness*? If one could cleverly arrange matters so that one's opponent had no chance whatever of survival, and oneself had every possible chance, why should any reasonable individual object? Why *shouldn't* the clever survive over the stupid? Wouldn't it improve the breed in the long run?

Maijstral waved an airy hand.

"Chugger," he said. "And let's not use explosive bullets or automatic fire. Far too vulgar." The point of a chugger duel was that each side got only one shot. He wasn't going to give Fu George more than one try at him.

"Very well."

"Anything you *won't* use?"

Everything! his mind squalled, but instead his voice was calm. "Axes. Clubs. Pole weapons. That sort of thing. Too . . ." *Brutal*, he almost said, but corrected himself at the last second. ". . . common."

"How about psych-scanners?"

Maijstral thought for a long moment. A psych-scanner in the hands of an expert could turn an opponent's brain into a mass of toasted cheese. Against a stupid or slow man, Maijstral would have had every confidence in using a scanner. Unfortunately Fu George was neither stupid nor slow.

He thought about the long nightmare that might result, with Fu George slamming at his brain for hours while he gibbered in terror and tried to evade the relentless psychic blast. No, he decided. Pistols were a lot quicker.

"I'd rather not," he said. "Scanners are an honorable

weapon, but too often they leave both combatants brain-dead. I'd prefer one of us survive this.''

"Bravo, boss. Only too.'' Gregor gave a laugh as he beat out a quick pattern on the bureau.

Maijstral looked at him bleakly. Gregor had been impressed by his chivalry, but Maijstral, to himself at least, meant only that he intended himself to be the survivor, and to hell with anything else. He'd rigged a chugger duel in his youth, when he'd been driven into an encounter during his last year at the Nnoivarl Academy; he wasn't sure he could work the same trick with a scanner.

"Any feelings about swords?'' Roberta asked.

Wrong phrasing, Maijstral thought. He had very clear feelings about swords, though none of them capable of articulation in this company.

"I would prefer smallswords,'' he said. "Or rapier and targe.'' Keep the damage to a minimum, he thought, with a light weapon. Perhaps he could manage to get himself scratched on the arm and pronounce honor satisfied.

"I would also prefer,'' Maijstral said, "that the meeting be postponed for a few days. I'd like to get to the bottom of this Shard business first.''

"Thank you, Maijstral,'' Roberta said. "I appreciate that.''

"I am at your service, your grace.'' Delay the thing as long as possible, he thought, which would give him a greater chance to fix the outcome. Perhaps, he thought cheerlessly, he could just poison Fu George in the night. Or get him arrested.

"What shall we do about the Shard?''

"If I were you, I'd try to buy it from Fu George. If you approach him privately, he may act differently than when he had my gun pointed at his head.''

She looked at him with a frown. "I suppose I should see him as soon as possible.''

"Right now, if you like."

"Yes. Thank you, Maijstral. I'll see Kotani as soon as the present crisis is over."

"Don't hurry on my account," Maijstral almost said. Instead he said merely, "Your servant."

"Yours."

Roberta bowed and left. Maijstral stared at Dolfuss's ceiling and asked it a long series of questions. There was no reply.

Viscount Cheng's captain, whom Khamiss was beginning to think of as Cap'n Bob, gazed in surprise at the unconscious body of the Tanquer.

"Er," she began, "is this somehow related to our problem?"

"Not really," Khamiss said. She turned to the console. "Ring the Duchess of Benn's suite," she said. "Then ring the White Room, the other lounges, each restaurant, the Casino, and all the shops on the commercial level. Give them the following message: should anyone see her grace the Duchess of Benn, Drake Maijstral, or Geoff Fu George, please have them call Khamiss at the central switchboard. Inform them that this is a serious emergency. End of message."

"At your service," said the console.

Kovinn answered the Duchess's phone. "Is her grace in?" Khamiss asked.

"I'm afraid not, ma'am."

"I need to speak with her right away. This is an emergency."

Kovinn's ears twitched. "Very well, madam. I shall inform her grace when she arrives."

"My name is Khamiss. I'm at the central communications

switchboard. Please beg her grace to call me as soon as she arrives.''

''I will give her your message.''

''Thank you.'' Khamiss rang off, then frowned and looked at the console. What next?

Cap'n Bob provided the answer. ''Does Baron Silverside know?''

''No.'' She turned to the console, an order poised on her lips, and then she hesitated, a clear picture rising in her mind of Baron Silverside having a fit of hysterics and tearing out hunks of whisker.

''Let's not,'' she decided.

''*Cheeseup!*'' called Dolfuss at the top of his lungs. By this point spectators' heads had ceased to turn at the sound of his roars, but instead had begun ducking between shoulders as if caught in an exploding hailstorm of bad taste. Dolfuss laid down his cards. ''And I've got the Emperor in what-d'you-call-it, and that's . . .''

''Cheddar,'' said Vanessa.

''Right. How many points?''

Vanessa laid down her cards. ''Sixty-four.''

''Right again.'' He beamed. ''I'm glad you suggested this game. Winning this one hand I've earned more cash than I get in sales commissions for a whole year.''

Vanessa rose from her seat. ''It's been a . . . *unique* experience, Mr. Dolfuss,'' she said. ''I regret I must leave you.''

''Too bad.'' Smirking. ''Sorry to see you go. If you could, ah . . . ?'' He took one of the betting chips and handed it to her. He looked at the score. ''That's a total of two hundred and forty-four.''

''Yes.'' She wrote the amount and signed it, then handed the chip back. *Choke on it,* she thought.

Dolfuss grinned and twitched the lapels of his green—yellow jacket. "Maybe I ought to travel to these sorts places more often. I figured I wouldn't be able to afford them, but maybe I can after all." He gave Vanessa a speculative look. "Where are you travelling next? Maybe can meet for another game, ha ha."

"I'm afraid my plans are unsettled; I really can't where I'll be. Good afternoon, Mr. Dolfuss."

"Afternoon."

Seething, her whole being shrieking for bloody vengeance, Vanessa began moving toward the exit, then checked when she saw Fu George walking toward her. She proached him and took his arm.

"I damn well hope you got the Shard," she said. "Somebody ought to be rewarded for my spending an hour the most repulsive individual I've ever met."

"Maijstral caught me." Simply.

Vanessa bared her teeth. "I could kill him."

Fu George raised a contemplative eyebrow. "You not have to, my dear. I may do it for you."

Roberta found only Drexler in Fu George's suite. The K alikh agreed to have Fu George call her as soon as returned, and Roberta began her return to her rooms. W waiting she could call the Marquess Kotani and agree u a time to meet and arrange the encounter between Maij and Fu George. As she entered her corridor, she saw Pa Kuusinen ahead of her, holding his walking stick me tively behind him with both hands. Her pace increase

"Mr. Kuusinen!"

He turned, saw her, and waited while she hasten him. "I hope things have been arranged satisfactorily, grace," he said. With some difficulty he matched her l legged stride.

"Things are wretched. Maijstral lost the Shard and Fu George was caught red-handed in the room. Fu George denied stealing the Shard, and now he and Maijstral are going to fight a duel. I'm Maijstral's second. I just tried to speak to Fu George privately to see if we could reach an arrangement about the Shard, but he's not home."

Kuusinen stopped dead, his eyes opaque. Roberta, knowing him, paused. "Yes, Kuusinen? What is it?"

"A moment, your grace." Lost in thought, he paused, touched his chin with the head of his cane. He looked at her.

"Where is Maijstral now? I need to give him some information."

"I believe he's in a room on the Green Level. I don't quite remember the number."

"Would you do me the kindness of showing me where it is?"

"Certainly." She began striding down the corridor again. Kuusinen, after a skip or two, matched her pace. Roberta looked at him. He was frowning at the carpet.

"Are you going to tell me what's on your mind, Mr. Kuusinen?"

Kuusinen was startled. "I beg your pardon, your grace. I was . . . lost in thought." He cleared his throat. "It's rather complicated. Let me begin at the ball, that first night."

They arrived at the door of an elevator, and Roberta touched the service ideogram.

Kuusinen spoke on.

"What other ships are in dock?"

Cap'n Bob called up the manifests. "*Count Boston* will arrive in three days. Other than that, there are only private yachts belonging to Miss Vanessa Runciter, Baron Silverside, and Pearl Woman.'' She frowned. ''The Baron's yacht is down for maintenance.''

''Runciter's probably vanished along with Fu George,'' Khamiss mused. She turned to the console. ''Contact Pearl Woman's suite.''

Maijstral was not pleased to see Mr. Kuusinen, with or without the Duchess. He had just got a handle on his nerves, and the presence of his second reminded him of things he preferred to keep safely buried in the back of his mind. After Roman let the pair in, Maijstral remained prone on Dolfuss's bed, asking rhetorical questions of the ceiling while Kuusinen prosed on.

''The press is restricted here, you see. No one reporter is allowed to control more than eight media globes at any one time. So when I noticed that there were only six at the ball, and then six at your performance this afternoon, it became clear that they were being used elsewhere.''

A flash of insight struck Maijstral. Quite suddenly he realized where this was going. He sat up abruptly. Hope floundered to the surface of his mind like an escaped convict pursuing daylight at the end of a long tunnel.

''Tell me more,'' he said.

Bells of doom tolling in his mind, pistol firmly snugged in a harness built into his jacket, Zoot walked with a cold, sepulchral tread toward the docks. A series of practical decisions had brought him here. He had been intending to kill himself in the bath, where it would be easy to clean up; but then he realized that the charge might go through his head into the room adjacent and do someone damage. He's decided therefore to kill himself in an isolated airlock, where the station crew would find it easier to clean up the mess and where no one else could get hurt.

* * *

Lord Qlp boomed on. Lady Dosvidern's expression alternated between despair and bafflement.

Pearl Woman, smiling triumphantly, seemed a bit surprised when she saw that it was Khamiss who called her.

"How may I help you, madam?" she asked.

"We have an emergency situation on the station," Khamiss said. "Lives are at stake. I wonder if we might meet you at the docks and perhaps ask for the codes to your yacht."

Pearl Woman tilted her head, permitting a view of the trademark that dangled from her ear. "Of course," she said. Her powerful shoulder muscles flexed. "I can be there in a few minutes." Her expression turned puzzled. "By the way," she added, "what's that *noise?*"

Khamiss hesitated. "Could I possibly explain later? It's part of our problem."

"Very well." She looked out of the camera's range. "Fetch the cutlasses, Advert. And some of our media globes."

Her hologram vanished. Lord Qlp's voice continued to roar from its speaker.

"Oh, no." Khamiss looked up sharply at Lady Dosvidern's tone.

"What's wrong?"

Lady Dosvidern's expression was stricken.

"Its lordship just imposed a deadline. We have one hour before it transmits its final message to Zynzlyp and blows up the station."

Khamiss rose from her chair, her hand resting on her holster. "Then I'll have to hurry," she said.

Once out the door she began to run.

Though she ran as fast as she could, she was possessed the while by a certain sense of futility. Once she got to the docks, she had no clear idea what she was going to do.

* * *

"Drake Maijstral's on the phone." Vanessa Runciter's eyes glittered coldly. "Trying to wriggle out of the encounter, no doubt."

Mild surprise overtook Fu George's features. "Odd. I wonder what he intends?" He and Vanessa had, just that moment, returned to their suite to find emergency lights blinking all over the telephone equipment—Drexler, crouched behind the sofa with detectors strapped over his eyes and a pistol in his hand, had steadfastly been refusing all communication. Vanessa had reached for the phone to check for messages just as a holographic Maijstral popped into view.

Fu George stepped to before the telephone. "Maijstral," he said, "are you certain this is quite regular?"

Maijstral's lazy green eyes, despite the bruising around the left, glowed with silent delight. "I'll confess to irregularity," he said, "but I think we find ourselves in an irregular situation."

Fu George raised an eyebrow. *"We?"* he asked. He'd take this gratuitous plural from Vanessa, but hardly from the man he expected to blast out of his boots in a day or two.

"I know this is an extremely odd request, Fu George," Maijstral said, "but would you do me the irregular favor of meeting me down on Mauve Level, outside room sixteen?"

Ignoring Vanessa's mime of outrage, Fu George gazed deliberately at Maijstral and assumed a look of gravity. "This had better be good," he said.

Pearl Woman was dashingly dressed in boots, pantaloons, a short-sleeved, quilted Quivira jacket, and her matched cutlasses. The butt of a Fantod Exquisite mapper protruded discreetly from the open jacket. Her private media globes, technically illegal onstation, orbited silently overhead. She listened to Khamiss's hasty story, then nodded.

"So you want to use my yacht to get some of your people across to the liner?"

"Right. Or, if necessary, ram the *Cheng* and disable it."

"Qlp will see you coming. He can't miss something the size of a yacht heading for him."

Khamiss's nostrils fluttered hopelessly. "I don't know what else to do."

Pearl Woman considered the question. "Maybe we could cross unobserved from an airlock to the liner."

Khamiss was in no mood to question the sudden gratuitous *we* in Pearl Woman's conversation, nor for that matter the illegal media globes that recorded the debate.

"*Cheng*'s got exterior cameras as well as detectors. If they're in use, its lordship will see us." Khamiss's diaphragm pulsed. "I may as well use the yacht. It will give me more options."

Pearl Woman frowned. "Do you by any chance have access to darksuits?"

Khamiss looked at her in slow surprise. "We confiscated darksuits from Maijstral and Fu George when they came on station."

"Excellent. They'll have antidetection mechanisms built in."

"The suits are in impoundment. Just over there."

Pearl Woman smiled. She drew her Fantod and spun it in her hand.

"Let's get them," she said, and her smile broadened. "You know, Miss Khamiss, I was planning on being bored today. It's nice to know I'll be disappointed."

* * *

Gregor and Roman, hopping and clashing elbows in their haste, were changing into their darksuits in the bathroom. Maijstral had adopted a more leisurely pace; he was letting the closet robot unlace his jacket and the sideseams of his trousers.

"Mr. Kuusinen, I thank you," he said. "I don't think you need be present at the finale unless you wish to be."

"I prefer to remain in the background, sir." Kuusinen bowed. "I wish you success."

Maijstral tore off his jacket, falling bands, and holster. "Your grace," he said as he unstrapped his knife from his forearm, "I thank you for bringing this to my attention."

"Pleased to be of help, Maijstral. Do you still want me to see Kotani?"

"Not until this business is resolved."

Roberta drew back her ears. "You wouldn't have a spare darksuit, would you?"

"Not here. My spares are impounded at customs."

"Too bad, Maijstral. I'd like to be in on the finish, but I'm afraid I can't be seen in your company—I can't afford the appearance of colluding with you in the theft of my own treasure."

"I'll give you first view of the recordings, your grace."

"It's not the same as being there."

"Alas, not."

The door opened. Roman and Gregor stepped out, darksuit hoods drawn over their heads.

"We're ready, boss," Gregor said.

"If you'll excuse me, your grace."

"Maijstral." She stepped toward him and gently sniffed his ears. "Good luck." Surprise stirred in Maijstral. In the parting handclasp, the Duchess had offered him three fingers.

* * *

Vanessa Runciter, fashionably ornate detector goggles over
her eyes, reached into the closet for her Nana-Coulville rifle.
"Nana-Coulville," as the advertisements read, "gunmaker
by appointment to His Imperial Majesty Nnis CVI," never
mentioning that the Emperor had been frozen stiff for two
generations and that even when he was alive he preferred
stalking insects with nets to shooting live animals for sport.
Vanessa's lightweight mapper was not precisely a sporting
weapon, being intended for driving large-caliber slugs through
force fields and into the bodies of sentient beings, whence
the victims' nervous systems would be mapped within seconds and permanently short-circuited by the single-minded,
homicidal, miniature intelligence concealed in the hard cas-
ing of the bullet.

Vanessa, pleased at the heft of the weapon in her hands,
formed in her mind the happy image of little jagged lightning
bolts running along the network of Drake Maijstral's nerves,
turning them black as charcoal. Cheered by the graphic
quality of the picture, Vanessa paused and smiled. It was
a pity that Maijstral was going to get his comeuppance at
Fu George's hands, not her own.

But maybe not. Perhaps Maijstral had lured Fu George
and Drexler off to Mauve Level in order to loot his suite;
in which case he would find Vanessa, Chalice, and a mag-
azine full of nasty homicidal bullets waiting for him.

Dwelling on this cheerful thought, Vanessa glanced up,
her detector goggles showing her the pulses of energy from
the alarms set in the false closet ceiling atop which Fu
George had stowed his loot. Vanessa's smile vanished. There
was something wrong here.

She leaned the gun against the wall, reached up on tiptoe,
and disengaged the false ceiling. Alarms failed to clang.
The ceiling was suspiciously light.

The loot had gone. Vanessa flung the false ceiling across

the room and sent crystal glasses hopping from the portable bar to the floor. Unsatisfactorily, none broke.

Maijstral! she thought.

"Chalice!" she shouted, and reached again for her gun. "To arms!"

"Boss," said Gregor. "I think I should tell you something."

"Later, Gregor."

"It's sort of important."

Maijstral looked at him in irritation. *"Later,"* he said more firmly.

Gregor shrugged and gave up. "Right," he said. "Like you say."

Maijstral, Roman, and Gregor stepped from Dolfuss's room, then rose on a-grav harnesses and sped down the corridor. Camouflage holograms blossomed around them. Dodging the occasional startled pedestrian, they soared straight to a communications main, entered, dropped three storeys to the Mauve Level, then raced onward. Mauve Level was devoted largely to storage of food, water, furniture, and other bulky items: the party encountered no employees or guests as they flew to their destination.

Geoff Fu George, his countenance displaying suspicion, waited with Drexler. Chalice and Vanessa, Maijstral assumed, were guarding Fu George's suite.

As Maijstral settled to the floor, Fu George folded his arms and gave him a cool look. "I hope you have an explanation for this, Maijstral."

"Yes. One moment." He gestured to his two assistants. They deployed media globes, stepped to one of the false walls, inserted passkeys, and swung the false wall up on its hinges.

A startled Kyoko Asperson hung in a hammock stretched inside the utility corridor. Media globes circled over her head. Loot was piled high around her. There was clearly no room left for the impact diamond. The Eltdown Shard glowed at her throat. She raised a hand.

"Hi there." Tentatively.

"Boss," Gregor said. "This was what I wanted to talk to you about."

The airlock door closed silently behind him, a gateway from the world Zoot had known to the world awaiting him.

He glanced over the empty airlock and gave a long sigh as he ran over a mental checklist, assuring himself that there was nothing left to do with his life but finish himself off. Apparently, he concluded, there wasn't. His diaphragm pulsed reflectively.

His farewell text, sealed in an envelope, made a crinkling noise in his breast pocket as drew his disruptor and set the selector to "lethal." He licked his nose and pressed the barrel of the gun to his temple just below the left ear. His heart beat a slow dirge in his chest.

His eyes shut tight, he commended himself ritually to the Sixteen Active and Twelve Passive Virtues, then conjured in his mind's eye the image of Lady Dosvidern, in whose name he committed this act. The image, he discovered, was maddeningly indistinct. The situation was too distracting for proper meditation. Zoot growled and concentrated harder. The image hardened. Better.

Goodbye, cruel world, he thought, and prepared to squeeze the trigger.

The door behind him opened.

Zoot yowled in surprise and jumped three feet, his pulse

hammering harder than it had when he was about to kill himself. He whirled and saw Khamiss and Pearl Woman standing in the airlock door, pistols in their hands.

Pearl Woman grinned at him. "Thought you were going to get away with it, eh?"

Zoot stared. "Your pardon?" he asked.

Pearl Woman stepped into the airlock. "You're not doing this alone, you know."

"I'm not?" He wondered briefly if he should ask them why they were doing away with themselves; then decided the question was in bad taste.

Pearl Woman laughed. "Thought you'd get sole credit, didn't you?"

Through his fog of bewilderment, Zoot became aware that his features were, once again, running through a long repertoire of ticks and palpitations. He drew himself up and summoned indignation.

"Ladies," he demanded, "what in heaven's name are you doing here?"

Pearl Woman touched the ideograms that controlled the airlock. "We're here for the same reason as you," she said. "Don't be naive."

Zoot looked at her as the door cycled shut. There must be some perspective on this, he thought desperately, in which all will make sense.

Khamiss stepped close to him. She put her hand on his arm and softly sniffed his ear. "Thank you, Zoot," she said. "I'm glad you're with us."

Zoot looked at her. His diaphragm gave a final, resigned spasm. "You're welcome," he said.

Hello, cruel world.

"Air's getting ready to cycle out," Pearl Woman said. "Turn on your fields."

For the first time Zoot noticed that the Pearl and Khamiss

were both dressed in one-piece garments, Pearl Woman with her swords belted on over her clothes. The two intruders blurred slightly as they turned on the force fields that would capture and preserve the air around them.

Zoot had built a similar field into his jacket, mainly to aid in river crossings or diving into predator-filled waters. With a push of his mind, he turned it on.

He was long past the point of trying to figure things out. He'd follow the others and hope, eventually, everything made sense.

He was too confused to feel relief.

"Good work, Kuusinen. I am in your debt."

"All in a day's work, your grace." The door to Roberta's suite swung open. She stepped in and glanced in surprise at her telephone.

"Look at all the emergency lights," she said. "I wonder what's going on *now?*"

"A common thief," Fu George said. "I'm surprised at you, Miss Asperson."

Kyoko reached into a pocket. "Hardly common," she said. "Here's my burglar's ticket. Read it and weep."

Fu George looked at it, then handed it to Maijstral, who saw that it had been issued three years before to a Michi K. Asperson by the Imperial Sporting Commission representative on Khovenburg. He handed the ticket back and turned to Fu George.

"Do you recall this name on the listings?" he asked.

"I'm ranked third from the bottom." Kyoko smiled. "Most of my jobs haven't received any publicity."

"I see," Fu George said. "You were going to release all the recordings to the Commission at once, then leap to the top of the ratings all in one go."

"Something like that. I figured that would be worth a lot of style points."

"And in the meantime you would be able to use your job as interviewer to get close to people and plan your jobs. Very neat, Miss Asperson. I congratulate you." Fu George had, while speaking, reached into the hiding place, removed bundles and boxes, and begun to sort through them.

"I don't have the advantage of gentle birth," Kyoko said. "I've got to make up for it somehow."

"Wait a moment," said Fu George. He looked up in surprise. "These are mine!" He brandished a handful of the Waltz twins' jewels. "When did you take these?"

Kyoko shrugged modestly. "About an hour ago."

"While I was in Maijstral's blind, being held at gunpoint."

She looked from Fu George to Maijstral, rising delight on her round face. "At gunpoint? Really?"

"At gunpoint," Maijstral said, narrowing his eyes over his pistol's sights. "Really." This woman, he realized, had almost got him killed. He stepped closer to her and, manfully resisting the impulse to strangle her, delicately removed the Eltdown Shard from her neck. She watched with regret as the Shard dropped into Maijstral's darksuit pocket. Regret changed to indignation as Maijstral's hand moved to one of her boxes, snagged Madame la Riviere's diamond necklace, and dropped it into the same pocket.

"Hey, that was mine! I didn't take it from either of you!"

Maijstral smiled delicately and opened another box. Emerald brilliants dangled from his fingers, then disappeared into the cargo compartment built into the darksuit's back. "You may object if you wish, Miss Asperson," he said. "You can even call for help if that is your preference. But if you summon the authorities, you will doubtless be apprehended for theft of the Shard and for what also appear to be numerous other items discovered missing in the last day or so, including personal property belonging to Mr. Fu George and myself. Fu George and I, of course, have the recordings that *prove* that the items were stolen, legally, by us, and are now our property.'' Dusky pearls glowed magically in air as Maijstral tossed a necklace to Roman, who caught it deftly and stowed it in a pocket.

Kyoko sighed. "Easy come, easy go," she said.

"Besides, Miss Asperson," Fu George said cheerfully, "Maijstral and I can steal from you if we feel like it. It's what we do for a *living*." Lady Tvax's glowstone bracelets disappeared into a pocket. He frowned at Kyoko. "Not only that, you've been going about asking provocative questions about our *duel,* as you put it, and I don't care for that. Theft is one thing, provoking antagonism quite another." He stripped the cover from an elastic box and tipped it to show the contents to Maijstral. "Quite a lot here, wouldn't you say?"

Kyoko gave a laugh. "I robbed the hotel safe." Smugly. "It was easy once I sabotaged the central security console during an interview."

"My congratulations. I'm sure Maijstral and I are duly grateful." Fu George handed the box to Drexler.

"Careful, Fu George," Maijstral said. "We should divide this evenly."

Fu George gave Maijstral a look. "You owe me one, I believe. For last night."

"Ah. How discourteous of me to forget. My apologies."

"Think nothing of it, old boy."

Kyoko's hoard gradually resolved itself into two piles. Maijstral's was the larger, mainly because of the considerable bulk of the Baroness Silverside's art collection. Pockets bulged with small items of sculpture and jewelry. "Gregor," Maijstral said. "Ask the station to send us a large robot. We'll take my collection to our room."

"I saw a cargobot around the corner. I'll do a snap-off on it."

"Very well."

Fu George holstered his weapon. "I believe Drexler and I will take our leave. It was clever of you to have worked out what happened."

Maijstral gave him a careless smile. "It was easy," lying cheerfully, "once I realized the significance of the media globes.".

"Still, a very impressive piece of deduction."

"Thank you, Fu George."

Fu George raised a hand to pat his famous hair into place. "As far as our encounter goes, Maijstral . . ."

"Yes?" Glee danced wickedly in Maijstral's heart.

"Do you think at this point a meeting is strictly necessary?"

Maijstral stroked his chin and feigned consideration. "I shouldn't think so," he said, putting a touch of reluctance into his voice. "I'll speak to the Duchess and ask her not to see Kotani after all."

"Very well." Fu George grinned whitely. "Your servant, Maijstral."

"Yours."

Fu George and Drexler made their congé and departed. Maijstral waited by his pile, his gun still trained deliberately on Kyoko Asperson—he wasn't about to be caught again. Kyoko, he observed, seemed a bit depressed.

"Don't be too cast down, Miss Asperson," Maijstral said. "You'll still get quite a few style points out of this adventure."

"I suppose I shall."

"I imagine your recordings will go for a very high price. Of course, the Silverside material will have to be spliced with mine and Fu George's to make any sense, but I suppose we'll all three get a sizeable advance, considering the, ah, sensational nature of the material.''

"Got the bot, boss.'' Gregor sailed into sight standing on the platform of a transport robot. The robot came to a stop and Gregor stepped off. "Robot,'' he instructed, "put this pile on board. Be gentle, since some of it's fragile.''

"Yes, sir.'' Invisible tractors and repellers began lifting the precious objects and placing them on the robot's bed. Gregor stood by, his fingers tapping a hesitant rhythm on the robot's skull.

"Boss,'' he said. "I'd like to make it clear that I didn't have anything to do with this.''

Maijstral looked at him in surprise, then remembered himself and returned his attention to Kyoko and his firearm. "I never thought you had, Gregor,'' he said.

"See, Miss Asperson and I have got sort of involved. But I never told her anything about our jobs.''

Maijstral concealed his surprise.

"That's true, Maijstral.'' Kyoko's face was earnest. "He never told me anything, though I did try to worm a *little* information out of him. I got most of my information by following you around with micromedia globes. I was careful, and you didn't detect them.''

"Ah.'' Maijstral contemplated Kyoko's round face over his gunsight and, mentally, squeezed his trigger repeatedly. "A word of advice, Gregor,'' he said. "Never get involved with the media.''

"Right, boss. I'll keep that in mind.''

The robot loaded the last of the loot. "Robot,'' Maijstral ordered, "take these to the elevator. At walking speed.''

"Yes, sir.''

Maijstral and Roman walked backward down the corridor

after the robot, their guns still drawn in hopes of discouraging Kyoko from an act of desperation. They rounded a corner and slowly headed for the nearest elevator.

"Well done, sir," Roman said.

"Thank you, Roman."

"Should I holster my gun?"

"Let's get in the elevator first." They continued their slow walk, arrived at a bank of three elevators, and stopped before the middle one. Doors opened before Gregor could touch the ideogram.

"Hello," Gregor said, surprised. "Good afternoon, your grace. Mr. Kuusinen."

Maijstral, still walking backward, snapped on his detectors. The pickups in the rear of his darksuit gave him a clear image of Roberta and Kuusinen, who had just appeared as the leftmost elevator opened. Both appeared a bit breathless.

"Your grace," Maijstral said.

"The emergency's turned very serious," Roberta said. "I'll need the Shard."

"Certainly." He plucked it from his pocket and held it out to her. She took it.

The doors of the elevator on the far right opened.

"Have you seen Fu George?" Roberta asked.

Maijstral smiled. "Taken care of."

"A-*ha!*" Maijstral turned in surprise at the sound of Vanessa Runciter's voice. She and Chalice had just leaped from the elevator, guns in their hands. Vanessa's mapper was pointed at Maijstral. Her face was torn by loathing.

"Assassin," she said. "I'll take care of *you*." And then, as Maijstral gaped at her in astonishment, she pulled the trigger.

The giant *Viscount Cheng* floated above, over the asteroid's close horizon. Khamiss's flesh prickled at the sight: three of them were going up against *that?* Followed by Pearl Woman and Zoot, she took cover behind a landing cradle and paused to consider the situation. The others clustered next to her, merging their force fields and creating a common atmosphere in which they could all speak.

"Zoot," she asked, "will your jacket hide you from detectors?"

"I'm afraid not. There isn't much call for that on unexplored planets. But I've got simple darksuit projectors, to confuse native predators."

Khamiss glanced at the vast liner once again and reminded herself that there was only one Drawmiikh aboard: even with five eyes he couldn't be watching everything. She pulsed a series of minor commands to her suit and found that it obeyed her with surprising speed and ease. It was easier to be a first-rank burglar than she'd thought.

"I'll try to provide a screen for all of us," she said. "Zoot, if you'll put your arms around my waist from behind, and Pearl Woman in turn holds onto you, I think we'll present a smaller profile."

"Very well."

Zoot maneuvered himself behind her, locking arms around her waist. His furry chin settled on her shoulder. The contact reassured her; she experienced a wave of thankfulness that she wasn't alone in this. Holographic camouflage appeared around them and they began moving.

Rathbon's Star rose blazing above the rock's horizon. Red light dazzled Khamiss's eyes. *Cheng* was getting larger and larger. Her darksuit informed her that the ship's scanners were active; but the suit also countered the scans automatically. The admiration Khamiss felt for the suit's builder increased. Her confidence grew. So did the *Viscount Cheng*.

Khamiss's half-blinded eyes perceived a dorsal airlock and she headed for it. As the ship grew nearer, her suit began to signal her, little abstruse symbols and numbers appearing in the visual centers of her brain. She tried to puzzle them out, but couldn't. The signals continued. An urgent audio tone made her jump. Rathbon's Star dazzled her vision.

"We're getting close," Zoot said, his tone a bit worried; and Khamiss's awareness rose from the darksuit's signals to observe the *Cheng* was very near indeed. Its size had confused her as to distance. She slammed on the repellers, but too late.

Khamiss went face first into the *Cheng*'s hull next to the airlock. There was another impact as Zoot slammed into her from behind, then a third as Pearl Woman entered the crush.

The repellers now reversed, the accordion rebounded, sailing backward into space. Cymbals crashed in Khamiss's skull. She tried to head for the airlock again, but symbols were still pulsing in her mind and she wasn't entirely used to the suit yet. The audio tone blatted in her aural centers, distracting her. The *Cheng* came up very fast.

Khamiss hit muzzle first again. Zoot knocked the wind out of her; Pearl Woman bent some ribs. The three bounded back.

Her mind thoroughly awash by now, Khamiss got one mental command confused with another and piled on the speed. The urgent audio tone startled her and she didn't notice the *Cheng* coming up until she went into it nose first.

Zoot slammed into her again.

Pearl Woman brought up the rear. The three rebounded once more.

"That was fun," Pearl Woman said. "Shall we do it again?"

"Madam, allow me," said Zoot, a bit breathless. Gratitude filled Khamiss's reeling brain as Zoot, using his own repellers, guided all three precisely to the airlock. Khamiss dabbed with her cuff at her bleeding nose.

"Sorry," she mumbled.

"How do we get in, precisely?" Pearl Woman said. "If we open the airlock, Qlp's going to see it on the control panel."

"I can get us in," Khamiss said, denasal. Her head was still spinning. "This suit has everything necessary to cut out the alarms. Just give me a moment."

Gradually Khamiss's spinning mind stabilized. The symbols and audio she'd been receiving, she realized dully, were meant to inform her of the swift approach of something solid.

"Live and learn," she muttered.

Pearl Woman looked at her. "Can we save the maxims for later?"

Khamiss opened Maijstral's belt pouches and surveyed the contents. Her job as a security officer allowed her to recognize most of the objects therein, but unfortunately she had never actually operated any of them before. Her ears twitched in puzzlement.

Pearl Woman stepped closer to her, merging air pockets. "I hate to impart a traumatizing sense of urgency," she said, "but if you don't open the door very quickly, we're all going to run out of air."

"A moment. I'm not entirely familiar with the equipment."

"I think that point has already been demonstrated," Pearl Woman said, "but thank you for the reminder."

Khamiss took a moment to smooth her rising hackles. Moving deliberately, she chose the detector she thought she needed, scanned the door, and perceived the energies operating in the door's lock. The lock was simple—this was a personnel hatch, not a security door, and its operation was as simple as possible for the convenience of the crew. She reached for what she recognized as a tossoff remote and placed it above the lock, cutting out the circuit that would report the lock's status to *Cheng*'s control room. Then, with an insouciant gesture, she triggered the circuit that would open the airlock door.

Pleasure trickled through her as the door began to open.

"Very professional, Miss Khamiss," Zoot said. He handed her a handkerchief, and Khamiss placed it to her nose.

Pearl Woman had already dropped into the airlock. Media globes recorded her movements. Her mouthed comments were fortunately inaudible through the vacuum of space.

Khamiss and Zoot followed. The door closed and air rushed in.

Pearl Woman drew her Fantod in one hand and a cutlass in the other. Her smile was cheerful.

"Now the fun starts," she said.

Vanessa Runciter had always suffered from an excess of passion. Her first slug therefore missed—she was so passionately angry that she fired her rifle from the hip, and the round went wide.

An electric shriek of fear crackled up Maijstral's spine. He forgot he had a pistol in his hand, forgot where he was and what he had around him—instead he slammed on his darksuit's shields, his camouflage, and his a-grav harness, and went skimming backward at full speed.

A blaze of Roman's spitfire charges fountained off Vanessa's shields. Out of the corner of his eye Maijstral saw Roman moving, Chalice charging, and then his vision went to hell as disaster struck. He had forgotten the robot and the pile of loot that were just behind him, and his lower body struck the robot with a numbing crunch. His velocity was such that, on impact, his feet were thrown skyward—his boots hit the ceiling and rebounded; and this impact, in turn, threw his head upward. Stars filled Maijstral's vision as his skull rang against porcelain-covered asteroid material. He hit the ceiling a second time. His gun clattered to the floor.

Maijstral threw his a-grav repellers into neutral. His velocity diminished. Through the galaxies that exploded behind his eyes, he dimly saw Gregor jump behind the robot while clawing desperately for his pistol, Roman flattening Chalice with an expert roundhouse kick to the head and then leaping vainly for Vanessa, and, most horribly, Vanessa shouldering her rifle and taking careful aim, pointing the barrel directly between Maijstral's eyes. . . .

A lunging form intervened. Roberta flung herself from the elevator in a perfect racer's pass, feet first, legs lashing out in a kick at the precise moment of impact. Vanessa's ribs caved in with an audible crack and she flew like a broken doll across the hallway. The mapper slug went into Baroness Silverside's collection and demolished a genuine Adrian bronze of Flashman Capone, the famous stage actor and swindler.

Roberta twisted in midair and landed, amazingly enough, on her feet. She reached for Vanessa's rifle, snatched it, and drove the stock of the Nana-Coulville quite deliberately into Vanessa's face. Vanessa fell to the floor unconscious.

"Hit her again," Maijstral wanted to say, "she might be faking." But he seemed unable to speak. Instead he floated near the ceiling and watched as Roman and Gregor relieved Vanessa and Chalice of their gear.

"Are you all right, sir?" The voice was Paavo Kuusinen's.

Maijstral willed off his camouflage and made an affirmative gesture with his ears. He looked down at Kuusinen.

"I believe so," he said, pleased to discover his voice working again.

He lowered himself to the floor. His found to his surprise that his legs would support him. He bent to pick up his pistol.

"If you don't mind an inquiry, sir," Kuusinen said, "what was that about?"

Maijstral looked at the two unconscious bodies and could only flutter his ears in bewilderment.

Chalice moaned. He stirred himself and opened his eyes to find himself staring into a circle of pistols. Gregor gave him a look.

"Isn't this a little overdone," he said, "just to escape a ten-novae debt?"

His mind aswim, Zoot stepped from the airlock into *Viscount Cheng*'s crew quarters. Khamiss and Pearl Woman, weapons in their hands, glanced fore and aft at the complex pattern of small rooms, then looked at each other. "Where's a service plate?" Pearl Woman asked. "We'll ask the ship for a path to the control room."

"That way," Zoot said, pointing aft. He wondered if he should draw his weapon, then decided to keep it holstered for the time being. He stepped out of the airlock and began moving toward the ship's stern. Pearl Woman looked at him suspiciously.

"How do you know?"

Zoot was offhand. "I'm familiar with the specifications of the Celebrated Noble class."

Pearl Woman's suspicion was undiminished. "How? Do you stay up at night studying ship architecture?"

"I travelled in the crew quarters of the *Baron Marbles* once, when I was on the Ottoman expedition."

"I see." Still unconvinced.

Zoot led them to an elevator and called for it. "The control room's a short distance from the elevator." He looked at his companions and a flood of doubt entered his mind. He still had no clear notion what he and the others were doing here. He gnawed his lip, then spoke cautiously.

"I wonder, ladies, how we're going to handle the, ah, problem."

Khamiss's tone was worried. "Lord Qlp's got five brains. It'll be hard to knock out."

Lord Qlp? Zoot wondered.

The elevator arrived and the party stepped into it. "If we can catch its lordship by surprise," Pearl Woman said, "we can put a volley into it. That should probably do the job. My mapper can burn its nerves in a few seconds."

Khamiss seemed undecided. "I'd hate to kill it. It's probably just crazy."

"It might well be Lord Qlp or us. Or even Lord Qlp and the station."

"I'd still prefer to give it a chance to surrender. Or stun it."

Danger to the station? Zoot thought. And then, Lord Qlp?

"That may not be possible," Pearl Woman said. "It may be armed. It may also have ordered the ship to dive into the antimatter bottle on oral command—it'd only need a second or two."

Antimatter bottle? Zoot thought. He drew his pistol and contemplated both the setting and the consequences of an accident with a large antimatter container. His diaphragm pulsed in resignation and he clicked the setting to "nonlethal."

"I would prefer to stun its lordship if possible," he said. "The three of us should be able to do that, certainly."

The elevator doors opened. Pearl Woman looked disgruntled, then holstered her pistol, which had no nonlethal setting. "Right," she said. "I've an idea." She stepped out of the elevator, glanced left and right, and stepped through an open office door labelled "Purser." When she returned it was with a small container.

"I'll tell it I've got the Shard," she said. "That should distract it for a few seconds."

Shard? thought Zoot.

"Good idea," Khamiss said. "Best speak in Khosali— its lordship may not understand Human Standard."

The hallway was far more sumptuous than the crew quarters: parquet flooring, hand-woven, sound-absorbent tapestries featuring scenes of festive aristocrats dining amidst exotic splendor. "The command center is just through those doors," Zoot said, pointing to a pair of doors made of mottled ceramic and decorated with reliefs featuring the high points of Viscount Cheng's colorful Colonial Service career.

"Let me check it." Khamiss stepped forward and deployed her detectors. She found the door locked and alarmed and, moving carefully, she deployed her unfamiliar equipment and took apart its defenses. "Ready," she said.

The Shard? Zoot thought. He looked at Pearl Woman and the box. An idea struck him.

"Here," he said. "Take one of my lights." He took a pencil flash from his inner jacket rig and gave it to the Pearl. "Turn it on and put it in the box. When you open it, the interior should glow. It may look as if the Shard is inside."

"Thank you, Zoot."

Pearl Woman brushed her leonine hair back from her eyes. One of her media globes circled to record her from a more favorable angle. "I'll go through the right door while you hide behind the left. I'll use the darksuit to fly across the room. When I've got its attention directed toward me, step into the doorway and open fire." She gave a devil-may-care grin for benefit of the recorder. "Let's go," she said.

Lord Qlp, Zoot mused, and the Eltdown Shard. Antimatter bottles, and a liner apparently stolen. Were things unusually confused right now, he wondered, or had life always been this way and Zoot not noticed?

"Very good," he said. Readiness coursed through him. At the worst, he reflected, he'd only kill himself in this adventure, and that was what he'd set out to do in the first place.

Zoot stepped behind the door and deployed his jacket's darksuit projectors. They were far less sophisticated than those built into the suits Khamiss and Pearl Woman were wearing, providing only a cloud of darkness that obscured his outline rather than causing it to blend in with the background, but he concluded that it might serve to confuse Lord Qlp even so.

Khamiss stepped behind him and triggered her own camouflage. She pressed close. Zoot could hear her heart thudding against his backbone.

"Good luck," she said.

"Same to you."

Pearl Woman took a breath, stationed her globes for best advantage, and flung herself through the door. Lord Qlp's sputtering, booming voice, formerly suppressed by the sound screens in the door, was suddenly very loud. Zoot could feel Khamiss jump in surprise at its lordship's volume.

"I've got the Shard!" Pearl Woman shouted, in Khosali Standard. "Put down the pistols! I've got the Shard!"

Pistols? thought Zoot, alarmed at the plural. For a frantic moment he considered changing his weapon's setting to "lethal," decided against it, then stepped into the doorway and braced his own pistol to fire.

The control room was very large and sumptuously appointed—travellers sometimes stopped by to chat with the captain, and expected the amenities. Pearl Woman floated against the far wall, shouting frantically, waving the bag under her chin. Ghostly light from the flash illuminated her face from below.

Lord Qlp had disdained the padded captain's chair and instead was reared up near the communications console at the front of the room. Two of its eyestalks had wrapped themselves around pistol butts and triggers, the eyes laid along the barrels in order to sight them. The guns were both directed toward Pearl Woman.

Zoot thought fast. Lord Qlp had a mouth at either end, and therefore both mouths should be stunned first in order to end any possibility of an oral command being given. That, unfortunately, would leave the pistols free to fire. Concern for Pearl Woman and Khamiss flashed into his mind. He overrode it with an act of will.

He fired for the upper end first. Lord Qlp gave a startled belch from its lower mouth and fell forward across the console. One of its pistols went off, and a chugger slug exploded off the wall near Pearl Woman. Khamiss's stunner crackled and Lord Qlp twitched. Pearl Woman flung the bag at Lord Qlp and commenced a zigzag path across the room while drawing her cutlasses. Explosive chugger rounds blew holes in the ceiling. Zoot fired for the lower mouth. Lord Qlp collapsed. One of its pistols trained toward Khamiss, and alarm flared in Zoot as his next shot missed.

Pearl Woman gave a shout and flung a cutlass. It sliced the eyestalk neatly and the pistol fell. Khamiss and Zoot fired four or five more times each. Lord Qlp thrashed and lay still.

Zoot stepped to the navigation console in three fast strides. "Display course plot," he said. The computer obliged, showing a trajectory plotted, sure enough, right into the magnetic bottle that held antimatter for the power station.

"Cancel plotted course," Zoot said, and the plot vanished.

Pearl Woman gave a triumphant laugh and performed a somersault in the air en route to the navigation console. "I did it!" she cackled. "That cutlass was right on target!" Her exuberance turned to shouts of joy. *"Yaaaaaah! Yaaaaaah!"* She touched the controls to the video unit and broadcast her image to Silverside Station. The hologram of a wide-eyed Tanquer appeared over the console, with the *Cheng's* captain peering anxiously over her shoulder.

Pearl Woman smiled and turned her head slightly to display the pearl dangling from one ear. She brandished her remaining cutlass. "This is Pearl Woman," she said. "We have retrieved the situation. All's well."

The Tanquer's eyes rolled up into her nictitating membranes as she passed out. There was an audible thump as she hit the floor.

"Send a crew to bring us to dock," Pearl Woman said to the remaining figure of Cap'n Bob. She peered into the hologram. "And who *was* that, anyway?"

"I'm not sure," said the captain. "Whoever she is, she's rather odd."

Zoot put his pistol in his holster and looked at Khamiss. Khamiss held his gaze for a moment. Zoot felt a glorious moment of internal warmth. Khamiss looked away. Confusion roiled in Zoot's breast. He turned back to the course plotter and felt something awkward in his breast pocket. He was surprised to remember that it was his suicide note.

He took the envelope from his pocket and looked at it

for a long moment. Then he tore it in half, then put it in the nearest disposal.

Lord Qlp gave a belch. Pearl Woman looked up, alarmed. Its lordship twitched, then spoke distinctly in Khosali.

"I'm bored," it said. "Bored, bored, bored."

Zoot and Khamiss weren't listening. They were gazing at one another in some surprise.

CHAPTER 11

Voices in the White Room were resonating perfectly once again. Five days after its disappearance, the giant impact diamond had been ransomed and restored to its place of honor.

"Yes. After all those shots, its lordship *was* a little scrambled. One of its brains began to babble uncontrollably."

"About the Drawmii's, ah, existential dilemma."

"Yes." Zoot gazed into Kyoko's hovering media globes. "It seems that the Drawmii's multiple brains provide sophisticated and subtle modes of converse unavailable to the rest of us. They consider us terribly unsophisticated by comparison."

"And their lack of interaction with the Empire was not the result of their alien thought patterns, but because they were, ah . . ."

"They found us incomparably tedious."

"Right." Kyoko gave a half-believing smile. "Who could find *us* dull? I ask you."

"The thought is a bit humbling, I must admit." Zoot frowned at Kyoko's loupe. "But be that as it may, the Drawmii concluded that if the Khosali and other member species of the Empire were the best the universe could offer them, they might as well destroy themselves before they were all bored to death. Lord Qlp was sent forth as an ambassador, hoping to find some token which might give his species hope.''

''And he found the Eltdown Shard.''

''It appears so. Perhaps we'll never understand its reasons for choosing the Shard; presumably we can all be thankful it found *something* worth living for. It intended to purchase the Shard with the unique . . . tokens . . . that it manufactured in its innards, but the Shard was stolen, and its lordship began to lose all hope. *That*,'' emphatically, ''was when Lady Dosvidern became alarmed and contacted me, as an expert in xenobiology. She and I tried for an entire night to make sense of Lord Qlp's cryptic remarks. Unfortunately I was unable to help her.''

Kyoko smiled thinly. ''That was why you spent the night in her suite.''

''And why I couldn't tell you the truth concerning why I was there. Yes.''

Zoot grinned at her, tongue lolling from a corner of his muzzle. He was pleased to discover that his facial muscles were obeying him this time, not betraying him with twitches and tics. Now that he had a plausible story, there was no reason to do away with himself. He was thankful for that, as by now he had other plans.

''Incidentally, Miss Asperson,'' Zoot said, ''I have another pair of announcements. Firstly, I intend to retire from the Diadem.''

Kyoko's visible eye widened. ''After your greatest achievement? Your ratings are certain to take a leap.''

Zoot allowed a touch of regret to enter his expression. ''I've enjoyed my time in the Diadem, of course, but I'm afraid I've found that celebrity is interfering with my true business, which is xenobiology. I intend to join the next plotting expedition bound outward.''

"Well." Kyoko appeared to be considering matters. "A vacancy among the Three Hundred."

"I'm certain it will be filled by someone worthy."

"Of course."

"Perhaps yourself. When Maijstral and Fu George revealed your covert activities two days ago, it created a sensation."

Kyoko gave him a look. "You said two announcements, I believe."

"Ah. Forgive me. And the most important announcement of all, too." Zoot grinned. "I intend marriage."

"Congratulations. Do I know the lady?"

"Miss Khamiss. She will be resigning her security job and joining me in the expedition."

Kyoko gave a laugh. "Interesting how the crises in Silverside Station have tended to resolve into romance."

"Has there been more than one?"

"Yes. But it would be inappropriate to speak of the other at this stage."

"Ah." Zoot grinned again. "In that case, let discretion reign. By all means."

Baron Silverside still frowned and flushed angrily at the provoking sight of Mr. Sun. Even the sight of Mr. Sun in a robe and cowl, eccentric dress even for a fashionable resort.

"My resignation, sir."

"Accepted."

So much for ceremony, thought Mr. Sun. Well. He must atone for his faults. Let the atonement begin now.

"I have taken second-class passage on the *Count Boston*," said Sun. "I will enter a New Puritan monastery on Khorn."

The Baron smiled. "Very good, Mr. Sun. You may rest assured that in the ensuing years I will often be comforted by the thought of your cleaning latrines and flagellating yourself."

Sun only bowed. Things had come about this way, he was certain, because of some fault within his character. He knew not what the fault was, only that it was there, and that somehow it had put him in dutch with the Almighty.

Now he would have many years—decades, perhaps—to discover what it was.

"Miss Khamiss has given notice also," the Baron said, and frowned. "Despite my offers of a higher salary."

"Mr. Kingston is perfectly qualified," Sun said. "He is a little frivolous in his parts, but I think he is solid enough."

Baron Silverside gave him a suspicious look. He was not prepared to accept any of Sun's judgements at their face value.

"Very well, Sun," he said. "If you are finished . . . ?"

As he stepped from the Baron's office, Sun was surprised to feel a blossom of happiness opening in his soul. Atonement, he found, had left him oddly content.

"It bothers me that I've been contacted about the diamond but not about the other. I'll increase the offer by a quiller."

"Thank you, my lord, but I think not." Geoff Fu George smiled placatingly at the holographic image of Baron Silverside. "Maijstral and I seem to have arrived at a delicate arrangement on these matters. I would not care to disturb it."

"I wish you would reconsider, Fu George." Baron Silverside scowled in thought. "It is a very pretty piece of money."

"Your lordship's offer has been kind," said Fu George, "but I think not."

"If that's your final word." Gruffly.

"I'm afraid it is. Your obedient servant."

"Yours."

Fu George turned from the telephone and stepped to his suite, where Vanessa was supervising the packing of his loot. Vanessa gave him a look. The look was odd, but Fu George couldn't tell whether the oddness was intentional or rather a result of the fact that Vanessa's face, at the moment, simply *looked* odd. The bruising had been massive, the nose had been broken, and for the last several days Vanessa had been in seclusion with a mass of semilife forms attached to her face.

"I wish you had accepted the Baron's offer," she said, denasal. She rotated toward him stiffly: the ribs were healing fast under hormone infusions, but were still giving her trouble. "I'd like to see Maijstral lose that art collection."

Fu George placed bits of foam packing around the delicate settings of an antique necklace. "I'd rather not try for Maijstral's loot again. Our working against one another has been fraught with more than the usual amount of hazard. Kyoko used our rivalry for her own ends. I'd prefer not to be rendered so vulnerable again."

She lit a cigaret. "Still," she said, "one last coup seems such a tempting idea. What with the collection *and* the Shard *and* that display with the diamond, Maijstral may end up with a lot of points in the next rating. He's certain to receive a promotion. He may even take first place."

Fu George closed the jewel case. "It had to happen sooner or later, Vanessa."

"I don't like the idea of our not being on top."

Our? thought Fu George. He sighed and turned to her. "We've got all the money and fame we could desire," he said. "It's been fun. But sooner or later someone else was going to take first, or I was going to get careless or unlucky and end up in prison somewhere. And very soon the Constellation Practices Authority may well recommend Allowed Burglary be *dis*allowed throughout the Human Constellation, which would substantially decrease the amount of enjoyment to be had from this profession.'' He spread his hands. ''Perhaps the time has come for a gracious retirement.''

Smoke curled disdainfully from Vanessa's nostrils. ''And do *what*, Fu George? Do you want me to spend our declining years on our back terrace, watching the robots trim the hedges while you write your memoirs?''

''Hardly that.''

''I like spice in my life, Fu George. Excitement. *I'm* still young, you know.''

Fu George ignored this reflection on his age. ''I thought the Diadem might be persuaded to renew their offer. That would guarantee us travel and celebrity.''

''Hm.''

''In any case, I have no intention of retiring as long as I'm still in first place.''

''*That* was why I wanted you to take the collection.''

''That subject of conversation,'' Fu George said, turning back to his jewels, ''has long ceased to be of interest to me.''

''Hm,'' said Vanessa again, and breathed in smoke. This was going to take some thinking about.

''I think not, my lord,'' Maijstral said. Baron Silverside glared at him stonily.

''It's a good offer,'' he said.

''I prefer to decline. Fu George and I are professionals, after all. We don't pursue foolish rivalries.''

''If that's your last word.''

''It is. Thank you, however, for considering me.''

The Baron broke the connection. Maijstral let the service hologram float in his bedroom and stepped into the front room of his suite. The Marquess and Marchioness Kotani were returning their drinks to Roman's tray.

"Another drink, my lady? My lord?"

"No, Roman," Kotani said, speaking for both. "Thank you."

"My apologies," Maijstral said. "A personal call."

Kotani lifted an eyebrow. "Not getting another bid, were you?"

"He doesn't know I have the collection. Not for certain, anyway. He keeps trying to hire me to steal it from Fu George."

"I'm afraid this last week has cost the Baron rather heavily."

"But not in custom, I daresay. After the last seven days, Silverside Station is certain to become established as one of the most fashionable resorts in the Constellation. Were I the Baron, I might well consider my losses justified."

"Quite." Kotani smiled thinly. "Lucky that I struck my arrangement with the Baron before that fact became obvious to him."

Maijstral bowed. "I congratulate you on your sense of timing, my lord."

"This means Kotani and I will revisit Silverside for the play," said the Marchioness. She looked at Maijstral from beneath her lashes. "The place has such fond memories for me, such . . . sympathetic resonance."

"I'm glad," said Maijstral, seating himself, "that your ladyship found your stay fulfilling."

"And," looking at him, "I shall be taking memories with me, in the form of the collection. I will delight in installing such a distinguished accumulation of artwork at home in Kotani Castle."

Kotani patted her arm. "This idea of yours was inspired, dearest," he said. "I barely had to make a single correction after all those negotiations with Maijstral."

"I think," she said, no longer daring to look at Maijstral, "the negotiations were my favorite part."

"And now, my lord . . .?" Maijstral held up a Casino betting chip and a molecular pencil.

"Certainly. My pleasure." Kotani wrote an amount, signed, printed. Maijstral took the chip and placed it in his pocket.

"I'll have one of my people deliver the collection this afternoon," Maijstral said. "In plenty of time for the departure of the *Boston*."

Kotani stood. "I have arrangements to make, alas," he said. Maijstral stood and the two men sniffed ears. "Your servant."

"Your very obedient. Oh. Beg pardon, my lord. My shoe caught in the carpet."

"Think nothing of it, Maijstral."

"My lady." Maijstral helped the Marchioness to rise.

"It has been a great pleasure, Maijstral." She sniffed his ears and clasped his hand. Maijstral stiffened slightly in surprise.

"Yours ever, my lady," he said.

After Roman closed the door behind them, Maijstral looked at the object in his right palm. It was a small jewelled pin, fashioned of silver, rubies, and brilliants, in the shape of the Rover of Hearts. The ideogram for Singh's Jewelers was stamped on the back.

"How very thoughtful of her ladyship," Maijstral said. He opened his other hand, which held the two diamond studs Kotani had worn in his left cuff. He had taken the studs off the right cuff in greeting, and the two securing the jacket while giving him his drinks. Stealing the studs hadn't been difficult: replacing them had. The phony diamonds would dissolve in a matter of weeks. Maijstral dropped the pair of studs in his left jacket pocket, along with the other four.

The Rover of Hearts he pinned to his lapel.

Shifting chromatics blazed from the three objects on Roberta's table. "The colors appears to be the result of bacterial action," Roberta said. "They do not seem to feed on anything but light, and most of that they give off as phosphorescence. Another drink, Kuusinen?"

"Thank you, your grace." Roberta signalled Kovinn and Kuusinen returned his attention to the three objects. "I have looked into the xenobiological files on the Drawmii," he reported, "and so far as I can tell these three objects are absolutely unique. Nothing like them as been reported—if others exist at all they are a very close Drawmii secret."

"They are valuable, then, these alien hairballs."

"Your grace," solemnly, "they are priceless."

Roberta took a sip of roxburgh wine. "Oh, dear," she said. "I've had to employ six people just to guard the Eltdown Shard. How many guards will I need for these?"

"I would keep the objects in separate places, your grace. You don't want to lose all three at once."

"I'll do that. I have enough vaults in enough residences, gracious knows."

"Thank you, Kovinn." Kuusinen took his glass from Kovinn's tray.

"Kovinn," said Roberta. "You may take the objects away and pack them."

"Yes, your grace."

Kuusinen looked at Roberta from over the rim of his glass. "What now, your grace?"

"The Special Event, of course."

"Yes. Of course. The Event." He sighed. "The other candidates have been dropped, then? It's to be Maijstral?"

"Almost certainly. But just in case, I desire you continue your inquiries elsewhere."

"As you wish, your grace."

"Send the reports to me—you have my schedule—and then, if you don't hear from me otherwise, take ship for Nana."

"And speak to Maijstral's father?"

"Yes."

Kuusinen sighed. "I hate talking to the dead. They're so . . . faded."

"I gather old Dornier was pretty faded when he was alive."

"And Maijstral's mother?"

Roberta's expression was cold. "I've met her, and once was enough. We can leave that woman out of it."

"I'll be happy not to see her. I tried to stay out of her sight that one time, but still she may remember me."

"Yes. Her memories on that occasion would not be happy ones."

Resigned to another half-year of travel, Kuusinen raised his glass and drank.

"Its lordship will be returning to Zynzlyp," Lady Dosvidern said. "It has swallowed the Shard in order to keep it safe, and will regurgitate it on Zynzlyp. I think even Fu George would have trouble stealing the Shard from the Drawmiikh's insides."

"It sounds quite secure," Zoot said.

"I'm given to understand that the Imperial Sporting Commission, at the request of the Colonial Service, is considering the placing of a ban on future theft of the Eltdown

Shard—they don't want a High Custom sporting event causing the suicide of an entire planetary population."

"Very wise," said Zoot. Despite the fact that he and Lady Dosvidern were having what to all appearances was an innocent conversation at a public table in the White Room, Zoot found himself jittery; he kept cocking his ears back as if to listen for people sneaking up behind him. He had difficulty keeping his eyes focused on Lady Dosvidern. Every time he looked at her, he kept imagining (with convincing realism) the pressure of a pistol barrel to his head.

"And of course"—Lady Dosvidern smiled—"Lord Qlp's return to its planet of origin will mean that I'll be free."

"You won't be taking up residence on its lordship's estate?"

Lady Dosvidern's ears turned down in disdain. "Its lordship's estate consists of three stone huts, two of which are filled with livestock. No, I had an arrangement with the Colonial Service. Now that my task is over, I'll be collecting my pension and leaving Zynzlyp forever. I won't be returning unless Lord Qlp leaves again, and I doubt it will be doing that." She smiled at him. "Perhaps we can meet somewhere."

The very idea conjured in Zoot an instinct to run from the room as fast as his legs could carry him. Zoot suppressed this and drew his face into a semblance of regret. "My lady, I am sorry to report that I'm really not cut out for adultery."

Lady Dosvidern seemed amused. "How odd. And this from a member of the Diadem. It's not as if my marriage to Lord Qlp were anything but a diplomatic fiction."

"Yet. Still."

"Zoot! May I speak with you?" Pearl Woman, hands on cutlass hilts, came swaggering to Zoot's chair. Relieved beyond all measure by the interruption, he stood and sniffed her.

"Pearl Woman."

"I wonder, Zoot, if Lady Dosvidern will let me borrow you for a few moments. I'd like to talk about my new project."

"Ah—with your permission, my lady?"

"Very well." Showing nettled regret.

Pearl Woman tugged on his arm, drawing him away. "I wanted to ask you about Old Earth pirates. Now that my stock's high, I'd like to make a good deal for my next feature, and I think a romance about pirates might be just the ticket."

Relief spread gratefully through Zoot. "Yes," he said. "I am entirely at your service."

"Deus vult."

Roman had made the security arrangements for Dolfuss's room, and Roman, as Maijstral had discovered over the years, was fond of passwords that reflected the life and career of Maijstral's alleged Crusader ancestor. "Deus vult" was his favorite, but "incarnatus" was high on his list, as was "crux mihi ancora." It was fully characteristic of Roman, Maijstral thought, to assign passwords based on a religion that he venerated for its part in the life of Maijstral's supposed forefather, but which, had Roman been left to himself, he would have found violent, simplistic, and distasteful—the ritual cannibalism aspect alone would have turned his ears back, had he given it any thought.

But Roman probably hadn't given it any thought. Because Maijstral's ancestors had taken sides in the Crusades, Roman, being loyal, would also take sides, even though Roman, knowing Maijstral, therefore knew to his sorrow that Maijstral never gave the Crusades or religion a single thought except when Roman reminded him about them. That, Maijstral concluded, was one of the comforting things about

Roman. He was predictable in his loyalty to Maijstral and the family, no matter that Maijstral strained the loyalty from time to time.

The door opened. "Hi, boss," said Gregor.

Maijstral stepped inside Dolfuss's room. Dolfuss was nervously covering the door with a pistol. "The collection is packed?" Maijstral asked.

"Everything's ready, boss."

Maijstral cast a glance over the room. All had been packed save for some of Gregor's equipment for monitoring the Cygnus robots. No lights were glowing on Gregor's apparatus: the robots had all been instructed to stop their opening the utility passageways and setting off alarms. All the security people would know was that alarms would cease —the stratagem itself was secure till next time.

"A good thing it's nearly over," said Dolfuss. He holstered his gun and sat on the bed. "Firearms make me apprehensive. I'm happy not to have to stand guard much longer."

Maijstral smiled at Dolfuss. "I didn't really think anyone would make a try for our hoard, but I thought an attempt would be a lot less likely if we kept two armed men here around the clock. No sense in handing anyone an irresistible temptation." His smile broadened as he opened one of his cases and dropped Kotani's studs into it. "We're just keeping Fu George and Kyoko Asperson honest."

"Happy to provide such a reinforcement to public morality." Dolfuss took the gun from his holster again and put it on the bed; he found the thing uncomfortable. "I'll be even more happy," he added, "to tread the boards again."

"That may be sooner than you think. Our thefts have turned out to be far more sensational than I ever envisioned, and in addition to your advance you'll be getting sizeable royalties from the sale of the recordings to the media. Your name will be placed before the public again. If you announce the opening of a new theater, here in the Constellation where the Imperial bureaucracy won't ban your works, I should think you'd have no lack of backers.''

"Thank you, sir,'' said Dolfuss. "Barring the element of gunplay, it's been a most enlightening stay.''

Maijstral smiled privately. He could only agree.

He turned to Gregor. "I think I'll accompany you to Kotani's suite,'' he said. "For the sake of public morality, if nothing else.''

"Great,'' said Gregor. He put a hi-stick in his mouth. "I sort of wanted to talk to you anyway.''

Maijstral donned his shields while Gregor asked the service plate to send a porterbot. When it arrived Gregor carefully stacked Baroness Silverside's collection on its luggage rack, then the two checked their pistols and left for Kotani's suite.

"The thing is, boss,'' Gregor said, "I don't think much of this polish is wearing off.''

Maijstral looked at him. "Beg pardon?''

"You've taught me a lot, boss,'' Gregor said. "Don't think I'm not grateful. I've got a lot more finesse than I used to have, but I don't seem to be absorbing much in the way of ton, if you see my point.''

"Such things take time, Gregor.''

"More time than I've got, maybe. I mean perhaps.'' He threw up his hands. "See what I mean? I keep saying *maybe* after three years. It's a dead giveaway.''

Maijstral looked at him sidelong. "I suppose Kyoko Asperson has something to do with this.''

"Yes. What I mean is, she's started with a background like mine, poor smashed-up family on a hick planet, and she's made it in the larger world. Not by trying to turn herself into a noble, but just by being herself.''

Maijstral frowned. "She is herself in a very studied way, Gregor. She works at it very hard, perhaps harder than I do at being a lord."

"You don't have to work at being a lord. You *are* a lord. Or at least you have the option of being a lord or not." Gregor sucked nervously on his hi-stick. "I'm not a lord, and I won't ever be mistaken for one. So what I've decided is that I shouldn't be working with a lord, but with someone who has the kind of style I can use." He gave a heavy sigh. "So I'll be leaving on the *Boston* with Miss Asperson, is what I'm saying. I'm sorry to leave you in the lurch, but you and Roman can do pretty well with all the stuff I've built for you until you can find a replacement. And that shouldn't be too hard—not with the way your rating's going to rocket after all this."

Maijstral considered this for a long moment. "You have style aplenty, Gregor. Not my kind, but it's there. I've known that all along."

"Oh." Gregor appeared surprised. "Thank you, boss."

"I don't think you need to work with Miss Asperson just to discover something you already know."

"Thanks anyway. But I've made up my mind. I'm still leaving with her."

"A delicate matter, Gregor." Maijstral pursed his lips. "Should you leave my employment, you leave with a knowledge of my techniques and apparatus. Miss Asperson has already demonstrated a regrettable tendency to take advantage of any inner knowledge. . . ."

"Boss!" Gregor was scandalized. "I wouldn't let her do anything like that!"

"I'm relieved to hear it."

"You should see the junk she's got. Ancient. I'm surprised she hasn't got pinched a dozen times over. And the maintenance!"

Maijstral sighed. He had enjoyed Gregor's company, the younger man's appalling lack of manners having struck him as thoroughly refreshing. Gregor, Maijstral knew, would be missed. He decided to surrender with grace.

"Very well. I wish you and Miss Asperson all possible happiness."

Gregor brightened. "Thanks. A lot. Really."

"You're welcome. Really."

"The return trip will be second class, unfortunately," said Zoot. "The Diadem paid for the trip out; I'll have to dip into my own funds for the journey back. Even then, we'll probably need help financing any expeditions. Fortunately," his ears flickering, "my ratings are up, and the media should pay well."

"I don't mind second class," said Khamiss. "That's how I got here." She turned from her closet and held up her uniform jacket. "Do you think I should take my uniform? As a souvenir?"

"If you like, dearest. Why not? You were wearing it when we met."

"Which reminds me that you still haven't finished the lesson in physiognomy."

His tongue hung amused from the corner of his mouth. "On the passage, then."

She folded the jacket, placed it in her suitcase. Her service pistol was already packed. She stood back. "There."

"Put your wedding clothes on top," Zoot said. "The first day out of port will be a busy one, and *Cheng*'s captain may only have a few minutes to marry us."

"And after all we went through for her and her ship. What an ingrate."

Zoot put his arms around her and tenderly took one of her ears between his canines. Khamiss stroked his furry neck.

"I still don't know her name," she said. "I hope I don't call her Cap'n Bobby by accident."

Zoot didn't understand that remark, but wasn't about to let go of her ear in order to ask. He was finding it quite pleasant here.

Goodbye, he thought, cruel world.

Advert stood on the customs dock. Her feet were unshod, and there were rings on her toes as well as her fingers. The idea had come to her only a few days ago: she'd used some of the Pearl's money to purchase the rings from Singh's.

Pearl Woman, having finished her interview with Kyoko Asperson, waved at her from across the room. Advert turned to the Marchioness Kotani, made her congé, and advanced toward the Pearl.

Pearl Woman grinned at her. "Have you said your fare-wells?"

Advert nodded.

"Good. Shall we take our leave? I don't feel like waiting for the *Cheng* and the *Boston* to leave first."

"As you like. It's not your style to wait, after all."

Pearl Woman took Advert's arm and began walking with her to the private dock nearby. She gave Advert a careful look.

"You know," she said, "there's something different about you, these last few days."

Advert smiled. "Is there?"

"Yes. You seem to carry yourself differently. I can't put my finger on it."

Advert put her hand in her pocket and felt the credit chip there, the one with Pearl Woman's money. "I can't think what it could be," she said.

"Still. It suits you, Advert. There's something much more . . . intriguing about you."

"I'm glad you think so."

"An air of mystery, almost." Pearl Woman gave a laugh. "You know, I'm considering skipping our next planned stop and heading straight for Kapodistrias. The plans for the pirate project are advancing, and I know I could line up some backing there."

"I've never been to Kapodistrias. Is there anything to see?"

"Not much besides a big ocean. I was amazed to discover that Earth pirates didn't have flight—they actually sailed from place to place on boats, powered by wind. But I expect you'll be too busy for sightseeing. I have plans for you, Advert. There's a part in the pirate project that's perfect for you, if you'll take it. An ingenue role." Pearl Woman grinned. "Perhaps I'll rescue you from a fate worse than death."

Advert looked at Pearl Woman and considered for a long moment. "I'd like a clearer idea of the nature of the part before I give a definite answer."

Pearl Woman laughed. She squeezed Advert's arm. "There *has* been a change, Advert. A very interesting one."

Advert's ears perked forward in a gesture meant to be modest. Pleasure welled into her. "I hope so," she said.

"It's been an interesting few days," said the Duchess of Benn. "I hope the rest of my journey will offer something to equal it."

"Personally," said Drake Maijstral, "I could do with a rest." He paused. "I thank you both again, your grace, Mr. Kuusinen, for your assistance here. I might not have survived without you."

"You're very welcome, Drake. I've had fun." Her violet eyes sparkled. "Perhaps I'll see you later. I'm taking the grand tour, after all, and we may encounter one another."

Maijstral inclined his head. "I desire nothing else, your grace." *Fun*, he thought.

Roberta turned to Roman. "I also hope I see you again, Roman. Take care of Maijstral, will you?"

Roman stifled his surprise. "I'll do my best, your grace." More surprise was stifled as she stood on tiptoe to sniff his ears. She turned to sniff Maijstral, giving him three fingers to his cautious two, and then headed for her berth on the *Count Boston*.

Paavo Kuusinen clasped Maijstral's hand—one finger each—and they sniffed farewell. Maijstral looked at him, his shuttered green eyes betraying a gleam of interest. "Mr. Kuusinen," he said. "You've rendered me considerable assistance on two separate occasions, and I regret that I know so little of you. For instance, I have no idea of your occupation."

"I am an attorney, sir. I work for her grace."

"Ah. Very interesting."

Kuusinen gave an offhand flick of his ears. "Not very, sir. I find the practice of law too predictable. The labyrinths of sentient nature are more of interest to me."

Maijstral paused a moment while wondering, precisely, how to reply to this strange remark. "As they are to us all," he said finally.

"Your servant."

"Your obedient."

Maijstral suppressed a minor tremor as he watched Paavo Kuusinen follow the Duchess across the concourse to the *Boston*'s dock. Despite the man's assistance, Maijstral was happy to be rid of him.

"Sir?" A diffident voice intruded upon Maijstral's meditations. He turned to see a tidy human in a nondescript brown jacket.

"Ah. Mr. Mencken."

"I am pleased you remember my name, sir. Your Very Private Letter."

Maijstral took the envelope and looked at the VPL seal. "Thank you."

"Your servant."

Mencken disappeared into the crowd. Maijstral glanced at the seal again, then broke it. The scented paper told him of its source before he unfolded the note. The message was curt, the calligraphy hastily-formed but recognizable. Maijstral had an image of her bent over a desk, Mencken or someone like him standing behind her, waiting for the letter.

Drake,

Troubled in spirit, alas. Navarre has blossomed, been offered Diadem membership. Myself have rediscovered the stage, find the whole D. business distracting. I'd like to go on, but a meeting would be better. Is possible?

Sorry about this, Drake. Honest.

N.

Maijstral read the message twice, first hastily, then not. He put it back in its envelope and handed both to Roman.

"Destroy, please."

"Yes, sir. I hope she is well."

Maijstral frowned. "Entering a depressed phase, I think."

"She recovers quickly, sir. I wouldn't be overly concerned."

"Still. I wish she had someone around her she could trust."

"So do I, sir."

"Someone like you, Roman."

Roman bowed. "Thank you, sir." Carrying the envelope, he headed toward the nearest disposal. Maijstral looked after him and considered how much better a place the universe would be if *everyone* had someone like Roman to look after them.

"Drake." Vanessa Runciter's voice, hovering just over one shoulder.

He turned toward her, brushing her gently with his arm. He stepped back, putting distance between them. A translucent veil, Maijstral was pleased to note, was drawn across her face to hide the damage.

"Hello, Vanessa."

"I just wanted to say that I'm sorry I shot at you. I thought you'd just done in Fu George, you see."

"It's forgotten, Vanessa." Politely.

She cocked her head and looked at him. "You're going to do very well out of this last few days, you know."

"That seems likely."

Her voice was harsh. "Fu George is thinking about retirement. It all sounds pretty ghastly."

"He has earned his retirement, to be sure."

"I never said he hadn't. Just that it wasn't for me." She paused for a long moment, staring at him, then finally spoke. "Perhaps we ought to meet, Drake."

Maijstral was surprised at the cool firmness of his reply. "I think not, Vanessa."

She took a few seconds to absorb this, still looking at him, then nodded briskly. "If that's how you want it."

"I'm afraid it is." Even more firmly.

She turned abruptly and was gone. Maijstral let out a slow, relieved breath. A few years ago, he reflected, he might well have given a different answer.

He was suddenly aware of Roman's presence. He glanced at Roman, then back at Vanessa. "You know, Roman," he said, as he handed Roman her gun and bracelet—not being foolish, he'd taken the gun first. "I hadn't perceived until now the resemblance in character between Vanessa Runciter and my mother."

"Really, sir? It was the first thing I noted about her."

Maijstral looked at him in surprise as the gun and bracelet vanished. Roman's expression was carefully opaque. Maijstral sighed and turned away.

"We should escort our baggage to the *Cheng*," he said. "I think we've said all our necessary goodbyes to anyone leaving on the *Boston*." He turned and began to walk back to the residential quarters, where Dolfuss, with his pistol, was still standing over the baggage like Marshall Wild Bill Hickock guarding a gold shipment.

"Maijstral! A moment!"

Kyoko Asperson, dressed in yellow and violet motley, was leaping up and down, waving her arms, media globes dancing over her head. Maijstral patiently awaited her arrival. She gave him a wide grin and, while sniffing him, bussed him on both cheeks.

Maijstral's hand dipped into her pocket, returned with something small.

"Gregor told me how nice you were about his leaving," she said. "I'd like to thank you."

"We'll be sorry to lose him, but—" He dropped the stolen object in a pocket and threw up his hands. "I'd hate to stand in his way. Or in the way of true love, for that matter."

Kyoko colored prettily. One of her media globes moved closer to him. "Any final comments for the record, Mr. Maijstral?" she asked. "Any last thoughts on the subject of Silverside Station and what happened here?"

Maijstral considered this for a long moment. His lazy eyes glittered.

"I'd say that events came perilously close to farce," he said, "but that fortunately farce was averted."

Kyoko was surprised. "Thank you," she said.

"Your servant."

Maijstral stepped toward his room, Roman moving silently behind. He reached into his pocket and came up with the object he'd removed from Kyoko's pocket: a pearl dangling from a broken chain. He'd seen Kyoko's altered media globe, with its force cutters and grapplers, hovering near Pearl Woman's ear during the last interview, and guessed the rest. He handed the pearl to Roman. Roman cleared his throat.

"Yes, Roman?"

Roman's voice was carefully articulated. "Farce, sir?" he said.

A memory of terror gusted through Maijstral's mind, followed by that of an argumentative closet door, a dark, glowing gem, a vanishing diamond, a playing card glowing with brilliants. . . .

"For example, Roman," he said. "Had I said yes to Vanessa just now, that would have turned this comedy to farce. As I said no, farce was avoided."

Roman digested this for a moment. "I understand, sir," he said. "Quite perfectly."

THE BEST IN SCIENCE FICTION

Buy them at your local bookstore or use this handy coupon:
Clip and mail this page with your order.

Publishers Book and Audio Mailing Service
P.O. Box 120159, Staten Island, NY 10312-0004

Please send me the book(s) I have checked above. I am enclosing $_____
(please add $1.25 for the first book, and $.25 for each additional book to
cover postage and handling. Send check or money order only — no CODs.)

Name _____

Address _____

City _____ State/Zip _____

Please allow six weeks for delivery. Prices subject to change without notice.

THE BEST IN FANTASY